THE ICE MAIDEN

Recent Titles by Sara Sheridan

Novels

THE LOVE SQUAD
ON STARLIT SEAS
THE ICE MAIDEN *

The Mirabelle Bevan Mysteries

BRIGHTON BELLE
LONDON CALLING
ENGLAND EXPECTS
BRITISH BULLDOG
OPERATION GOODWOOD
RUSSIAN ROULETTE

* available from Severn House

THE ICE MAIDEN

Sara Sheridan

Severn House Large Print
London & New York

This first large print edition published 2019
in Great Britain and the USA by
SEVERN HOUSE PUBLISHERS LTD of
Eardley House, 4 Uxbridge Street, London W8 7SY.
First world regular print edition published 2018 by
Severn House Publishers Ltd.

British Library Cataloguing in Publication Data
A CIP catalogue record for this title is available from the British Library.

ISBN-13: 9780727829719

Severn House Publishers support the Forest Stewardship Council™
[FSC™], the leading international forest certification organisation. All
our titles that are printed on FSC certified paper carry the FSC logo.

MIX
Paper from
responsible sources
FSC   FSC® C013056
www.fsc.org

Typeset by Palimpsest Book Production Ltd.,
Falkirk, Stirlingshire, Scotland.
Printed and bound in Great Britain by
T J International, Padstow, Cornwall.

Part One
Virgin Snow

'Searchers after horror haunt strange, far places.'

HP Lovecraft

'Of all ghosts the ghosts of our old loves are the worst.'

Sir Arthur Conan Doyle

One

Karina waited till it was almost time for the tide
before she opened the door and slipped onto
the track that led to the dock. The moon hung
like a lamp in the darkness. It illuminated her
slim fingers as she fumbled with the catch, closing
the door behind her. Not that she was coming
back. They could have it all – the thin scatter of
straw, the cup, the grate and the seaweed she'd
left drying on the rafters. And her old dress with
its single browning petticoat, cast aside now.

On the track, the wooden houses were not yet
silent for the night. The lamps cast patches of
buttery yellow – the only time the island ever
seemed warm. From one homestead, the sound
of a violin snaked through the air as if it was
reaching for something. Further down, on the
dock, men's laughter carried and the smell of
hops mixed with the stench of whale fat from
the smelting trawlers. Nervously, Karina looked
at her ankles, a pale line of flesh protruding
between the hem of the breeches she had pulled
on and the worn tops of her husband's old boots.
Poor Thebo, she thought, he died in his good
ones and they never brought his body home.
Inside the ragged woollen jumper, her heart was

3

pounding so hard she wondered if it might break out of her chest. She was skin and bone these days. Unexpectedly, it had made her stronger.

At the front, she hesitated outside the company store, closed for the night. She owed money here, like everywhere else on the island. But if she stayed, she'd starve. It had been almost two years since Thebo had died and slowly she'd worn out the islanders' patience, along with what little money Thebo had left her and last of all, her teetering line of credit. She'd sold everything that would fetch a price – the furniture, Thebo's compass, her thin wedding ring and the little row of books the two of them had dragged around the world. 'My sister is sending my passage and coin. She's married to a merchant in Amsterdam,' she said, every time Van Kleek pointed to the bottom line on his damn ledger. But it had been too long since she had written begging for help, and Karina was terrified that something had happened to Marijke.

The last months, with no employment available for women, save the chances she had turned down to sell herself, she'd lived on eggs foraged from the cliffs half an hour to the north and the pickings of shellfish scavenged from rock pools. Nothing grew easily in this forsaken place, though last year there had been a few wild berries. Karina's stomach shifted at the thought of food. These days she rarely taunted herself with such imaginings.

The ships were still on their moorings. Her preference had been for a Dutch vessel but these would do. They were flying the jack. She spoke

4

some English, she comforted herself. That was what had given her the idea she could sneak aboard. It had come to her that afternoon when an English sailor had leaned over the side, beckoning her closer to the ship. He winked and said something suggestive, first in Spanish, then in Dutch. Karina had stared blankly and pretended she didn't understand. 'Where do you think she comes from?' the sailor asked his fellow. 'I want to get her aboard.'

'Well, she's blonde. No point in trying Spanish, mate,' the other man pointed out.

Karina turned on her heel and stalked away with her mind whirring. To go aboard with the knowledge of one of the crew meant she would be put off before they sailed and there was no measure in that. She'd thought of stowing away before. She'd considered it a few times as she slid further into destitution, but had decided on balance, that she still held out hope. That hope had now diminished and yet, for hours that afternoon she had remained unsure as she paced the little cabin and turned over the possibilities, though there were only two. The next day might bring the long-awaited banker's note from Marijke. Or it might not.

Now she surveyed the ships by moonlight. The cocky sailor had called to her from aboard the *Erebus*, so she chose the *Terror*. Two men stood guard at the gangplank, or rather, played cards on a barrel to the side. A lamp creaked above them but the moon was so clear, they must hardly need it. Karina cursed the brightness as she skirted the ragged line of shacks along the shore and slipped across the stones. The great ship was moored with a thick curl of rope.

She'd seen boys climb these when she was a child. Marijke and she had watched over the harbour where they grew up, on the island of Ven. 'Like little angels,' their mother had said, and the two little blonde girls must have looked that way. Most of the visitors had been summertime tourists on a jaunt from the Danish coastline across the sound. Older, Marijke had challenged Karina from their vantage point on the tiled roof as the visitors arrived.

'If you can name even one of them, I'll do your chores for a week.' The line of her freckled nose crinkled to underline the challenge.

Karina tugged distractedly at a yellow lock that fell across her face, defying her mother's attempts to pin it.

'Johann Oesterund,' she had tried, spotting a po-faced curate picking his way up the jetty with a woman she could only assume was his elderly mother or at least a dowager aunt.

Later, she was never sure why she had assumed Marijke knew the visitors' names. The older girl was, to her mind, endowed with magical powers and simply knew everything.

'Soren Masterson,' she tried. This one a doe-eyed honeymooner in a pretty pale blue smock embroidered with sprigs of daisies. 'Her husband's name is Pieter,' Karina pronounced, the childish assertion utterly confident. She thought if she believed what she said it would make it true. She thought, perhaps, she could divine the names if only she concentrated hard enough. There was

6

no telling of course if the incomers were Danish or Swedish or Norwegian. But the English were a different matter. You could spot them straight away.

Now, like the boys Marijke and she had seen, Karina clambered quickly up the rope. She balanced a tentative foot on an outcrop and hauled her thin frame over the side, falling silently onto the deck. Her blue eyes darted, sure she would be caught and marched down the gangplank. Certain that someone aboard must have seen this momentous event. Or someone on land, out for a stroll. Anyone could raise the alarm. But there was only the sound of the water slapping against the side. It seemed too easy.

Behind her, Deception Island continued its evening pursuits, unaware that Karina Lande was no longer resident. On board, the crew of the *Terror* knew no more – they ate their rations and worked their shift, the same as sailors the world over. Somewhere below there was the sound of a squeezebox being played and a man singing. Karina rose warily and dusted down her tattered-edged sealskin breeches. Then she stalked like a felon behind a pile of coiled ropes, scurrying to find somewhere to hide among the barrels, polished cleats and furled sails.

There was no hope she'd make it to port without being discovered. She tried not to think of what they might do when they found her. Seamen were cruel. 'The sea shows man no mercy, why should we?' Thebo said once. She could not recall what it was she had accused him of that elicited this response. Still, her husband's words rang in her ears as she peered from her hiding place and waited. She hadn't realized it would be so difficult to hold her nerve. After all, she was only trying to get home. She'd send them their money. She clung to a vision of a place of warm cinnamon biscuits and feather beds – the thin house off the Herengeracht where Marijke lived with her wealthy husband, thousands of miles away. Stowing away like this was forbidden and though dressed like a man, Karina would be the only woman aboard. The only woman. She'd decided and she must stick to her decision, she told herself as she clutched a rough rope, soft fingered in terror, as if she had to restrain herself from vaulting back over the side.

It didn't take long. A whistle sounded, a commotion burst on deck and she realized it was time. The men shouted orders in the moonlight and the ropes that tethered the ships to the bleakness of Deception were taken up. The tide was ready. Then, like a bell, there was a woman's voice – almost familiar. Karina raised her eyes just enough to see the squat Brazilian who ran the brewery offloaded down the gangplank in a flurry of flying bodice laces and the clinking of a bag of coin. The crew cheered as she strutted away with her earnings.

'All right, lads, settle down.'

Order was reinstated by a steely-eyed officer and all at once, it was suddenly too quiet, the wooden planks creaking as the *Erebus* and the *Terror* cast off onto starlit seas.

Two

When she woke, it was light again. Karina clutched her empty stomach and shifted on the hard surface below as she remembered what she had done the night before with a sense of disbelief. Had she really escaped? But here she was in the sealskin breeches, the knitted pullover and Thebo's old boots. She raised her hand and sure enough, her hair was shorn. She ran a finger from root to tip, stopping at her ear and marvelling at the strangeness of the empty space around her jawline. Above her the sky was moving. Her heart fluttered. *London would do fine*, she thought, and allowed herself a smile as she settled.

The spot she had chosen was auspicious, warm in contrast to the icy air, for, she realized, there was a stove directly below. Karina had not lit a fire in weeks. There had been no wood and no money, not even for whale oil which on Deception Island was cheaper than anywhere else the whole world wide. She hugged her knees to her chest, and slipped a single foot out of Thebo's old boot to warm her bare skin by the little chimney that jutted through the boards. What luxury. This occupied her only a minute or two before curiosity got the better of her.

Peeking around a stack of kegs, she positioned herself to watch the deck, alive with activity in the sunshine. Two boys, far younger than her twenty-four years, played some kind of ball game. From a distance, at the other end of the vessel, three men in smart uniforms studied the sky, pointing towards the horizon to illustrate whatever they were saying. She raised herself on her haunches, her eyes skimming the top of the barrels that were shielding her from view. Carefully she scanned all directions but there was no sign of the familiar shape of Deception Island's pale cliffs looming out of the spray. There was no sight of land anywhere. She breathed out slowly in relief and dropped down, instinctively curling her fist into her belly. That way it felt as if there was something inside. The smell of fish cooking in the galley taunted her nostrils but she was too afraid to reveal herself. They'd have to find her.

As she waited, her ear settled into the sound of English. Karina had always been adept at languages. When Thebo had been given his captaincy, they had spent two years in Maine. He had rented rooms that seemed more a dream now than a memory. There was a sofa upholstered in green velvet with tassels around the hem. There was a wrought-iron fireplace with a stack of logs to one side. She liked sitting there to read, when Thebo was at sea. 'Norwegian, are you?' the landlady had questioned, loitering by the door as she delivered the mail.

'Swedish,' Karina replied.

The old woman had nodded as if this was what she had meant. Some afternoons, Karina visited her in the downstairs parlour. The place smelled of petitgrain and beeswax and quickly her English had improved as the two women sat over a hand of cards, the tea cooling beside them. By the time the young couple had left for Thebo's new position at Deception Island, her English was better than her Spanish or her Dutch. Now it came back.

Men marched up and down the deck, cleaning the already sparkling brasses and uncoiling and recoiling piles of rope. They climbed the rigging and trimmed the sails. They hoisted flags to send messages to the *Erebus*, sailing in the ship's wake. On one side, junior officers carefully practised decoding the *Erebus*'s replies. The boys laughed when they got it wrong. 'Seven bells, imagine!' one said. 'Lord, Robert, you'll have us up early.'

Several times sturdy shoes and boots stopped so close that Karina could smell the polish, and yet, nobody hauled her from behind the barrels. Nobody noticed a thing. Two sailors fished over the side and an old man whittled wood, whistling an unfamiliar tune until he was called to the mess. Perhaps, she thought, they will be kinder than they need be.

By nightfall she had almost stopped worrying. It was as if she was invisible and instead of holding her breath whenever a sailor came within feet of her, she daydreamed of the island of Ven – the place she'd started out all those years ago. Her first home. The one she and Marijke had vowed to run away from so they could make their fortunes. It was Marijke who had fired the ambition. 'The island is so small,' she complained. 'How can Mother bear it?'

Other girls were content to play with dolls but Karina and her sister were strange creatures from the outset and the truth was Marijke was right: their mother was not entirely happy. With their father dead, she worked all hours, the little town's seamstress, sewing by such low light that she squinted even outside, when the sun was high. Their mother had taught them to embroider, but Karina had never taken to it. Marijke, on the other hand, worked flowers and birds onto their skirts. Sometimes when Karina woke and pulled on her clothes there was a new tattoo on her petticoat. A love heart or a key. 'The key to the world,' Marijke announced grandly.

'But what will we do when we leave?' Karina implored her sister.

Marijke shrugged. 'Trade what we have,' she replied.

Come the winter, the girls set up a snowshop on their doorstep selling snowballs and snow-bottles to the neighbours' children. Once there was even a snowcake which they rolled out of bed early to fashion from *fyklen*, the soft first falling, which holds together best of all. The children paid with buttons and occasionally suggested a special commission for the girls' pink fingers to fashion. Once they spent the afternoon making a snowdog that looked like a wolf for Sverre, the butchers' son. The next morning, he sneaked them a sausage to share, hot from the oven, as they joined the line of youngsters carrying *lykta*, the little candles that lit their way to the village school. Children came from all sides, specks of light in the darkness, joining together

12

on the old track. Still, Marijke had been determined to leave. She could not have been entirely sure of what lay beyond the little village but she knew it would be better. 'Soon we will be women setting out to cast our magic on the world,' she announced. She dreamed of cities with busy harbours and a panoply of adventure. Of people she didn't know a thing about. Of setting up a stall where the customers paid with coins, not buttons. The unknown.

On the *Terror*, Karina was hauled out of her daydreams by the neck. She had fallen fast asleep with the vision of Ven before her eyes and now it was dawn, she realized in a rush – her fourth day without a scrap of food. As rough-skinned fingers curled around her throat, her limbs lashed out and she struggled like a sparrow trying to fend off a hawk. The man who had hold of her was a giant. Her mind raced and if she had hoped for kindness, she realized now it was a forlorn notion. Across the open space of the deck she could make out the sailors she'd been listening to all these days – the men she'd seen only in snatches – a torso here and the rim of a hat there. They seemed suddenly huge, clustering in a mass as the sky lightened, calling for the mate, struggling to see the stowaway who had been uncovered. There was a whiff of stale rum and sweat on the air.

Round her neck, the fingers didn't loosen and Karina panicked that the man who had laid his hands on her was set on murder. He squeezed her windpipe and she wheezed as she steadied her limbs and forced herself to slow down and concentrate on breathing – staying alive. There was no measure in struggle. He stared glassy-eyed, as she made him out – a hefty black seaman with an immoveable jaw and fingers carved of stone. Another squeeze and her shoulders rounded and her knees gave way. The man sighed almost inaudibly as if he was bored by her fragility. *If he kills me, he kills me*, she thought, flat as if it meant nothing. A man like that could kill you by mistake.

The others, gathering behind the negro sounded increasingly bloodthirsty as she showed her weakness. Karina knew a thin, shivering lad by the ropes was only an occasion for sport. Men like these valued the entertainment in flogging a man or hauling him under the keel. Thebo's voice sounded in her head. *The sea is not kind, why should we be?* 'Go on,' the crowd jeered. 'Do for him. Do it.' Her eyes flared. For all the reputed English sense of fair play, she could feel the baying crew turn mob-handed and there was nothing she could do. Would they decide to hurl her overboard into the icy ocean? There were blocks of ice floating on the swell. No one could last long in that.

'What have we got here then?'

The voice was easy to discern. Later she would come to realize that the words of the officers were easier to follow than the words of the men, except one seaman who she would learn hailed from the Orkneys. The way the man formed his words sounded almost Norwegian and she picked out what he said more easily than the others.

14

'A stowaway is it? A stowaway?' This voice like cool air, like clean water – refreshing somehow.

The crowd was still growing. They came from all quarters. Karina scrambled again, though it was useless. She knew it would come to this. She could not stowaway for months of the journey without being discovered. Eventually she would have to eat.

'Well, let me through.'

The crowd parted as the young officer pushed forward and took charge. He was only a midshipman. The boy was dark-eyed and wore a cruel expression. His slick, pink mouth opened in a moist sneer like an oyster as he sized her up.

'This one is set to piss himself,' he said. 'And quite right. We do not take kindly to thieves and stowaways on board this ship.' He waved a hand as if conducting an orchestra. The black man loosened his grip and set Karina down, gasping.

'Well, what have you got to say for yourself?'

'I have stolen nothing, sir,' she scraped the words out.

'I have stolen nothing,' the midshipman repeated, aping her accent, playing to the crowd. 'Except your passage. Where are you from, boy?'

'I am Swedish. Here by way of Chile.'

'We did not dock in Chile, my fine gentleman. Play fair.'

She swallowed audibly, her mouth dry as sand. 'Deception Island, sir.'

'The whaling not to your taste?'

'I want to go home, sir. I want to work my passage.'

He circled, sizing her up to see how useful she

15

might prove. What he saw was a mere wisp of bone and muscle but there was no saying that she was not strong. 'Well now, let's see.' The midshipman was relishing this. He paused, about to pronounce judgement when, called by the commotion, the captain suddenly appeared behind him. Every man stood tall. Karina shifted. The midshipman's tone changed. 'Captain Ross, sir. We have a stowaway. The lad came on at Deception Island.'

Ross took in the scene. They allowed him space, Karina noticed. But then a captain always stood alone. It was, she realized, not the first time this man had found a stowaway on board his ship. 'A sharp dozen,' he prescribed without hesitation, almost as an aside.

This was the least she was expecting. It would be impossible to take her onto the crew without administering punishment for deserting her last station, whatever it might have been. She felt a sense of relief that she endeavoured to hide. The captain glared.

'It's a while before you'll see home, laddy.' He sucked his teeth.

Her eyes darted. 'Yes, sir. England will do as well.'

'England?'

Behind him the crew laughed, only barely managing to control themselves as Ross cast his eyes to silence them.

'England? We are not for England, boy. Nowhere near. We are for Antarctica. Did you not check before you stowed? There's no turning back. That will teach you!'

* * *

16

Karina coughed. She reeled in shock. She had taken this risk – this huge risk – and this little fleet was sailing in entirely the wrong direction. No one ever goes south, she thought, trying to take it in. No one. And yet these ships, the only ships in months . . . Her eyes filled with tears and she struggled to control herself. Her limbs felt weak. This meant no Marijke. This meant no Amsterdam. She had failed.

'Antarctica?' she croaked.

The captain did not reply. The matter was not up for discussion. 'Mr Bevan,' he called the cook. 'Could you use this one in the galley? He looks too scrawny for real sailing.'

Si Bevan stepped forward from the huddle of onlookers. His huge belly attested to the man's passion for his position. Karina, her mind still racing, could feel heat radiating from his body. The cook's skin seemed too pink, as if a child had drawn him. It struck her that she wouldn't be hungry any more. They weren't going to keel haul her. She would live. But here, not in the green, easy north. She would be further from home than before.

Bevan grinned, revealing a startling paucity of teeth. All but four or five were missing.

'Yes, sir,' he managed. 'I can always use a pair of hands in the galley.'

'I helped in kitchens before, sir,' Karina managed.

A snort emanated from Bevan's throat. The captain gestured to one of the crew. 'Well, first things first,' he said, and strong hands came down on her shoulders as she was taken away.

All she could think was *We are heading south.*
She had been so stupid.

At the mizzen, the bo'sun was ready to dispense twelve lashes without ceremony but still she kept thinking on what had happened. It made no sense. *South? There's nothing there. Why on earth would they want to go south?*

The bo'sun was half-hearted. He didn't remove her sweater. She was glad of it, though she was so thin now, she might as well be a boy. There was not a scrap of fat on her, not even there. It was months since a man would have noticed her breasts.

Most of the crew, already bored of the discovery, descended to the comparative warmth below decks. Only a handful clustered, lingering to see if the stowaway might scream. Karina contained herself, determined to show no weakness. She made herself focus on what was important – how long it might be until the ship turned northwards? *A while*, the captain had said. She fixed her jaw so no sound could escape. *At least I am moving*, she thought, *albeit in the wrong direction.* Saan er det bare. *That's just life. If I work, they will feed me.*

The bo'sun's first lash sliced the icy air and caught her unaware, but her jaw held. The man didn't put his back into it, but the leather still stung. Nauseous, she steeled herself for the next blow. The bo'sun struck in a perfunctory fashion but she counted the punishment carefully. *Two. Three. Four. And breathe.* In five minutes, she told herself, it will be over. In four minutes. In three. *Eight lashes, and a pause. Nine. Ten. His arm is*

18

tired, she thought. *Eleven.* She gasped out loud at the last of the dozen for which the bo'sun allowed himself a final flourish. She felt sick as she was untethered, but there was nothing in her stomach to vomit. Her head reeled.

'Here, lad,' the bo'sun said, nodding at the black man who had found her. Karina looked up and realized the fellow had a ring in his ear. She wondered how she hadn't noticed before. 'Hepworth will see you to the galley.'

The negro said nothing. Not then or any time after. Without even checking whether she was following, he led on. She couldn't help thinking that she didn't require an escort. Any fool could find the galley on a ship, let alone a fool who hadn't eaten in days. The corridor smelled of baking bread.

'Ah.' Bevan looked up as Karina stepped into his domain. His skin glistened by the light of the lamp. The smell of boiled pease hung in the air. The galley was dark, the walls lined with planks of wood the colour of well-toasted bread. 'We'll make a fine pair. A fat old cook and a half-starved scrap of a boy, eh?'

Hepworth nodded. His job completed, he disappeared down the corridor. Bevan cast an eye over the sorry state before him. He motioned for her to turn around and lifted the thick knitted top to inspect her injuries.

'He hasn't drawn blood,' he diagnosed. 'There's a bruise, is all. A graze really. It'll settle down. You took the beating well, lad.'

'How do you know?'

'You think you were the first down here?

19

Everyone knows everything on a ship such as this.' Without asking whether she was hungry, the cook handed her a horn cup of milk from one of the ship's goats. 'You could use some feeding.'

She didn't argue. The milk was warm and a thin wisp of steam rose, as the cup quivered in her hands. She couldn't stop quaking. Bevan ignored it. *Kindness at last*, she thought, as she slurped. It was difficult to restrain herself from gulping the rich creamy fluid without swallowing. She could have bathed, almost, in the smell of it.

'What did the captain mean, Mr Bevan?' she asked as she surfaced. 'We're not returning to England?'

'Not directly.' He spoke slowly. His accent it would transpire, was from the West Country and over time she would learn to discern it. 'We are for the Far South, boy. Captain Ross has led two expeditions to the Northern Circle. The Arctic, that is. And now he is set upon the southern continent. We have spent the last three years hereabouts. Half the year on the ice and half for resupply. He is gathering the measurements for a map, see.'

Her heart sank, even as Bevan handed over a chunk of rye bread with a thick crust. She dipped it in the milk and tried to slow her pace further. The food tasted alien. It had been a long time. A burst of malt opened on her palette as she relaxed enough to taste it. The feeling of warmth in her belly was both compelling and unsettling. It felt as if she was drunk and this exchange was some kind of heady dream. But

20

the dream was Amsterdam. The dream was Marijke – her sister's freckled cheeks and blonde hair. The way she smelled of fresh hay and silk still warm from the iron.

'How long will we stay in the south?' she asked.

The cook shrugged.

'We've food for more than a year on board as long as there's fishing. But we can restock near enough by. Deception Island or the Shetlands, I guess; the coast of the Australias or Van Diemen's Land, if we have to. We've done it afore.'

Her heart sank further. This meant that she might end up exactly where she started or, worse, even further away. Whatever happened, it would be a long time before she would see Amsterdam's wide harbour. That was sure. The food lulled her and sated now, her temper flared only slightly. Such bad luck again.

'But the ship will go back eventually. Home? Northwards?' she said.

Bevan had lost interest. 'What do you call yourself?' he asked.

Karina thought for a moment. She had no idea. She cursed herself for not planning better. For not checking where the ship was headed. For dozing like a fool, daydreaming about childhood days that were impossible to recover.

'You've got a name, haven't you, boy?' the cook checked.

She nodded. 'Karl.'

There it was, arrived out of nowhere; as close to her real name as she could muster.

* * *

She had a cousin Karl. Her mother had nursed the boy through the fever and then fell ill of it herself. She lasted only three days when her turn came. And that had been their escape in the end. A service was held in the little church. The priest gave a sermon. He said her mother had had heaven on earth. *Himlem par jorden.* Afterwards Karina had asked Marijke what that meant. 'Well,' her sister squared up, 'she's in heaven now, I suppose, wherever that might be.' The girls looked around furtively, for there was no saying.

Her uncle expected them to live with him. The death had transpired, after all, from the saving of his son's life. But he was their father's brother and Marijke swore their mother had told them to go and live with her cousin in Copenhagen. Karina nodded, sagely, backing up her sister's story. It was her mother's dying wish, the little girls held their ground. It was her instruction. Only thirteen, Marijke turned down all help. She had refused to listen to advice or reason. The village bustled, but there was nothing they could do. In the end, their uncle bought their tickets.

Efficiently, the girls sold everything and Marijke boarded herself and the eleven-year-old Karina onto a trawler and took passage across the sound. It had felt like she knew what she was doing. The two of them stood on deck holding hands as they watched Ven get smaller. This was how the summer visitors left. This is what they had been watching all the years. Karina hugged Marijke, nuzzling her sister's skin. That day she smelled of the island in summer, of grass and berries.

*   *   *

'You know how to make posset, lad?' Bevan asked.

Karina nodded, blinking as her mind swam.

'Show me.'

She put down the cup of milk and set aside the bread. 'The captain's partial,' Bevan chatted. 'He'd have posset every meal if we had the cream for it.'

The only way in life was to work hard. She lifted a bowl and began.

Three

Life in the galley was familiar. When the girls finally reached Copenhagen, Marijke secured a job with a dressmaker. She had inherited their mother's skill with a needle. The shop was five minutes' walk from Amalienborg and was frequented by women from the palace, though not the Queen. Still, it was a start. Marijke showed her embroidery folio and was immediately given room, board and a wage. Karina, however, had no aptitude with a thread. It always seemed to her that material (even fine material) was not malleable enough. With the help of Marijke's new employer, she found a job as a kitchen maid five minutes away, in the house of a French family who owned a string of bakeries. And there she encountered her first love – a meek and adoring thing that never came to fruition. Monsieur Albert came from Lyon and he ran the kitchen.

On the *Terror*, the first time Karina pulled a fruit pie from the oven, Si Bevan cut a slice and sank onto the galley stool. His eyes clouded.

'Where did you learn to fashion pastry?' he asked.

'My mother taught me,' she lied. The galley would hide her well, she realized. It kept her away from the sailors.

Si eyed Karina with dubiety. 'Well I never, lad.'

'I know what to do with cacao and honeycomb.'

24

She nodded towards the storeroom where she had found the potted fruit and a myriad of other culinary treasures. The sheer scale of the ship's supplies had quite overcome her. The storeroom smelled of malt and butter.

'Cacao? And where did you learn that?'

'Chile, sir.'

'Don't you sir me, boy. Si will do fine.' The old man laughed and paused before taking another bite of the pie. 'Extraordinary,' he proclaimed. 'My mother was considered a baker, but this . . .'

Ross had a sweet tooth, it transpired, and the new cabin boy made his mark at the captain's table. Hepworth took up the dishes – baked fish and rice. Cheese and cornbread. And then Si Bevan grinned as he handed over the final plate.

'Baked chocolate cream,' he announced. Hepworth raised a single eyebrow. Bevan sat on the stool, amusement emanating from his quivering frame. 'Go on then, take it in,' he instructed. 'Karl made it.'

The galley was cleared for the night and Karina was alone. Bevan slept in a hammock below, with the other men, but he'd given dispensation for the boy to sleep on the floor and mind the oven. After her bones being permanently chilled on Deception Island, on this first night the galley felt too hot and Karina struggled to sleep. The ship creaked, wood on wood, and there was no conversation or activity to distract her mind from falling into these cracks. It would take time to settle. Still, the work was hard and it felt good to be tired out after a long day. Here, she realized, she wasn't a burden. She had felt herself a burden too long. Slowly, the heat from the oven soothed her and creaking of the wood became a strange kind of lullaby.

It was after midnight when there came a knock on the frame of the door. Karina got up and pulled it back. The hard-eyed, dark midshipman stood in the passageway holding a candle. Karina caught a whiff of spirits as he leered drunkenly in her direction. Her heart skipped. 'Karl, is it?' he checked.

'Yes, sir.'

'It's the pastry.'

'Sir?'

'I was on shore leave in Argentina and they had this tart.' The boy gestured and Karina pulled back into the shadows. The midshipman laughed heartily. 'A tart. A baked tart. I'm not that way, boy. I prefer women.'

She felt herself blush.

'John Pearse,' he held out his hand.

She hesitated before she shook it. Pearse didn't appear to notice her reticence.

'It was crisp. Sweet. Made with custard. A small thing – only a mouthful or two but delicious. Dusted with cinnamon.'

'Like the Portuguese fashion them?'

'Ah. Portuguese. Yes. Maybe. It might have been a Portuguese hostelry, now you come to it.'

'They call them *pastel de natas*.'

'I see.' His tone was serious. 'It was very good. I wondered if you might . . .'

'I can try, sir.'

26

'Yes. Thank you.'

She smiled as she drew back the door. Perhaps it wouldn't be so bad here. She was fed, after all. And fed first, if it came to that. She'd get back to Marijke and life in a skirt, if only she could wait it out and keep herself to herself. It seemed somehow possible, in this odd situation, to get on.

Below decks the days passed. During the day with the oven fired up, it was boiling in the galley and noisy too. The *pastel de natas*, when she tried them, were a roaring success. 'Lad,' Si Bevan said, as if the word itself was a wonder.

Occasionally he sent her to fetch goat's milk. The animals were kept below. There were chickens in a coop – for eggs and for the meat. 'We'll keep them alive as long as we can,' Bevan told her. In the store, there was cheese stored in a wire-fronted cupboard to which he kept the key. And jute bags of sugar piled up. 'More than I thought we'd need,' the old cook admitted. He let her make what she wanted, instructing only a dessert for the captain or a soup for the men. He was speechless sometimes as she laid her offerings on the warmed metal plates.

'Where in heaven's name did you learn . . .' His voice trailed.

'Paris,' she replied smartly. Or Haiti. Chile. Lisboa.

Thebo had taken her around the world.

The news spread and a week after the chocolate cream and two nights after the *natas*, the officers of the *Erebus* rowed over to dine with their counterparts on the *Terror*. From below deck, Karina heard the rowboat clattering against the side of the ship.

'Permission?' they called up from the dark waters.

So strange, she thought. As if their friends had not invited them. As if the flags had not been raised. As if here on the blank waters, with nothing around, permission might be denied.

Ross kept fancy bottles of port among his many other luxuries and he released three for the dinner. Bevan had a pig slaughtered and roasted the belly, but it was Karina's spun sugar that was the object of the evening. A tranche of lemons was donated to it. She spent hours that afternoon creating a sculpture as fine as lace to tower over the citrus posset, as Bevan fussed around her, boiling rice and salting flesh. Even Hepworth stopped in his tracks when he saw what she had made. He grunted. The only sound he ever made.

At the end of the night, the plate came down clean but the last of the port was sent to the galley. A gentleman's thank-you. Bevan swore he preferred buttered rum but still, he splashed the rich red liquid into one of the captain's silver tumblers that had been returned for polishing. The cups were rounded on the bottom and didn't fall, no matter the keeling of the ship. The old timer downed a tot, then poured another a measure and passed it to Karina. As he watched her sip, he shuddered. The ovens had fired down, and the old man's blood was thin. 'It's cold where we're going,' he said. 'Cold! That's an understatement.'

Already the air seemed to eat the heat the further south they sailed. She gave him back the tumbler and Bevan smartly finished off the last of the bottle. 'Well done, lad,' he said, as he stumbled out of the galley for the night.

The next morning he arrived as pink in the face as ever. The dishes were cleaned and put away. Karina had already set the dough aside to rise.

'That's right. We mustn't forget the common men,' Si sounded almost relieved, as if her success with the spun sugar might have turned Karina's head. 'All this fancy cooking is one thing but the crew need to eat too.'

The men had taken to gathering above the stovepipe, where she had first stowed away, to smell the food in anticipation. There was, after all, little entertainment on board. Karina baked cornbread, which was both buttery and light. She became a curiosity, she supposed, but still, her days were busy and the galley and the storerooms became her world.

Eventually, when she had the confidence, she ventured above deck. It was late one night. Dinner was over and the crew were sleeping. The air was like cool, black silk on her face, the darkness punctuated by two lamps hoisted at the end of the ship so the *Erebus* could make them out. Across the water the other ship's lights moved smoothly in the *Terror*'s wake and beyond them only a wide well of darkness, the moon a mere sliver reflected on the surface of the water.

Karina shivered, relishing the freezing air as it filled her lungs. It was all but silent bar the wash of the tide. It felt good to be above decks, more or less alone in the darkness. No clattering of pots and pans. None of Si's chatter. She reached over the side to catch the breeze and wondered where on the map of the world Thebo had carried with him the *Terror* might end up. There had been nothing marked to the south of Deception that she could remember. Was it possible there was another country? And if so, what kind of men might live there?

'You're the stowaway,' a voice said suddenly behind her. She jumped and swung around. It was another officer, by the sound of him. But still, she could hear a little twist on the vowels.

'Sir,' she said, struggling to make out the man's face.

'Can't sleep, eh?'

'No, sir.'

'Nor can I. I thought I'd keep an eye out for the whale. He's been swimming alongside all afternoon. Did you see? I think it's too dark to catch sight of him now. There's no moon to speak of. Fascinating creatures.'

Karina shuffled. As her eyes adjusted she made out the man's frame. He wasn't wearing uniform – there was not a scrap of gold braid or button to catch what little light there was. The figure settled against the wooden rail.

'Did you work on a whaling ship?' he asked. 'Before?'

She wasn't sure how to answer. Thebo hadn't talked much about his work except there was no thrill like being the first to have his spear hit home. He'd had a strong arm and he was brave, by all accounts. That's what had done for

30

him. The one time he had misjudged it, he'd fallen foul of everything. Or that was what Van Kleek had told her when he came to deliver the news. 'He died just over halfway through the voyage,' he had said. What he meant was that he was not going to advance her the captain's bonus that was due on return from a successful whaling trip because Thebo had not completed what he set out to do. Van Kleek paid her from his purse – a derisory sum but there had been no point in arguing.

'I'm not a whaler,' she said, deciding she couldn't keep up the conversation if it turned that way.

'Shame. You might have been able to reckon them for me. I'm the botanist, you see. The zoologist.'

'Botanist?'

'I record the plant life and the animals. I collect samples for the herbarium at Kew. Back at home. Near London. And for the Royal Society too.'

'I have never been to London,' she admitted.

The officer warmed to his subject. 'Oh, it's a wonderful city. The biggest and best in the world.'

Karina did not tell him she had heard it was a stinking, rat-infested hole and that the river that ran through it was as good as slime. Thebo always said you cannot trust the English. Danish sailors had not forgotten the war, the battle of Copenhagen. Nelson and Napoleon were as bad as each other, Thebo had sworn.

'You're from London?' she turned the conversation back on the man, with a sting of resentment that he had intruded into the luxury of the dark silence.

The officer remained bluff. 'I'm from Glasgow. It's to the north. The name means Green Meadow.' He laughed. 'Sorry. It's just so dark.' He paused before continuing. 'You were a lucky find for us, boy. Standards at the captain's table have risen considerably since you came aboard. Ross said he almost regretted the flogging. The ship you left must certainly mourn your loss. What's your name?'

'Karl, sir.'

She loitered, deciding she must not come up like this again. It was too dangerous. The officer waited but there was nothing more to say.

'Well, Karl,' he ventured. 'I'll go to the heads, I expect.'

'Yes, sir.'

'Goodnight.'

Karina thought no more about it, but the man in the darkness called for her the next day.

'Mr Hooker asks you deliver his plate. He has it in his cabin,' Si Bevan announced.

'The botanist?' It was a guess but a fair one.

'Hark at you. Yes. And the ship's doctor, if it comes to that. You're quite the favourite. Well, don't dawdle.'

Hepworth usually served the food. He had a jacket the captain had supplied which he wore for the purpose. He was, she'd heard it said, the image of a famous footman who served the royals. There was a portrait – not of Hepworth but of the other man.

Hooker's cabin was the second largest after the captain's own. Karina knocked smartly and entered. Inside, several lamps were burning, positioned round the botanist's desk. Every surface was covered with books and sheaves of paper laid untidily about. In the eye of it all, the botanist was cataloguing a pile of fish bones over which a brass magnifying glass was set on a pole. He was the same age as she was, she noted, now she could see him in the light. His hair was brown, almost nondescript, though he sported extravagant sideburns and had a sensitive face, she thought. The doctor was bent on concentration. As he peered at what he was doing, his spectacles slipped slightly down his nose.

'The bone density changes as you get further south,' Hooker said absentmindedly, gesturing her to come in and pointing at the only clear space in the room, beside him. Carefully she laid down the tray and peered at the skull of a large cod.

'You're probably good at filleting 'em, eh?' Hooker said.

'No, sir. My skill is with the oven. Pastry, mostly. And some sugar.'

He sniffed in the direction of the food and lifted the fork, only with difficulty taking his eyes off the magnifying glass. 'Smells good. Well, as good as I can make out. Have you noticed that the colder it gets, a fellow's sense of smell is impaired? It must affect your cooking, I imagine. I would make a study, but it's almost impossible. No standardization, you see. You can't measure it.'

Karina hovered but he didn't dismiss her. She felt her curiosity piqued. 'Why don't you dine with the other gentlemen, sir?'

Hooker paused. He sat back in his chair. There

33

was something elegant about the doctor. He pushed his hair off his face and she took in the thick nap of his velvet jacket. He wore a scarf bundled at the neck. The scarf was silk.

'I'm sorry.' Her eyes plummeted to the boards at her feet. Her question had overstepped the mark. 'I'm sorry,' she said again, and edged towards the door.

'No.' Hooker stopped her. 'It's a fair question, boy. Conformity, you see, is normal in the navy. Not only in the navy. We are queer creatures, we men. We like to ape each other.'

'Creatures, sir?'

'I dine some nights with the other officers but sometimes it does not please me and the truth is, I am the only one with an excuse. I have my work and I am not strictly speaking an officer. That is, a naval man. So if I say that I must catalogue fish bones or see to a sailor with the fever, I can go my own way.'

Karina's eyes landed on the pile of fish bones.

'Science,' Hooker said. 'And before you question it, I asked for you because Hepworth does not speak. He never utters a word. You've never heard him, have you?'

Karina smiled. Men didn't talk to women this way. They didn't include them in their scientific endeavours or gossip about the crew. 'No, sir.'

'I have examined him. There is no medical reason I can make out for his silence but he will not be encouraged. In any case, this seemed an altogether more pleasant arrangement.' Hooker slid his fork into the slice of pie.

'Sir,' she cut in, 'that is the pudding. The dessert.'

The doctor grinned. 'A fellow can eat whichever way he prefers. In his own quarters.'

'Yes, sir,' she said.

'All right then,' he waved her off.

As she turned for the door she caught sight of a leather case, open on the bunk. Inside there was a saw and several other surgical tools.

'I haven't had to use that yet this year,' Hooker said, swallowing his first bite and shifting back towards his desk. 'Let's hope I don't have to use it at all.'

Four

She was woken first by a whistle and then by a bell – an unholy racket from above. Outside the small porthole it was light but still too early for Bevan to have lumbered in and taken his place by the stove. They had fallen into a routine over these first few weeks. Si prepared the meat or fish and Karina bent over the block making pastry or bread, rolling it out when it was ready. Si had always kneaded in a bowl on his lap before. Karina shook her head slowly when he showed her.

'None of your cheek, Karl,' he had insisted with a smile.

In the evenings, Karina turned out some kind of confection to delight the officers. The brioches and nut pies had become so commonplace that Bevan had ceased to remark on them. Then, once the officers' table had been served, Karina would deliver the doctor's tray. It was the same every day. But this racket was unusual. In the morning the ship was generally quiet.

She jumped to her feet, stretching out the stiffness in her limbs after the night on the boards. She had filled out a little, but not so much as to betray her and in this weather the men went around swaddled in any case, even doing their business at the heads. Above, the sound of whooping started on deck – the men cheering and shouting. She put aside the blanket she had been given. It had got colder as the journey had worn on. And then colder, still. The captain had ordered heavy greatcoats to be cracked out for every man and day on day, the crew who had business visiting the galley seemed wearier. A week further in and the use of hats, cuffs and collars was ordered. They were issued as uniform, but it was still difficult to get warm right through and even if you succeeded, it didn't last – the weather went from freezing to even colder and back again. There were more blocks of ice than open water and a watch was mounted for icebergs, day and night. The pace of the ship had slowed.

Karina's eyes darted as the noise above became more insistent. Then the galley door burst open and Hepworth looked in.

'What is it?' she asked uselessly.

He motioned and turned tail, setting off down the corridor. There was nothing else for it, she realized, and fell into step behind him. Above, the sky was bright. In the chill air, the port side thronged with men. Hepworth pushed his way through with Karina still in his wake. Bevan was at the rail and she slipped into place beside him. Ahead was a jaw-dropping coast of white cliffs – stark and thrilling. After weeks of all but vacant sea, they rose like a blue-and-white cathedral that glistened in the oncoming sunlight – a strange and deadly sculpture.

'Is that it? Is that where we're going?' she asked.

The men's cheers seemed to disappear over the side, swallowed by the piercing silence. There was a kind of glamour, a magic hanging in the chill air. She felt it draw her in from the first – the sheer emptiness of the place. It seemed too clean.

'Aye.' Bevan nodded. 'That's it all right.'

'And nobody knew it was here?'

'I wouldn't say that. There was never a map. There were sailors' tales of course. But we are the first to take proper soundings.'

'Where do we port?' she asked. 'What is the town called?'

Bevan laughed. 'Town? Nobody lives here. This is the summer, boy. Think what the winter must be like. How could anyone live here? No, there's nothing but ice and snow and a few lousy birds. You'll see. It's the emptiest place in the world, and that's the truth.'

Karina gasped and then shuddered. There was something majestic about the ice cliffs ahead. Something ominous.

On the *Erebus*, they had hoisted flags but she could not read their meaning. Below the cheering, though, she discerned a low grumble, no matter that with the great white continent came the prospect of limitless fresh water melted from the ice. The men knew the dangers. Around her they enumerated them in a low chatter. There were treacherous, submerged icebergs and the lottery of distinguishing between what was land and what was only frozen brine. The seawater was always in rotation – freezing and melting so that deadly plates of ice peppered the surface close to the land and, the men said, even in summertime, the weather beggared belief.

'She's like some beautiful whore who puts

38

you through misery,' the ship's carpenter, Archie, said to Bevan with a sigh.

The cook nodded. These men had followed Ross to the Northern Circle and signed up again, for this tour of duty in the south.

'There ain't no snow bears, which is a crying shame. Down here the birds are useless for eating and the seals ain't much better,' Bevan complained. 'Some days it seems almost warm and then out of nowhere the wind rises.'

Karina turned away. At the other end of the ship some of the able seamen were whooping into the silence and laughing. Then, last on deck, ever one to make an entrance, Captain Ross appeared and the men parted. The grumbling abated and so did the cheering.

'It's a veritable fiesta,' the captain commented regardless.

Behind him, Hooker, resplendent in a large fur hat that rested low on his brow, pushed into the space created by the captain's wake. His eyes were shining and his cheeks glowed with the cold.

'Back again, eh, Joseph?' Ross said. 'And we are to start at Penguin Bay, so you shall have your way.'

'The Royal Society will be most exercised,' Hooker replied. 'We must collect as many as we can.'

'Indeed. Well, let's get her to anchor.'

An order was called and the men dispersed. It was impressive, Karina thought, like some kind of machine. Up till now she had only caught sight of the running of the ship now and then

– as she peered out from behind the barrel or noticed something underway as she passed. She had sailed the world wide but never on a vessel like this. The English were famous for their navy.

'Karl,' Bevan called her, as he turned to go below, but she lingered alone at the rail, drawn to the whiteness of the vast plain, almost glad that she was here to see it as the men scrambled to their duties.

Below, the bread was baking and hard tack and hot rum had been issued by the time Karina got back to her station. She set herself to preparing pease broth in an iron tub.

'You took your time,' Bevan said without looking at her.

'Sorry.'

'Never seen anything like it before, then?'

She shook her head. 'What will we do here?'

Bevan laughed. 'What will we do? Well, you, my fine lad, will cook.'

She hunched over the pot and poured in some barley. 'And the rest of them?'

'They'll do as they're told. Lord, you're like a woman, fussing so.'

This comment silenced her. Thebo used to complain the same. 'You're like an old woman,' he'd say when she asked him for details about his boat or took an interest in the flora. If she asked about money, he sulked. As a result, they used to squabble. It was easy, in the intimacy of marriage to annoy each other, she'd found, especially towards the end. He had taken the commission on Deception Island for the money alone. Van Kleek offered good wages. Their plan was to stay for two years and save enough to return to Copenhagen – Thebo's home town. 'You can go to Amsterdam, to your sister's house,' he said, ever the captain and in charge.

What he meant was, that once they were across the Atlantic she could leave him and start again. Unsaid, it was what they both wanted. There was no ill will, but the marriage was over.

When Thebo went to sea that last morning, Karina had been almost relieved as he slammed the front door. There was a moment's silence in contemplation of a couple of weeks alone to read, to enjoy, to explore and make the best of it. Then a sting of annoyance as the door opened and he came back. He had forgotten his sweater – the thick one that she had knitted when they decided to come so far south.

'Yes, yes,' she said, as she fetched it in the candlelight.

She was always a dutiful wife, but Thebo hadn't laid his hands on her in months. Not even in the night. Not even fast asleep. Not even if she asked him with her eyes. She wasn't compliant enough for him. She asked too many questions. She had tried to contain her curiosity but there was only so much disinterest she could feign.

'Goodbye,' she had nodded.

No touch. No kiss.

The truth was she hadn't cried for her husband when he died. She didn't hate him but she didn't love him either. The memory made her feel guilty. The marriage had ignited in a flurry of passion

41

and at first the intrigue of travelling had fanned the flames. Thebo had liked her questions then – when he had been the one who could hold her spellbound with tales of streets lined with lilac trees in the south of Spain, of drinking cacao hot and spiced, sitting in the dappled shade. She had been slack-jawed at the horrors of the slave markets on the African coast that still abided, despite being outlawed. At the beauty of carved conch shells. At the money to be made. But then she had seen it for herself, Thebo was no longer a man of the world, and she started to ask questions he couldn't answer.

That last morning she had turned away from the shadowy sight of her husband heading towards the dock, knowing he would be whaling for almost a month. They had made a deal and were in it together until it was fair for them to part. In the meantime, Karina's duty was to wait. She curled under a blanket and read Holberg from a tiny tattered-edged book that had accompanied her on all her travels. She knew the text by rote but she liked to hold it anyway. The thick leather bindings felt comfortable in her hands, adding weight to the poetry. Thebo walked alone to the harbour. She never saw him again.

In the *Terror*'s galley, Karina tripped against the stove and pulled back from the heat. Bevan laughed and the sound jolted her guilty imaginings. Sometimes an idea got a grip but there was nothing she could do to change things. Not now.

'Giddy, are you?' the old cook asked. 'We've anchored, lad. The boat's not moving.' Carefully she found her feet as Bevan eyed her. 'You're not much of a sailor,' he commented. 'You look white as a ghost. Take a turn on deck. Go on.'

She stumbled out of the galley. She hadn't thought of Thebo for weeks. Now she tried to haul her mind back onto the *Terror*. Ross had ordered the ships anchored close to shore. On deck, the crew were moving as one, the *Erebus* its mirror image. One lad, dallying by the rail, received a sharp lash from the bo'sun and jumped back to his duties with a last longing glance at the other ship.

'It's his brother,' the bo'sun said. 'On the *Erebus*. I wonder we shouldn't unite them, but they are needed where they are.'

Karina did not reply. The bo'sun was not so much cruel as lazy. 'You got the still sickness? Land legs?' he asked, seeing the state of her. 'Bevan can't have you being sick into the soup, eh?' An amused expressed played across his mouth and disappeared as if his skin had absorbed it.

Karina settled by the bowsprit as the men collected ropes and boxes of instruments. Joseph Hooker fussed around a bundle of jute sacks. 'Mind yourself, Karl. The frost will get you.' He nodded towards her boots, these days fortified by navy regulation stockings and a pair of socks that Bevan had supplied. She understood the dangers. Ven was cold in winter, though, it struck her, it had never got colder than she was now, here, in the polar summer. She knew the dangers. If you did not stay warm, your extremities went white, which was called frostnip. If

43

this was not tended the affected areas blackened and died.

'I doctor the men as best I can but last year five men lost fingers. It's all in the education. Be careful,' Hooker warned her. 'You have to learn to watch for it.'

'Will it kill a man, sir?'

'You cannot carry dead flesh with the living. Not for long.'

At the portside, three midshipmen, Pearce among them, were taking measurements with the glacial jagged white vista behind them. 'This is where we stopped taking soundings last year,' Hooker explained. Now we must chart every nautical mile to the south from here on. For the captain's map, you see.'

'So we will go further south?'

'Not today. Today,' Hooker grinned, 'I shall have a shot at my penguins.'

'And on shore, sir, you will move on foot?'

'Yes.'

'At home, the men use dogs in such conditions. Dogs and sleds. In the far north, the Sami use reindeer.'

'As cold as this?'

'In the winter,' she confirmed.

'We won't go inland. We're not equipped for it. But dogs, eh? That is an interesting idea. You must tell me more when you bring my tray. You're a bright young fellow, Karl.'

Hooker tied the last of his bundles and the men who were chosen for the mission piled into two crammed rowing boats lowered for the purpose and loaded with equipment. Karina stood with the rest of the crew and watched as they set out slowly across the sound. On land, such as it was, the colony of birds teemed with life.

'Strange-looking creatures,' one fellow observed.

Karina nodded. They were odd – almost human-looking as they waddled across the ice.

'Penguins,' the sailor said sagely and turned away.

On deck, several of the men fetched sketch-books and settled to draw their observations as they kept watch over the exploratory party. The stunning scenery proved difficult to capture on paper and soon became reduced to a solemn series of measurements, scientific theories and superstition. Going ashore was dangerous and it was considered a grave duty – part honour, part forfeit. At any second, the landscape or weather could change. Those left behind felt some kind of guilt, it seemed. What was the point of guilt, she wondered. What was the point of it?

'Last year we near lost Harry,' one commented.

Harry, a thick-set northerner, took a penny whistle out of his pocket and blew on it. 'Well, I am alive, aren't I? But I wouldn't go ashore again. That ice shelf could crack easy. Any time.'

'Did you see your end?'

'Near as. I was lucky, I got a hold,' the man said and not wanting to talk about it, he settled to play an air. Karina tried to stop herself wondering what Thebo had seen at the end. Did he regret setting her aside? Had he thought of her at all? Really, this wasn't helpful, she scolded herself and instead, she settled on a barrel to watch the shore party.

From this vantage point, watching the men

45

move among the birds made for entertainment. Pearce stood with an eyeglass, holding the brass just shy of his skin lest the cold burned him. He barked a laugh now and then at the comic goings on as Hooker and his men disembarked. When they got close to the colony the birds pecked the party fiercely. The penguins might look as if God made them for the sole purpose of amusement, but their beaks were deadly.

Next to her, one man took in a sharp breath as the first bird made an attack. 'I got caught by one last year,' he said. 'That'll nip.'

All afternoon the sailors observed the birds' splashing, squabbling family lives while Hooker and his party carefully measured and inspected the flock and its rookery. Karina lingered, astonished to hear Hepworth giggle as the Adélie penguins jostled at the water's edge. The men wagered their rations on which bird would be sent tumbling into the jaws of a predator by his cruel fellows, for they tried to trick each other into diving into the water to see if there was a predator waiting. Gales of laughter echoed from below, a cheer going up when one of the birds tipped into the jaws of a seal.

'It gives you something to look at,' one man declared.

Two of the sailors whittled the distinctive squat shape of the birds out of old bone. Below deck, Bevan's friend, Archie, had composed a song that became an on-board favourite called 'Old Fellows on the Ice'. It seemed, Karina thought, quite jolly.

Then the killing started. The penguins had no idea of the men's intentions and neither had she.

She put her hand to her mouth to stop herself crying out. She wasn't squeamish. She had been brought up on an island among fishermen. Then she lived on Deception where there was no indignity spared God's creatures. She had throttled razor-billed gulls with her bare hands, when she was hungriest, those last months. But the penguins, in the main, were trusting little things. It was a shame. Still, she could not take her eyes off the slaughter as the ice was peppered with red and the pile of bodies grew. Beside her two men gambled on whalebone dice. She wondered how they could ignore what was happening.

When it was over, and Hooker had what he wanted, the shore party came aboard, proud to have been this year's first on the virgin ice. Hooker directed the men as the cargo came up. Pearce helped him, seeing the ropes recoiled and stowed and the rowing boats secured in place. The doctor took a shot of spirits from a silver hip flask in a leather case and surveyed the carcasses to make sure they were not damaged.

'Here,' he called Karina.

She hung back. She did not want to touch the dead birds at her feet. They were too large – somehow too solid. From far off they had looked tiny. Hooker thrust his leather bag into her arms. 'Put it beside my desk,' he ordered, and she fled.

In the galley a few of Bevan's cronies gathered to gossip. Karina set herself to preparing fish soup. Her hands shook as she cut the flesh. The men ignored her. Clearly nobody aboard was shocked by what had happened. Perhaps they had seen it all before.

'I wonder could you skate on it?' Bevan asked, as if the Antarctic was only a vast, village pond frozen over at Christmas. He had never been off the ship here to try for himself.

Archie shrugged. In pantomime fashion, he held his nose, all the cockier for being the one who had had the experience.

'It looks pristine but the birds stink, Si. I was brought up on a pig farm and I never smelled the like. You don't expect it here. The whole place gives me the shakes, and not only for the cold. 'Tis an eerie old outpost,' he pronounced. 'Once you're off the water. Out there. It's like you're being chosen for death. God knows what spirit's hanging over the old place.'

It was not the first time that Karina had heard talk of a ghostly spirit on the ice. Rumours circulated and some of the crew declared they did not want to go ashore. There was a whisper that the men who had had the ice underfoot had been somehow touched and were now part-wraith.

'I can hardly sleep when we're this close,' Archie admitted.

Karina listened silently. She had never believed in ghosts. Marijke hadn't either. On Ven, the children had told stories on the dark nights but Marijke had just laughed. 'There is nothing but you can touch it,' she swore. And, as in all things, Karina had formed her view likewise. What point was there in scaring yourself? Once or twice, after Mother died, Karina wondered if she might not see her again, but *Mor* never appeared. She

48

didn't like to think of it. She turned towards the cooking pot. Archie was right about the birds. Her sense of smell was not so impaired that she hadn't caught a whiff of them. Poor things.

That evening, when Karina delivered the doctor's tray, Hooker was bluff. He had enjoyed himself. 'I'll preserve one of these successfully. I'm sure of it,' he said as he rolled down his sleeves and turned towards his food.

'You tried before?' she asked.

'The carcasses rotted. They seemed to rot no matter what I did. I bought more alcohol for pickling them this time,' he said cheerfully, as he picked up a soft chunk of bread and bit into it.

Her eyes must have betrayed her or perhaps her skin had paled.

'Are you all right, boy? Not squeamish are you?'

Karina ignored the question. 'They say there is a ghost. Some kind of Valkyrie. On the ice.'

Hooker snorted. He had no more truck with superstition than she did. He was a man of science and a stolid Scot. But at least it might divert him from uncovering her weakness. 'Nature scares people,' he commented. 'It is the majesty of it. They want to put a word to their fear.'

He scarcely stopped working as he ate, throwing her a few details here and there, as if he was feeding a puppy from his plate. Carefully he notated the details he had taken of the landscape and the birds' behaviour. 'Interesting,' he said. 'The females seem independent.'

Karina ventured a question. 'How do you tell a female penguin from a male one?'

Hooker laughed. 'It is tricky,' he said. 'They are

49

almost identical, but the males are larger, more or less. Body and beak. Even I can't always be sure.' He seemed satisfied that she was taking an interest. 'They must be very ancient, don't you think?' he said. Karina only murmured.

After he had finished eating, the doctor let her carry his things up on deck where he unfurled his surgeon's kit on a barrel. The sky was still light – the darkness retreated more each day and soon there would be no night at all. The ice mountains in the distance cut the air like a knife. 'I have to get to it before they freeze solid,' he said.

She made herself watch while he skinned the carcasses. He was strong for a gentleman, she thought, and competent. He seemed to be enjoying himself though the unravelling of the birds' anatomy was ghoulish. This was a particular kind of butchery. Karina had never killed anything that wasn't for food. She felt like escaping into the warmth of the galley but the spectacle of gristle, bone and bill kept her rooted to the spot.

Two sailors scrubbed the deck around the doctor with seawater, their hands raw and pink. One flung a brush in Karina's direction. 'Too hoity-toity, are you?'

She fell on her knees, one eye still on the doctor's work, and helped them.

Afterwards, Hooker collected the constituent parts. He ordered the pelts to be dried on wooden airing frames positioned around the stoves in the men's quarters. This proved a point of contention, for to have a place so close to the fire taken up by a dead creature was never going to be popular.

50

The officers ignored the men's complaints and prioritized the penguins. One or two of them, the captain included, came to survey Hooker's work.

'It's for the greater good,' Ross insisted, and hushed below decks, out of the officers' hearing, the men aped him.

Last of all, flecked in blood, Hooker washed in tepid seawater warmed in the galley. It was well beyond midnight. She wondered if he regretted the killings.

'Another day you must tell me about those dogs,' he said with a yawn.

Five

For the most part, cold or not, Karina found
herself content aboard the *Terror* as the ships
made their way down the coast. The slaughter of
the penguins over, business proceeded as before.
The midshipmen were constantly on deck over-
seeing the taking of soundings and the recording
of measurements. The first week the weather was
fine. 'Clear as a bell,' Bevan proclaimed. When
they could, they fished for food – drawing aboard
their prey of lumbering seals, as well as smaller
sea creatures. Prompted by hunger, it wasn't long
before the crew attempted to kill a whale, but
it was a particular skill. No man on the *Terror*
had Thebo's deadly aim or, Karina thought, his
determination.

Ten days in, in the absence of other game,
they anchored once more and resorted to another
penguin cull, though this time to better purpose.
Si stood over the carcasses in the galley, his
filleting knife dripping in blood and his woollen
jacket flecked with gore.

'Last year we did this,' he said, his tone making
it clear that he held out little hope that the meat
would be palatable. 'Maybe you can make it
better.'

Karina tried. She melted blubber and then
fried over such meat as there was, which seemed
mostly comprised of fat and gristle. It was bound

to be tough, she thought, adding a small beer and averting her face. After half an hour she dipped in a spoon. The concoction tasted meaty and fishy at once and the smell of the Old Fellows on the Ice as they bubbled in the pan was pungent to say the least.

'I think the birds smell better alive,' she said.

'Come now, every animal is better cooked, surely,' Bevan laughed. But still, his face crinkled when he tasted the stew. At length, they decided it would turn stomachs more delicate than those of Her Majesty's finest. Nothing was to be wasted though. The men were served the penguin with hard tack and the officers had it in a pie with a blubber crust.

Both treated the novelty of the meal like a scientific experiment. Even the common men might have been discussing dinner served in a fancy restaurant, as if the tough hunks of fatty flesh were a delicacy imported from Paris.

'Archie says a little sauté might make it better,' Bevan noted. 'Or a sauce.'

Karina shook her head. There was nothing that could improve the meal. 'It's foul flesh, even freshly slaughtered,' she proclaimed. 'They are having their revenge on us.'

Bevan nodded sagely, as if it were possible that the birds might decide to taste unpalatable through sheer force of will. Karina did not argue with him. She did not eat that night. 'Let's hope the fish and the seal hold out,' she said.

Two weeks in, the ships hit their first storm and it became apparent that the weather in the deep south hit hard and without warning, as the blizzard obliterated the blue above and all visibility with it. The *Terror* anchored in a bay, men working at the double as the cry went up to batten down the hatches. At anchor, the ship rocked violently and everyone kept below decks bar two lookouts – who lashed each other to the mast so the wind could not take them.

Below, the whisper went up that they had lost sight of the *Erebus*. The wind was howling like a banshee.

'Sound the bell and light the lamps,' came down the order from Ross himself and the men sprang to it.

The weather ate the chimes though, as if they were the tiny tinkling of a child's toy. There was no hope for the lamplight either as the thick air swallowed it. Below, hot rum was served in the mess and the men huddled together as the ship creaked and strained.

Karina had the strangest sensation of being alone. It was a whisper of what it might be to be dead, she thought. Everyone on board had the same eerie sensation as they sat together, waiting. It was the *Erebus* that was absent but the *Terror* that was lost. The boy whose brother sailed on the other ship, wept. Karina pulled a biscuit from her pocket and offered it to him but he waved her away.

'Come on, lad,' one sailor offered. 'We should pray.'

And together the men recited the Lord's Prayer.

When finally the blizzard died and the water settled, the whole crew streamed on deck. The last of the watch were given blankets and hot toddy. Pearce ordered the bell tolled once more. And they waited, in sight of land. For an hour there was no sign. Silence fell over the crew and the bell sounded melancholy. And then one man spotted her. He screamed, 'The *Erebus* ahoy! The *Erebus*!' and everyone came hammering across the deck to see for themselves. The bell picked up its pace and it was as if there was a carnival as the ship sailed back into view. The flags were raised hurriedly. 'All's well,' the men shouted as they saw the reply. 'All's well. We survived the storm.'

Ross came to see for himself as the crew danced to the hornpipe, all movement swaddled by thick clothing, but still they danced and their fellows danced back from the other deck. Two men with broken limbs were rowed over for treatment and welcomed like kings, hoisted aboard and transported to Hooker's cabin.

'If we'd lost the other ship,' Si started, but could not finish his sentence for the prospect was too dreadful.

As the polar summer wore on, darkness disappeared. In the unrelenting light, the glare from the snow affected men's eyesight. Without darkness to mark the nights and with the place engulfed in immense silence, it was easy to feel awash in time. No one slept the night through. The endless frozen sun was unexpectedly troublesome. For some reason it felt as if the never-ending light was the men's greatest difficulty – or at least the easiest one to admit.

'Men are animals who wake in the light and

sleep in the dark. At least that is what we are used to,' Hooker declared privately as Karina served him. The doctor's cabin became more piled with books and bones, day by day. Through the window the sky was the only clear space. She couldn't take her eyes off it. 'You never know what you might learn by studying these conditions, Karl,' the doctor said sagely, peering over his spectacles at the wooden bowl of stewed fish she had laid before him.

For herself, Karina struggled to see the purpose in the doctor's notes. The information seemed impossible to classify – a strange jumble of facts and observations.

As the cold wore on, the men's eyes ached from the glare and lack of sleep. Hooker kept a log of medical complaints. He did not note, however, that below decks there was dissent. The men grumbled incessantly.

'Nothing is as it seems – the sea turns to ice, the ice is land and the night is bright as summer,' Karina heard one man complain. 'I'll not come back another year. You don't know where you are here.'

The light affected her less than the others. If anything, it seemed natural. In Ven, celebrations had been held at the summer's sunny midnight, though on the island her childhood summers had been hot. She slept easily, the only one on the ship by all accounts. That said, there were other changes. As Hooker had predicted, Karina soon found she could smell nothing and yet food still tasted good. She had become accustomed to eating. After the privations of Deception she put on weight though not everyone was so lucky and for some the pain of the cold (for in such conditions there was inevitably pain) was terrible. Not everyone spent their days in the warmth of the galley. Hooker dispensed advice. In the evenings, when she delivered his tray, there was often a sailor being treated in the doctor's cabin. On these occasions, she became his assistant – passing bandages and dispensing rum.

The doctor clearly cared about the welfare of the crew and she noticed that when he treated them, he did so with such kindness that she found herself well-disposed towards him despite his brutality in the matter of the penguins. The glassy-eyed medical men she had known in other ports showed their patients little care. She hardly recognized the man who had ripped the bird flesh to pieces as she watched him spooning hot soup into his charges. Two men lost toes and one a finger, but it would have been far worse had the doctor not been so kind.

One evening, Karina laid down the tray on his desk and hovered. Hooker had given an injured sailor his seat. It was odd for him not to be at his station. The man looked afraid. She smiled to comfort him as he held out his hand for Hooker to inspect. He was quivering.

'It's an ice burn,' the doctor diagnosed.

'Burned, sir?'

'I know it sounds odd. But ice will burn just the same as fire.'

'I was on fishing duty. It was so cold my fingers felt like they were made of wood.'

'You mustn't hold onto the ice blocks. Even if

you need to clear the net. It's painful now, I bet. But you'll live.'

Hooker rifled his shelves and handed the man a pot of salve.

'Put that on it, and no more fishing until it is healed. Tell them, those are my orders.'

The man looked satisfied. He had come to see the doctor thinking he might lose his hand. Now he saluted.

'Thank you, sir.'

As he left the cabin, Karina laid the cutlery. She had come to enjoy the time she spent in Hooker's cabin. She liked tidying the bandages and fetching hot goat's milk for the recent amputees, as Hooker chatted about botany and geology. Si said the store was almost out of feed and the animals would be slaughtered soon. She wondered what they would give the invalids then.

'Poor chap,' Hooker said. 'This cold almost makes you wish for a fever. Can you imagine the winter?'

Karina had been given a woollen waistcoat from the stores and wore it over her other clothes. It was impossible to get warm right through but you could stave it off. 'Reminds you of home, I expect?' Hooker said, as he inspected the tray.

'The winter can be cold where I come from.'

'An island, you said?'

'I left when I was young.'

'The islanders are good men.' Hooker smiled. 'At least, that's what they say where I come from. Men and women from our islands are tough.'

Karina laughed. 'I don't know about that.'

He rubbed his eyes and pushed his hair off his

face. Then he searched the desk for his glasses. 'Very good, Karl,' he said, dismissing her as he picked up his spoon.

As Karina walked down the corridor she wondered why he'd sent her away. Perhaps tonight he was tired. The doctor's cabin was the most interesting on the ship. Once she had arrived to find he had bottled a penguin in a chemical solution, sealed in a large glass jar. The bird's little body bobbed with the movement of the ship, an eerie spectacle. She wondered where he had got it, for they had not been ashore that day.

'Don't ask,' he advised, reading the question on her face.

Perhaps it was this – that he seemed to know her. In time, they had become firm friends or at least as much as might be tolerated across the ranks. He found her useful – an extra pair of hands. Some days the doctor wrote his journal, scribbling in tiny writing, hardly looking up. 'I swear I need to get this onto paper,' he said. 'I worry that the ink will freeze and I shan't manage.' She laid down the plate and peeked over his shoulder. It struck her she had never known a gentleman who worked so hard. On the page, there was a jumble of scientific symbols between lines of text. *The pastry is tremendous. Butter?* He had written. And *Late night seals like old men swimming for their health.* And then calculations, scattered freely and small diagrams. His writing was tiny, but then paper was scarce. From the corner of the desk, the doctor noticed the line of her eyes.

'Can you read, Karl?' he asked.

Karina hesitated, pulling back. Most sailors did not have their letters. Still, she didn't want to lie.

'I didn't mean to snoop,' she said. 'I learned to read as a child. My mother insisted.'

This was true. Not all girls were sent to the village school but Marijke and Karina never missed a day, even when they could have helped at home.

Hooker pulled a book from his shelf. 'Here,' he said, opening it at the fly leaf. 'Show me.'

Karina weighed the book in her hand and then read the words. 'A handbook for travellers on the continent being a guide through Holland, Belgium, Prussia and Northern Germany, and along the Rhine, from Holland to Switzerland: containing descriptions of the principal cities . . . with an index map,' she said hesitantly at first, and then finishing smartly. It had been a while and the book was in English.

Hooker looked impressed. In England, reading in the lower orders it was rare. 'Well, I never,' he said. 'My mother bought me that book. I think she hoped it would encourage me to travel closer to home.'

'Where is she, sir?'

'Mother? Glasgow, I expect. I miss her, to tell you the truth. Do you miss yours?'

'My mother is dead.'

'I'm sorry.'

'Don't be. If she hadn't died, my sister and I would still be on Ven,' Karina smiled.

'And would that be so bad?'

'Would Glasgow?'

Hooker laughed. 'Everyone needs somewhere

to go home to. Somewhere to keep in mind. Though for me, it is probably London that is closer to my heart. You would love to see it,' he swore, still unaware of Thebo's warning. 'I shall show these specimens there and Ross will deliver his charts to the Society. If we can calculate the pole, we might even be famous, Karl!'

Karina didn't care about fame. What was the point of that?

'For me, the place I think of is Amsterdam,' she cut in. 'My sister lives there.' It was the first time she had said it out loud since she boarded. She stared, vacantly, as if she did not recognize the words.

'Amsterdam?' The doctor sounded almost impressed. 'I have never been.'

Karina's eyes warmed. Here was somewhere that she was the more experienced. 'It is a fine city. They say the canals are like Venice. And there is a library.'

Marijke loved the library. When they arrived from Copenhagen it was the first place she had visited. They allowed women members. Later, when she had married, Marijke sold the business she had set up at the bottom of one of the grand canals. She had become famous herself in some small way, and several society ladies had been disquieted at her quitting but her workshop continued to prosper and Marijke took tea there once a month to dispense advice to the woman who had bought it. Or at least she had done so when Karina had left to return to Copenhagen, which was, by her calculation now almost six years ago. She had been called back to run the kitchens of a former mistress. The money had been good. As she sailed out of Amsterdam, she had felt her stomach turn for the first time. She'd miss Marijke, of course. But she'd miss the city too. It was an unfamiliar feeling. She'd never once felt homesick for Ven.

'What kind of library?' Hooker enquired.

'There are scientific papers. Religious texts.' Marijke read about the stars. She had always been fascinated by the night skies – a map as important as the world below, she said.

'You have read such books?'

Karina shifted uneasily. She did not have the same interests as her sister. 'Poetry,' she admitted.

The doctor laughed. 'What manner of poetry?'

'Just poetry.'

He regarded her slowly in the candlelight. 'Well I never.'

Some days later, when Hepworth was incapacitated with stomach cramps, Hooker suggested the kitchen boy serve at the captain's table. Bevan thought this a hilarious development. Half the size of the black man, Karina could not wear the footman's uniform.

'Why can't someone else do it?' she objected.

Bevan stared. 'It's the captain's order,' he said baldly. 'And you'll do as you're told.' Then he tittered. 'Have you ever given service?'

Karina shook her head. 'Not at table.' She had served beer in a tavern. She had served a lady in a private room. But a table of English officers was a different matter. In the dark passageway, she loitered with the tureen of stew in her hands, listening to the long, low creaking of the ship, as if it was laughing at her. Bevan had slaughtered the goats at last and the meat she was holding in her hands was markedly better than anything they had served for weeks. Still, she hesitated before slipping through the door.

The room was lit with candles so that it looked warm. There was a stove at one end, which gave out some heat, at least. The men wore full dress.

'Ah. Excellent,' Ross declared, his voice booming.

Karina made the rounds and each man served himself. They ignored her; a shadowy shabby nobody from the galley. The conversation turned to home and the new queen on the throne. She was called Victoria. Captain Ross was dismissive. Far from respectability and beyond all reach of her majesty's dominions, he spoke his mind.

'She'll never last,' he said. 'Not to be disloyal,' he checked himself, 'but a queen. And so young. Rule is too much for such slender female shoulders. It is as well that she is married. She will defer the business of monarchy to Prince Albert. She must.'

There had been news of the royal engagement as the ship left England some years ago. The last time the expedition made land or, more accurately, the last time it made civilization, the captain had found an old copy of the *London Illustrated News*, which confirmed the royal wedding had gone ahead. That was the way of it at sea – a sailor was always behind on events. The news was a queer patchwork to be assembled out of sequence and peppered by a dash or two of word of mouth. Queen Victoria might have had a child by now but it would be months before the men of the *Erebus* or the *Terror* would hear of it.

Karina laid the tureen on the side. The men tore into the food, passing cornbread between them. Silence fell as they savoured it. Hooker caught her eye and she looked down.

'Our progress has been excellent,' the captain said. She realized he was speaking about their mission. To one side, a desk covered with papers and scientific instruments attested to the officers' efforts. 'The crew is working well despite the conditions. We will finish this year, I think.'

'And the pole, sir?' Pearce asked.

The officers hung on this.

'Our instruments are unreliable, I fear. What do you say, Joseph?'

Hooker looked up from his plate. 'The only way would be to go inland, sir. And we don't have the means. We can make calculations but we will not be able to prove them.'

'But the Society will be happy with calculations, will it not?'

'They are an improvement on the current situation.'

'The men say there is a spirit at the pole,' Pearce stated.

Ross laughed. 'The men believe there is a spirit almost everywhere. I heard one terrifying another as we crossed the equator – voodoo or somesuch. They all believe in it. Boy,' he motioned towards Karina, 'do you believe in ghosts?'

'I was not brought up to, sir.'

The captain grunted. 'Fine fellow,' he said.

'Karl can read,' Hooker chimed in. 'He also has some experience of expeditions across snow with dogs.'

'Dogs, eh? Excellent.' Ross poured a glass of wine. Karina felt her skin prickle. 'A most unexpected fellow, our kitchen boy. Though we have not had one of your custards for a while.'

'Supplies are running low, sir. The goats . . .'

Ross waved dismissively. 'Well, I'm sure you'll manage something. You're in the navy now, boy. Have Bevan trim your hair. You look like a bally female.'

She almost ran out of the cabin as they started the cheese, clutching the empty tureen to her chest and heading for the galley where she slung the pewter into the washing bucket and scrambled to hand Bevan the shears. She ran her fingers through her hair.

'Cut it,' she said. 'It's too long.' All she could think was that the captain had said they were finishing this year and then, surely, they would sail north. Bevan stumbled. He had had one rum too many to be clipping hair. As the strands fell at her feet she had a sudden vision of herself in a dress of Marijke's making – a silk concoction that swung as she made her way down a European street, the scent of baking bread on the summer air. A secret star stitched into the bodice and a velvet purse on her wrist.

'Are you all right, Karl?' Bevan squinted at his handiwork.

'I want to go home,' she said.

* * *

65

The next night, Hepworth was reinstated to good health. Karina felt a flood of relief when he appeared as usual at the galley door in time to serve dinner.

'I don't know. It was an honour to be asked. It was a promotion,' Bevan muttered, as he spooned fish onto a pewter achette. 'You should try to continue, Karl. Maybe they'd have the two of you at the table.'

'I don't like serving the officers,' she insisted.

Hepworth looked gratified. Silently, Karina had spent the afternoon making an ice with sweet ginger for the table. Bevan was dubious about the wisdom of it. 'What fool wants cold food?' the old cook declared, rolling his eyes as if it were his own fault for giving her the freedom of the stores. It was too late now to make something else, and wasteful besides. So, along with the rest of the meal, Hepworth set off with the ice in a wooden bowl.

'Here,' Bevan passed Karina the doctor's tray. 'You'd best take it to him.' But the captain's comment the night before had shaken her and she felt fretful going down the corridor. The secret weighed heavily. At Hooker's door she ran a palm over her hair. Bevan had done a good job of cutting it in the end. More by accident than design. *They are all too busy to mind me. Nobody knows*, she told herself and knocked smartly.

As she entered the cabin Hooker was carefully cataloguing penguin bones so that a skeleton could be reconstructed. Already in a state of nerves, Karina took fright at the little white figure he had laid out. She almost dropped the plate

66

onto the wooden boards. As it was, a thick splash of stew slopped over the edge.

'I'm sorry, sir,' she said, straightening the dish at the same time as she bent to clean the floorboard. She chided herself that she should be calmer. That was no measure in fear. If anything, this was the time to hold her ground.

And then it happened. As Hooker got to his knees to lend a hand, he touched her fingers, and just that moment it felt as if the whole world had stopped. Karina pulled back as he looked up. She had never felt anything like the doctor's touch. There was a connection. To the bone. She felt her heart race as the air in the cabin became somehow vivid. Then she caught a particular look in his green eyes, only just realizing that he did not understand his arousal was natural for she was a cabin boy. A sixteen-year-old scrap of nothing. The doctor flushed and pulled away.

'Get out! Get out!' His tone was harsh.

She burst out of the cabin and ran. It felt as if she tumbled into the galley.

'You're quick tonight,' Bevan commented, smoking his pipe by the stove.

Karina shrugged. Her hand found her stomach, as if somehow that would ground her. What had happened was dangerous. Forbidden. Silently and sadly, she vowed she'd never visit Hooker again. She would cook his food but have Hepworth deliver it. The black man could be bought for the payment of a slim slice of the officer's tart or a peeling of cheese. Her cooking had some currency at least. She was not a woman who delighted in playing with fire. The cold summer stretched ahead and the galley suddenly felt like a coffin. But she'd rise again. She'd get to Amsterdam. She swore it.

'I wonder what they made of your ice, lad?' Bevan took a deep draw of shag as he considered this.

Karina set to cleaning the pots in a bucket of seawater that had been left on the floor.

'Maybe it'll ginger them up,' the cook chortled. 'Ginger them up, eh?'

Six

The further south they went the worse the weather. The storm (as with all weather in the Antarctic it seemed) blew up out of nowhere. The wind was like the heavens shouting. The temperature plummeted. Freezing air crept along the ship's passageways in an icy wave, cold on cold. Inside the captain's cabin. three dishes slid off the sideboard. Hepworth went to tidy them.

'Go!' the captain urged one of the lieutenants. 'Take a look and report back.'

If the storm seemed set, the ships would make for the coast and weigh anchor. There was no point in risking being driven onto the ice. With the table unsettled the remaining officers poured more drink, but they gave up eating. It was difficult to stomach food with the room lurching. Hepworth scooped a platter of ships' biscuits back into place while the officers argued about a mathematical equation that might effect their calculations.

'Nigger,' Ross periodically forgot Hepworth's name. 'Send the kitchen boy to get Hooker from his cabin, would you? He's the man to settle this.'

Hepworth laid down a pewter jug and stumbled out of the cabin.

At the door of the kitchen he gestured the captain's order, pointing in the direction of the doctor's cabin, mimicking the doctor's spectacles and sideburns.

'No,' Karina said immediately. The galley had to be cleared. With the jerking of the ship, a measure of flour had tumbled already and Bevan had ordered her to scoop it back into the sack. 'I'll make you a rhubarb tart,' she promised. 'You go for me.'

Hepworth looked as if he was considering this, but then one of the lieutenants appeared behind him. 'More brandy,' he ordered. 'Well, hurry up, man.' And Hepworth disappeared, the brass buttons on his jacket jangling as he stumbled from side to side along the corridor like a drunkard in the swell.

'You better fetch the doctor,' Bevan said over his shoulder. 'I can manage.'

Karina hauled the jute sack against the wall and secured it with rope. She had not been alone with Hooker since their hands had touched. This, however, was a direct order from the captain and from Bevan too. With the ship caught in the vice of the weather, she knew she'd find it difficult to find someone else to do the task. The storm was rising.

'All right,' she said.

Along the dim corridor a man was vomiting into a bucket. As she made her way she was flung twice hard against the wall. Three deck hands headed for their stations at the double, arrayed in regulation oilskin. They pushed past and hammered upwards, as she continued below. The men banged the hatch open and an icy slash of water sailed through the air and caught her unawares soaking her, shoulder to knee. The sheer cold took her breath away and she paused before she could move on. At the doctor's door, she steadied herself, already shuddering. Then she knocked.

'Come!'

She did not cross the threshold. 'The captain requests you, sir.'

Hooker nodded curtly and Karina left. He had no more desire to see her than she had to see him, clearly.

Her teeth already chattering as her wet clothes chafed her skin, she made for the galley to dry out. Behind, Hooker followed her up the corridor at a distance. It would seem they had a tacit agreement and he mentioned nothing of her sodden state, though she knew the cold water would be deadly if she did not get dry. She must be quick. Then suddenly:

'Karl!' he shouted. 'Watch out!'

She didn't have time to look up before it hit her. A piece of jagged wood shattered by the vicious swell flew down the corridor and caught her squarely in the legs. She tasted a tang of blood as she keeled over. It happened so quickly that it felt like flying. There was no pain even when she heard the bones crack. The last thing she saw was Joseph Hooker's anxious face over her and then everything went black.

When Karina awoke it was to a piercing, sickening pain in her side. It felt as if she had been knifed. She tried to swallow but that only made it worse. The best thing, she understood quickly,

71

was to stay still. Moving only her eyes, she could tell she was below, in Hooker's sick bay, on a makeshift bed. The doctor's other work had been packed away and instead the leather bag with surgical tools was open to one side. She had seen him remove a man's toe here once. Silently, she checked that she could still feel her limbs.

'You awake?'

The unknown voice came from her right. She steeled herself not to look, for she knew if she did so the pain would stab her.

'Mmm,' she tried.

'You caused a right rumpus, milady!'

The thick voice cackled. Then the sailor limped into her line of sight. It was Michael Farmer, an able seaman. He helped Si slaughter the animals. Now his shoulder was bandaged. She had never heard him speak before.

'They told me to keep an eye on you, as I'm no use for anything else.'

'I'm not going anywhere,' she managed.

He cackled again. 'I'd say that's right. You got broken ribs and that pretty face of yours had a beating. You fell flat on it. Poor girl, the doctor called you.'

'He knows, then?'

Farmer looked as if he might explode with delight. If they'd reached the pole itself, he could not have been more excited. There had been no news on board for months – nothing like this. Gossip beyond imagining. Riches.

'We all know, my pretty. Doctor had to bandage you, see? No wonder you cook like a right madam!

You is one! Not right, though, is it? It's unlucky to have a woman on board.'

She had not the energy to reply and defend herself. There was no point, besides. Sailors were on perpetual lookout for things to brand unlucky. She took a painful breath that at least cut into the shame turning in her belly. Then she heard the door click open and the doctor entered the cabin in conversation with the captain. As he came into view, Hooker did not meet her eyes. The captain, on the other hand, glared at her, sheepish and angry at once that the stowaway boy he'd sheltered was in fact, a woman. Ross was a gentleman in the English sense of the word. In this state and given her sex, he could not have her beaten. He berated her however, whipping her soundly with the birch of his words.

'Madam,' he started, 'you have been playing some game. Dr Hooker discovered you in the most horrifying fashion.'

Karina glanced at the doctor. Tears pricked her eyes. She had thought if she was to be uncovered it would be by instinct – that someone would simply see her for what she was. Not that she would be injured and stripped bare while she was unconscious.

'I am sorry, sir,' she said, fighting the impulse to cry.

'We will face a mockery. De Bougainville is considered a fool.'

'De Bougainville, sir?'

'His cabin boy. Turns out she was a bally woman too.'

'I'm sorry, sir.'

73

'Well, I cannot see what we can do about it, boy.'

The captain checked himself. Able Seaman Farmer took a deep breath as he tried not to laugh. Karina drew herself up in the bed, though it stung.

'My name is Karina Lande. And I am very sorry for the trouble, sir.' *That surely is some kind of start*, she thought. What else could she do but introduce herself and apologize? Ross was not to be appeased.

'Madam,' he burst out, 'it is an abomination to have you on board but a worse one for you to be dressed in breeches. We shall array you appropriately for your sex, Mistress Karina.' The captain pronounced her name carefully, almost spitting the word. 'I understand that somewhere there is a dress of some description.' His hands flapped as if to illustrate ribbons or lace around the neckline. 'Unless you have something suitable in your possession?'

'No, sir. I left it behind. I feared it might uncover me.'

Ross bit his lip. 'Deception,' he muttered and she couldn't tell if he meant the island or the leaving behind of her gown.

'And shall I remain?'

The doctor stepped forward. 'You should not move for some time,' he cut in.

'But,' the captain was eager to make matters clear, 'when you are well, you shall work for your keep, madam. No one aboard either the *Erebus* or the *Terror* enjoys a pleasure cruise. It is entirely appropriate for you to continue to work under Mr Bevan in the galley.'

'Thank you, sir.'

'You can thank me when we deposit you elsewhere. Which I intend to do at the earliest opportunity.'

Hooker interjected. 'James, what might become of her? The girl is, I imagine, trying to get home. She must have been in straitened conditions to—'

Ross spluttered. 'My ship,' was all he managed but it silenced the doctor admirably. Then he stalked away.

Hooker sat by the bed on a low stool. 'Well,' he said, 'you're a turn up for the books.'

Karina turned painfully towards him.

'Do you think he'll really put me ashore? I have to get to Amsterdam. I am returning to my sister.'

'So that is true?'

'I'm not a liar, Doctor Hooker.'

'Except. Karl, was it?'

'It was my cousin's name. I had to get back and I had no money. I was widowed.' A tear leaked out. She cursed herself – he'd think she was crying over Thebo or that she was making a tawdry attempt to milk his emotions. But she couldn't help the tears. 'I had nothing,' she burbled. 'Perhaps a gentleman cannot understand, but I was left with nothing. Less than that. And this. This is a humiliation.'

Hooker handed her his handkerchief. It was crumpled but clean.

'Shhh.' He tried to soothe her. 'I'm sure it was terrible. I mean, no lady would stowaway in this old tub if she didn't have to. Look, first, we must get you well, Karina Lande. We are already missing your cooking. Ross will come round.

And if the captain puts you ashore, I shall see to it myself that you have money enough for a passage home. Please do not concern yourself.'

Karina smiled. She sniffed. '*Etter regnet kommer solen,* my mother used to say. After the rain there comes sunshine.'

'Yes. Why not? Farmer,' the doctor called the seaman. 'Fetch a sheet. We must screen Mrs Lande's bed.' The man jumped to. 'There is a requirement for modesty,' the doctor said, as if it had only occurred to him.

Day by day, the pain subsided and Hooker let her read from his library of books, which they discussed, one by one. Carefully, she made a list of words she couldn't understand and just as carefully Hooker explained them. *Pall Mall* and *balloon* and *classification.* Through the porthole she caught sight of a shard of ice now and then and the flash of clear blue sky. Twice a day, Si Bevan delivered food from the galley and hovered uncomfortably watching Karina eat, as if she was a wonder.

'I wasn't sure if I should have added more seasoning,' he said.

The fare was not bad, but not good either and his cornbread was heavy as if it was made of rubber. Still she ate as much as she could. Si loitered over the empty plates, his pink face perplexed.

'If you have a question . . .' Karina offered. 'The captain says we are to work together again once I am well.'

'But you are a woman.'

'There is no denying it.'

'Don't you get smart with me.'

Karina sighed. 'I had to come aboard. It was my only way home.'

'Plenty woman find themselves in difficulty and don't dress up as a man, I'm sure.'

'There is nothing I can do about it now, Si,' she said.

'It's not natural,' he pronounced as he swept away.

At his leisure, the doctor quizzed her more gently. He shared his views on Lord Byron's poetry, some chatter about his family – a niece newly born before he left. He asked her how she had managed when she assisted his operations. 'And you did not mind the blood?' he checked, and looked contented when she declared that she had not. Then he broached the subject about which he was really curious.

'Your husband?' he asked. 'You were widowed, you said?'

Karina regarded the bedclothes lying over her legs. She took a breath and then told him about Thebo's death, or as much as she knew. Van Kleek hadn't divulged a great deal.

'It must have been difficult news to bring,' she started, remembering that morning. The bang on the door. Asking him in. Van Kleek had glanced towards the window of the dark cabin as he said the words and handed over the little purse. What had happened wasn't his concern and it was clear he wanted to get out of there, back down the muddy street and out to the cabin he kept on a trawler moored in the bay. A solitary type, he always seemed a man of extraordinarily little appetite. Perhaps that was how he had lasted so long at the whaling station – neither women nor food nor drink meant anything to him. Nor company either. He was a rock of a person. A craggy island outpost. 'The company representative just said it was an accident,' she said slowly. 'He told me that Thebo had fallen into the sea and drowned. They were after a whale, you see.'

'They must have tried to rescue him. Was there a storm?'

Karina shrugged. 'I think he went too far when he was harpooning. I think he slipped.' She knew it could have been anything. Going to sea was a dangerous occupation. Men simply fell out of the rigging and plummeted to the deck, dead immediately on account of a misjudgement or misstep. At least for Thebo it had been quick. An injury might fester – a bad scrape with a hook or perhaps not even that – a small abrasion could prove mortal, let alone a broken bone that pierced the skin. Seafarers died. Officers and men alike. That was the way of it. She knew she had been lucky.

'But few drown so quickly that there is no attempt at rescue,' Hooker objected.

'I expect they tried. Thebo was the captain. All I was told was that there was a whale. He had been harpooning. His second-in-command wrote me a letter later, but it did not say any more than that, only that he admired Thebo, what little he knew of him.'

'Did he not visit you?'

'No. He was promoted. He went to Brazil, I think. Or maybe to Argentina. Afterwards.'

'And your husband was a captain?'

'Yes.'

'You must miss him.'

She did not want to meet Hooker's eyes.

The doctor waited a moment. 'He was young?' he pressed.

'He was thirty when he died.'

'I'm sorry. You are too young to be a widow.'

'Many are widowed as young as I was, doctor.'

'Well,' he said. 'Why don't we see if we can get you on your feet?'

The pain felt as if it might rip her skin. Her ribs were still healing. She sat on the edge of the bed like a child dangling her feet in a freezing pool. Hooker held out his hand. She took it, afraid only momentarily of what such contact might release. He smiled. 'Now then, I know you are brave,' he said.

The boards were cold. She shuffled like an old woman, each movement a fresh cut, but he helped her as she made it to the porthole. Through the glass, the sun hit the ice so that it was almost blinding. The water was choppy, a dark reflection of the sky.

'I expect that's enough for today,' the doctor said.

Karina struggled back and hauled herself into the bed. She sat up and he handed her the book she had been reading.

'You are healing well. It takes longer in the cold. I have noticed it with the men. I shall check on you later.'

He proved as good as his word. The ship kept the doctor busy and Karina was not his only patient but he visited a couple of times a day. They talked. At first it was awkward. Not like before, when she was a boy.

'Do you miss home?' she asked.

Hooker almost shrugged. 'The house in Glasgow – my family's place – is built of russet stone. There is a balustrade and the gardens are lush. I miss the smell of growing things. The tick of the clock as I sit by the open window. In the summer, you know.' He looked abashed at saying so much. The men didn't talk like this – about what they wanted. She knew that he'd not have admitted these things to Karl. It made her smile. Perhaps things were settling. She did not want to overburden him by saying she was so homesick, she missed places she hadn't visited. She considered Rome a moment. Yes, she was homesick even for there and she had only once seen a picture of it. 'I didn't mean to come here,' she said.

Hooker got up from the stool. 'Oh, it's not so bad,' he said.

The truth was, as she watched the ice through the porthole, she lost herself a little. It was like being a child and watching trees in the wind. She followed the line of the cliffs against the sky and strained to see the dark water that reflected them. And there was peace in that, she supposed. Just a little.

After a fortnight, he arrived with a brown paper parcel. He laid it on the desk and cut the string.

'Ross sent this,' he announced, pulling out a shabby grey gown with a stiff bodice that laced at the front. 'Goodness,' he held it up. 'I wonder where he got it.'

Karina reached out and took the dress. 'A governess. That's what it looks like.'

She had never been one for fancy clothes. In Portugal, she had arrayed herself in a feather headdress one night and Thebo had laughed at her. They both preferred when she was simply herself. Better a governess than the other kind of woman.

'It'll do,' she said. 'Though I shall still need my woollens, I imagine.'

He waited while she changed behind the sheet.

'I'm sorry,' she kept saying, for it took a while. Still, the bodice fitted and not only that, it felt good to be contained. Her newly knitted ribs settled comfortably into the proscribed shape. She pulled back the sheet and he smiled.

'When your hair grows, you'll look fine,' he said.

Karina ran her fingers through her shorn locks, Si Bevan's efforts now in vain.

'There is no hat, I'm afraid.' Hooker lifted the empty brown paper and turned it over as if by magic more feminine attire might appear.

'I can use my knitted cap.'

'It will look strange.'

'It'll have to do.' She leaned against the bed. Her ribs were painful still, but not as cutting as they had been. Besides, the pain was not her only worry.

'What's the matter?'

'It's them.' She motioned upwards.

'You will have to face the crew. We cannot confine you forever.'

Karina brushed her hand along the surface of the thick cotton skirt. The dress was slightly too long. It obscured Thebo's old boots, at least. 'Well,' she said, hauling herself off the bed, 'perhaps I should just get on with it.'

Hooker accompanied her along the corridor, up through the hatch and into the light. The men stopped work and stared with no regard for her modesty as she stepped on deck. There was silence and then, in a clatter she heard them coming up from below as news spread that the woman was on show. Far off, on the *Erebus*, she sensed there were some fellows sharing an eyeglass.

Hooker whispered, his tone that of a man she'd heard once, soothing an unbroken pony as he slipped on the reins. 'They will get used to you. You look like an English lady now.' She shifted, pulling her shoulders back and he offered her his arm. After weeks in the gloom of the sick bay with only a porthole-sized circle of light, the full vista of the glacier was so dazzling it almost blinded her. There was a lack of colour in the south and an abundance of whiteness – a shock to the unaccustomed. The air was so fresh it would sober a drunk man in seconds. It felt good on her skin. Below deck there was a perpetual fug from the men's pipes and a heavy, musty air that lingered, ingrained into the wood.

At the mizzen, pink-faced and proud, Pearce stood in defiance as the doctor and his patient approached. Behind him two seamen lined up shoulder to shoulder.

'Dear God,' the midshipmen said, 'what have we here? Our little cookie?'

'Mrs Lande is almost well enough to return to her duties and I know, you for one, will be glad of that, Pearce.' Hooker did not drop Karina's arm. It was as if he was promenading with a woman of worth in his beloved London.

'I'll make you a tart, sir,' Karina said.

The midshipman snorted. 'Not dressed like that.' She blushed.

'For heaven's sake man.' Hooker sounded exasperated. 'Have some manners.'

They continued to the bowsprit and she sat for a moment. On deck the men shifted, one or two getting back to work. Karina closed her eyes and breathed deeply. 'You look bright,' the doctor said. 'Like some strange spirit.'

She wondered what he meant. Her hair was pale and now arrayed in grey, she must match the landscape along the coast. She remembered a fairy tale Marijke had once read out loud. A woman with skin as white as snow. 'Like you,' she had said because her own skin was peppered with freckles. Karina was the pretty one. The one easily led. Or, she had been. Now, her clothes were an odd jumble and she looked no lady. She might be able to read, but this was something different entirely. After all, a woman's first duty was to look well on a man's arm. That was why Thebo had fallen at her feet that day in Copenhagen when they first met. What had it been about him that she had let him?

83

'Don't worry,' Hooker kept his voice low. 'Give it time.'

'You are too kind, doctor.'

'Somebody must be kind,' he said and held out his hand to escort her below.

Seven

Hooker was right. The men gradually settled. Daily, Karina promenaded on deck, more than when she was a kitchen boy. The light seemed to nourish her and the sky was stunning. There was something majestic in the roll of the icy hills and all the shades of blue that faded in and out on the changing weather. Now and then there was even a touch of orange – the ripe apricot rim of the sinking sun and the flash of a penguin's beak. There were lights in the sky some nights that glowed golden, purple and pink. There was such clarity and vividness but, she realized with a pang, no green. She missed it. There was not so much as a patch of weedy ground or some velvety moss on the freezing stones. In time even the muddy outcrop of Deception Island developed a kind of glamour with its rough scrub. She ached for it with a visceral kind of longing. Green – the colour of life.

Hooker, it transpired upon coaxing, missed his garden for the same reason. He eulogized the hills beyond Glasgow. 'The fertile, dark earth of Argyll,' he said, as if the words were poetry. 'Plants that live and die and live again.' When he visited her in the evenings, he took to bringing a botanical dictionary and intoning the names of the species in Latin, pronouncing them as if they were the names of delicious morsels. He pointed at the illustrations, describing them in detail – feathery ferns that were almost yellow and the thick, dark tongues of the greenhouse exotics. He talked fondly of the orchid houses at Kew.

Karina longed differently. Her desires were less exotic – for the verdant pastures of her homeland with the bright sparks of wildflowers for which she know no Latin. The Scandic grasslands of the fallow fields of Ven where the *fjällfibbla* and *polarull* grew in summer. 'My sister and I used to take a picnic,' she said. Where they sat, the grass it released a clean scent onto the warm air. It seemed a hundred years ago when the world was ephemeral. In the far south, everything had an eternal quality – the glacier moved so slowly. The white and blue hardly changed and the mountains creaked without moving. 'This place is forever. That's why it has no smell,' she said. Who knew that green was necessary for the soul?

It was no shock when it happened. She was almost completely better and no longer in pain. He had held off sending her back to work and she knew it. Once or twice she had thought to ask if she might go to the galley but something kept her waiting. That was a woman's place or at least, as she understood it, that was how English women behaved.

They had eaten together that evening and were at their leisure. She was bending to read a book when Joseph laid his hand on her waist. He stroked gently and she realized she could scarcely breath. Time stopped. It was the same feeling as that evening all those weeks ago. But now it was allowed. She hesitated, trembling, and turned to meet his eyes. Here at the end of the world there was no hurry.

'Don't worry,' he said.

'I am older than you are,' she pointed out.

'But I am wiser,' he smiled. Then he took just a moment too long.

'What is it?'

'Do you think of him?' he asked. 'I mean, your husband.'

With Thebo, in the beginning, it had been different to this – frantic almost. With Thebo there had been the world to excite them. All the places they had been and those left to visit. They had met in Copenhagen when Karina had returned to run the kitchen. When she arrived, it transpired that the job was to run the household. Marijke wrote daily and Karina replied by return. She negotiated an extra payment and every second Sunday off.

One Sunday, as she strolled along the Strogert, Thebo struck up a conversation as she stared in a shop window. He was wheeling a bicycle – an odd contraption. It had made her laugh out loud. 'You should try it,' he insisted. He was studying navigation. His father was a mapmaker, but Thebo longed to leave his family's dusty library and see the world for himself. He asked if he could walk her home, but she refused. In the five years since she had left Ven, Karina had advanced but she was still in service. Her Sunday best, hand sewn by Marijke, made her look like a lady.

It had been pleasant to return to Copenhagen.

The job was easy enough. She liked organizing the accounts and checking the linen and some evenings she would make little pastries stuffed with cinnamon and almond paste because it pleased her to cook. She took to plaiting her long, blonde hair and putting it up in a complicated bun. And it was that caught Thebo's eye, he said. Hair like spun gold. By the time he found out she was a housekeeper, it was too late.

The affair was forbidden. They met in secret and that fired their passion. Stolen moments at the market – a chart mapping their desires. They talked of the Brazils and the countries along the Mediterranean coast. They talked of escaping the grey skies of winter and of being free. The irony that they ended up on Deception Island was not lost on her. They had passed all the colours and kept going. Did she miss him?

'There was nothing more to come between us,' she said. 'You are a different passion. A different man.'

He blushed at that or perhaps it was the way she was staring now, quite openly in desire.

'English women do not speak that way,' he declared.

'It is the truth. You probably saved my life, doctor. Do you want me to play games? To make you wait?'

And then he kissed her and the world stopped again.

Like the ice, she realized, love removed her from the human concerns of time and place. Amsterdam could be a few months away or a few years. It didn't matter. She waited for him to want her naked. She waited for him to ask for more. To fumble. To unlace her. But he didn't. They kissed for a while. That was all.

That night, she moved back to the galley. She walked along the corridor without as much as a twinge. She half expected Hooker to come after her and drag her back to his cabin. But he didn't. She lingered at the galley door. Si Bevan jumped, aghast, when he caught sight of her. 'I'll never get used to it,' he declared. 'A kitchen boy in a dress. What are you doing?'

'I am returning to duty.'

She slipped the dirty dishes from her supper into the old seawater tub on the floor. Hepworth appeared and disappeared again, hovering at the galley door only momentarily before he sped off down the corridor with a look of delight on his face.

'You'd think a dumb man could hold his counsel,' the old cook declared. 'Well, what am I to call you now? Milady?' He chortled. 'I can't say I am not glad you are back. I held off using the last of the jarred fruit so you could bake it. You can treat them to a pie tomorrow.'

As Hepworth's silent news spread below decks, Archie appeared in the galley to gawp.

'For God's sake, man,' Si snapped. 'Is this what we're to have? A royal progress, is it?'

Archie grinned. He had even fewer teeth than Si. Karina laid her hands on her hips. 'If you're coming in, you best be useful.'

89

Archie removed his cap and loitered away from the stove. He reached into his pocket. 'Here,' he said, bundling a parcel into her hands.

'Is it for me?'

'Go on, girl.'

Karina split the brown paper. Inside, a scarf of fine wool nestled in the centre. A merino, she would guess. She lifted it between her fingers. It took her breath away. A sigh escaped her lips. It was the colour of wet summer grass. She lifted the material to her cheek, to bathe in its greenness. 'It's so soft,' she said.

'We missed you, girl.'

Momentarily she thought she might cry.

'Missed her? Missed her skill with the stove, more like,' Si snapped. 'What's wrong with my damn cornbread anyway?'

Archie looked bashful.

'Where did you get this?' Karina asked as she ran the river of green between her fingers.

The old man shrugged. 'I bought it for my missus when we docked the other side of the equator. I'll get her another. It goes with your dress, doesn't it?'

Karina looked doubtful. Nothing would ever match the old, worn, governess's frock. 'Thank you.'

That night she settled down to sleep, holding the scarf in a patch of moonlight so she could sleep in sight of it. The colour of his eyes. She was used to a bed now – albeit a hard one – and her old station on the floor made her ribs ache again. There was a creak in the corridor and she wondered if he might come for her, but it was only the ship shifting as the *Terror* cut through the swell. When she woke up it was morning and Si arrived into the galley, waking her late.

'None of that,' he said. 'You'll work as hard as before or you'll not work at all, milady.'

Later, when the bread came out of the oven, he tasted it. 'Ah,' he let out a long sigh. 'The boys'll be happy.'

And from there the day stretched. Bread and pie and brose. The grog was doled out. The stew bubbled in the pot. Perhaps she simply wasn't used to it any more, she thought. Her arms ached but it felt good to have something to do – a strange kind of homecoming that left her still missing something. Not green any longer. Him. Oblivious, Si was in his element, clattering pans and feigning disinterest.

By the time the captain's dishes were sent out that evening, Karina found she was singing, low, under her breath. Still, she kept a weather eye out. Not a day had passed since she was first injured that the doctor hadn't tended to her. It was strange to have to wait and wonder if he would come. Si took out the tray and laid it. He spooned a dollop of stew and a slice of tart.

'You better take this to Hooker, girl.'

Carrying the tray along the corridor her heart beat at a pace. She knocked on the door and waited for his call. 'Ah, Karina,' he said, as if he had expected her. The cabin was familiar but he had folded away the bed. She laid the tray on the side and waited awkwardly.

'Will you share the food with me?'

She shook her head. 'I have eaten,' she admitted. 'Bevan and I ate first.'

'Galley privilege.' Hooker motioned towards a stool and she pulled it forward. 'How are you feeling?'

'Good.'

'Back to work?'

She wasn't sure what he was asking. The way English women behaved clearly made life more complicated.

'Don't you want me?' she asked.

He shifted in his chair. 'What kind of question is that?'

'An honest one.'

'I cannot . . .' His voice trailed off. His teeth looked white and sharp and she felt as if he had torn her flesh. She wondered what it was that he seemed so ashamed of. Not *that*, surely. It didn't feel that way to her. She got to her feet.

'I don't wish to trouble you,' she said. 'It must be irksome to have a woman aboard, and last night . . . It doesn't matter.'

She turned to go but he caught her fingers and pulled her back. His eyes lit on the green scarf, then his gaze travelled down.

'I want to show you London,' he said.

'You are a romantic, then?'

'And you are very direct.'

'Are you scared of what they'll say? The men?'

Hooker let out a bark, half laugh, half yelp. 'No.'

She waited, one more time. He ran his finger across her palm and it came to her – the thing she wanted to tell him. She felt afraid but the thought of not saying what she felt and returning to the galley did not lie easily.

'I have been a married woman. I almost starved to death. Then I might have been keelhauled. I might have been thrown overboard. I was injured and you nursed me back to health, but I could have died of what happened to me. Sailors have died of less. I am lucky, Doctor Hooker. I am here at the end of the world and it is a miracle I have survived. Any day one of these storms might do for all of us. Do you think I want to wait like an English lady? To talk of drawing rooms and dressing rooms and of shopping in Piccadilly for a new bodice and a green dress. A fox cape to keep me warm. How many times do you think I must dodge death before I learn to grasp life when it shows itself?'

She could feel her cheeks burning. Hooker's eyes were stern. 'No one has ever spoken to me like that,' he said, low, below his breath.

She reached out, a pulse of fury running through her. She slapped him hard.

'Wake up,' she snapped. 'What's wrong with you?'

Hooker grabbed her wrist. 'My God.' She flinched as he reached in her direction but he only laid a long finger on her lips. Then slowly he began to stroke her face.

When it happened, making love felt as natural as the gentle seasons of Europe – an escape from the harshness of the polar extreme. One stroke leading to another, once they had started. It was an exploration.

'Joseph,' she whispered, trying his name for the first time. She had only ever heard the captain

93

use it. He fetched furs from his trunk and stretched a thick bearskin over the bed. Then he laid her on it.

'You are my ice queen,' he breathed, as he helped her remove the grey dress and regarded her snowy skin as it emerged.

'We are like Esquimaux,' she teased him.

Joseph did not like that. He had not been to the north, but he had read Ross's journals.

'You are not a native woman. You are not a country wife.'

She had no idea what he meant, but he had used the word *wife* and that felt promising. She nuzzled his neck. She wondered if here, in the most unexpected of places, they might have a life. She lay on the fur, luxuriating in it and watched him watch her as he removed his clothes and bent to stroke her hair. Then he clambered on top and set her alight so she forgot everything except her desire.

Afterwards he said he had drowned in her.

'Do not say that,' she whispered. 'No sailor should ever think of drowning.'

Hooker laughed. 'When I was inside you, I swear you smiled.'

'Of course.'

What strange kind of women had he had before, she wondered. They kissed until he fell asleep and for a while she watched his breath rise and fall, his lips rosy as a girl's and his hair parted to one side, flopping onto the pillow. His body was taut, like a working man and yet he was still boyish. Her newly reinstated curves were by way of contrast. With Thebo, she had run away. It had been a carnival from the day they were married at the sailor's church in Lisbon. But this was a long, slow dance and she realized there had been times when she hadn't been able to tell her own body from his.

'Karina,' he breathed in sleep, and reached out to hold her.

She stretched under the cover. He moved, caressing the curve of her hip and the line of her stomach. Then he nestled into her neck breathing in the scent of her pale hair. There had been a shift, she realized.

Outside the porthole she followed the line of blue sky till it met the ice and she felt no need to be anywhere else the whole world wide than with Joseph Hooker. Drifting to sleep she dreamed of skating across the ice.

When she woke, his dinner lay uneaten on the desk. She slipped out of his arms and pulled on the shabby grey dress. Then she lifted the tray and took it back to the galley, careful to be in place before Si Bevan arrived to set the kettle boiling and start the round of cornbread and pease porridge.

'What are you smiling at?' he asked.

She hadn't been aware she was smiling.

'It's a beautiful day,' she said, nodding towards the porthole.

'Beautiful day,' Si muttered under his breath, dismissing such madness. 'I'll give you a beautiful day. We just have to get on with it, don't we?'

Eight

That night, Karina moved into the doctor's cabin. She did so without announcement. Nobody commented upon the new arrangement. The British, it seemed, preferred not to say anything and having few possessions meant that the matter could be managed discreetly. She waited for some kind of outcry or backlash or judgement, but the cold made thinking a slow process and gradually outrage had become all but impossible. The crew were more interested in warm bread, fish stew and scalded rum than in the rights and wrongs of wedlock. The affair was a private matter. Life on board, she thought, now she had settled to it, passed as easily as when she was a boy and was far more diverting.

At night, the doctor and his mistress took to swathing the furs from his trunk on top of their greatcoats. They tripped up on deck to glory in the canopy of the bright sky and make out what they could of the stars. There, at the end of the world, it felt as if they were alone, the crew sleeping in hammocks below, the outline of the sun and the moon hanging in the sky at once.

The days were full of activity but the nights felt empty of everything except the landscape and the bearskin flung across his berth when they went back below. As the season turned and darkness began to bleed further across the sky each night, the ships turned back and the officers of the *Erebus* came aboard for a celebration dinner to mark the start of the trip northwards. The way the men eyed her, she could tell they knew everything. She wondered if a junior officer had sent the news to the other ship, and which flag might have declared her a woman and the doctor's lover.

Hanging back, she avoided their glances, content to be the girl in the shadows, as she passed them in the dark corridor or scurried to fetch a bottle from the store. An officer as blond as she was sniffed the air in her wake. 'Violets,' he pronounced. 'Can you almost smell violets?'

'It's your imagination, Harry,' his fellow cajoled him. 'None of us have smelled a thing since God knows what bearing.'

'They say she can cook almost anything,' the first man said wistfully. 'Makes you wish she'd stowed away on our side.'

But nobody said a word to Karina's face and after the cheese had been finished and the port drunk, the officers returned to their ship and the course was set northwards.

From then on, Pearce and the other midshipmen were taken up making a fair copy of the map and the rest sailed hard for they must get out of these waters before the winter hit. The crew talked of warmer climes, of drinking beer at port and of crossing the equator.

'We'll resupply,' Bevan sounded excited as he stood filleting fish. He could not write but verbally he repeatedly ran over the list of provisions he'd buy. Fresh fruit, vegetables and meat. The lemons were gone and needed to be replaced. And the coffee and the tea. In warmer weather, food spoiled more easily but they would put in periodically to resupply as they sailed up the coast. 'Brazil for the cacao,' he announced. 'Then Tobago.' The words lolled around his mouth.

And galley to sick bay, Karina continued. She cooked and helped the doctor tend to the men. When one of the seamen died, she sewed the canvas around him and the crew gathered to sing a hymn and slip his body into the icy sea. As they turned back to their duties, the men deferred to her, she noticed. They let her walk ahead.

The weeks passed. The map was almost finished by the time the ships arrived back where they had started, at the penguin colony. The anchor was weighed and the bells were rung. Then whistles sounded. Some kind of ceremony was underway. 'We'll stay a day, I expect,' Si Bevan said sagely, as he handed Karina a tray to deliver to the captain's cabin. It was a dish of sweetened rice pudding. Ross ate at his desk during the day. He called it 'nursery food'. The captain waved her in.

'Thank you.' He motioned her to leave the dish and she hovered waiting to be dismissed. But the captain hesitated as if he had something to say.

'Sir?'

Ross cleared his throat. 'A lady shouldn't work,' he said.

He had realized, it seemed, that Karina was not the shabby illiterate he had first assumed.

The compliment sent a prickle down her spine but she did not want to be confined. Working in the galley was better than having nothing to do.

'Oh no, sir. How else might I be occupied? I am happy.' She realized as she said it that it was true. She was happier than she had ever been – even those first heady months of running away with her husband. Even then.

'It has been difficult for the men,' the captain continued. 'And you have done admirably. Do you remember, Mrs Lande, what I said to you in the sick bay?'

Karina nodded. Her fingers quivered. She put them behind her back. 'You said you would put me off, sir. First place we came to.'

'The first place will likely be Deception Island.'

Fear must have flickered across her face but he sought to comfort her. 'Do not concern yourself. I could not be so cruel, after the service you have given. We will hide you aboard if you wish, when we pick up our first supplies. But I cannot allow you passage, Mrs Lande. It is not fitting. Hooker tells me you have a sister.'

'In Amsterdam, sir.'

'You wish to return to her?'

Karina hesitated. It was what she had always wanted but now Hooker had stroked her hair and promised her London. She had a sudden vision of it – his world, the two of them strolling down Pall Mall. 'Your skin is like silk,' he had said the night before as he slipped inside her. And then, for the first time, 'I love you.' The words had made her gasp as they tumbled from his lips and she wrapped herself around him tighter.

99

Ross glared, waiting for a reply. What visions flickered in front of his eyes, she wondered. What did the captain long for? 'Amsterdam, Mrs Lande?' he offered again.

'It is what I hoped for when I came aboard,' she replied.

'There will be Dutch ships at Maranhão. We can put you ashore there. The doctor will pay your passage.' He said it as if the matter was settled.

Karina eyes flicked towards the door, the corridor and Hooker's cabin. 'That is what he wishes?' she asked.

'I am the captain, Mrs Lande. It is what I wish.'

She bit her lip. It was on the tip of her tongue to promise him custards and nut cracknel and choux pastry but he wasn't a junior officer or a negro servant. 'Please, sir—' she started but Ross cut her off.

'Madam,' he said, 'do not try my patience.' Then he waved her away.

She burst like a bullet into the corridor and headed straight for Hooker's cabin. The doctor was not there. Inside, she paced up and down wondering if he knew this was what the captain had intended. Had they discussed it? And if so, why had Hooker said nothing? Outside the porthole the ice continued eternal but it could not calm her. At least he did not intend to put her ashore on Deception.

On Hooker's desk lay a pile of papers, a book about Linnean classification and the doctor's journal. Karina hesitated as she moved towards his leather-bound notebook and then pulled back.

She itched to open the pages and see – did he know? And if so, how long had he plotted with the captain to send her away? She restrained herself. That wasn't love. Instead, she slumped into his chair and wiped a tear from her cheek as the door opened.

'My love,' the doctor said lightly, as his greatcoat brushed against the door frame. He laid an eyeglass on his desk and removed his hat. His glasses had steamed. It was not warm below, but it was warmer than on deck. He wiped them and then laid the palm of his hand on her shoulder. She wrapped her fingers around it.

'Did you know, Joseph?'

'Know what?'

'Captain Ross will put me ashore.'

Hooker did not reply straight away. He simply sighed. 'I'm sorry,' he said at length. 'There is nothing I can do. But I will pay your passage, Karina.'

'And London? You said you wanted to show me London. You talked of home?'

She realized she had entertained a vision of her cooking for him. A halfway position between housekeeper and lover. Something, now she thought of it, that was unspoken on his part. He had talked of shopping. Of going to the theatre. Of plants. Of exhibits. Never of them living together. 'You do not want me?'

'In England,' he started, 'there is no place . . .'

'We shall go to Glasgow, then.' She knew she sounded simple. For a man like Thebo to marry a servant was almost acceptable. But for a doctor. A botanist. A gentleman.

101

'I have thought about it,' he said slowly. 'I could set up a household. A place in the country. Kensington, perhaps. I could visit you there.'

Karina felt her heart shift. If the ice shifted the same, it would surely crack. She got to her feet and got to the door without making a sound. In the corridor, she whimpered as she leaned against the wooden planking. She had been a fool.

Hooker stood in the open doorway and peered after her. 'Come back,' he asked. 'Please. I haven't finished.'

Karina turned. 'Finished?'

'Damn it, woman.'

Sheepishly, she turned. *Hope will make you go back*, she thought. Hope was what had kept her on Deception too long. She might have stowed away on another ship. She might be home by now. Her heart sank further. Hooker closed the door behind her.

'I know you can't take me to a ball. To an opening. To your la-di-da. I know that.'

'La-di-da?'

Bevan had used the word the other day and she had liked it.

'You want me to be your mistress?'

'Look, do you have to always be so . . . direct?'

'I thought you liked that about me.'

'I do. Sometimes.'

'You like it well enough in bed.'

He grinned. 'I can pay for you to go to your sister's. From Brazil it should be easy enough to find a packet to take you there. And then, if I was lucky, I hoped you might come to me.'

'And I would be a secret?'

'Many men have such secrets, Karina.'

'You are ashamed of me.'

'I worship you.'

'And what would I do?'

'Do?'

'All day? What would I do with my time? Between these visits?'

He was about to say something when a sharp rap came on the door and Pearse popped his head around. 'Sir,' the midshipman said, 'come quickly. There's been an injury. Fulsom has fallen out of the rigging.'

Hooker shrugged in her direction only a fraction. His eyes betrayed a sliver of relief. Then he grabbed his bag and disappeared in the boy's wake. She wondered if he might say, 'Dismissed,' as Ross did with his officers when he breezed off, but the doctor was more abrupt even than that. She glanced at his journal once more as the door banged behind him. Riffling among his papers lacked grace. Instead she returned to the galley.

Her jaw set in determination, she found a task to do. At least it would keep her occupied. Above, men were running this way and that, as she decanted wine for the captain's table. She followed their motion, guessing what was happening above. She felt part of the ship and the truth was that here, she had been useful and Hooker had made her feel loved. Was it all an illusion? Holding up the bottle to check she was leaving only the dregs, she drank a mouthful in defiance, putting down the decanter just in time as Bevan bustled in.

The old cook hulked a leg of smoked ham onto the block before raising his knife. 'I'd forgotten about this,' he said. 'If only we had eggs. Or leastways, if I hadn't killed the chickens. One of the young ones fell, you know. It's a broken leg, they say. The doctor is setting it now. What's wrong with you?'

'Nothing.'

'Nothing will come of nothing, boy,' he chortled. 'Love's young dream, is it?'

She flinched. 'They will put me off at Brazil.'

Bevan looked taken aback. 'Put you off? The best thing that ever happened aboard this ship? And what am I supposed to do? It was bad enough when you were poorly.'

All afternoon she kept thinking of the difference between them. What Hooker had to go back to. London. Family. The honour of lecturing about the pole and the penguins. It felt by contrast as if she had very little. Maybe she'd get to Amsterdam and Marijke would be gone. She'd need to find herself a position. A new life. It was dark in the galley and walls began to close in. The logic of the captain's decision made her stumble as she mixed the dough for a baked pudding and sprinkled raisins into it, folding the paste till the little black dots disappeared. The ship could be a coffin, she thought. It was only a box of wood and they might as well bury you. A deep sting of betrayal cut through her. Betrayal by Hooker most of all. It was the people and the place that were important and she felt that she had neither.

When the doctor asked for her that evening,

she refused, buying off Hepworth with a savoury strip of toasted cheese spiced with mustard powder so he would deliver the message that she was busy. Then, before Hooker could reply, she wrapped up and took herself on deck. The white nights had long receded and the cliffs ashore glowed blue in the darkness. The air was so sharp it felt it might cut the skin. Winter was coming and it would be fierce. A long stream of smoke trailed from the galley into the night sky and below decks there was the sound of dice being thrown and then cheering.

She wondered what she had expected of him. Did she think she might become a gentleman's wife? It struck her that she had always wished for what Marijke had, but Jakson, Marijke's husband, was no gentleman. He was a stolid burgher and wealthy but that was quite different. He valued Marijke's business sense. Her way with people. Thebo had been a captain, and she had been only a pretty adventurer, for that is what he wanted on his arm. Neither of these men were like Hooker. It seemed he had no place for passion in his public life. The English were confusing. Their ways seemed harsh. Had she made a mistake in choosing him? If that were true, it seemed late to be learning of it and besides, she knew he wasn't truly cold. She knew it.

When she was only eleven, Marijke had taken a passion to one of the boys at the village school. After class, she'd wait for him by the window at home, hovering in the hope that he'd pass. He

105

was called Anders and he was older than her –
thirteen perhaps.

Marijke had loitered endlessly at that window.
If ever Karina and she had to pass Anders'
house her temples reddened and she'd giggle
at whatever Karina said. When it became clear
Anders was sweet on Barta from Landskragen,
who was some kind of distant cousin of his,
Marijke was furious. She tried to ignore the
window, tried not to look for him, but even at
nine years of age, Karina found her sister's
bravado unconvincing. She did not understand
Marijke's interest. Anders, as she recalled,
smelled of milk and onions. Maybe passion
always seemed foolish from the outside. And
yet what else was there?

She quit the galley and went above. It seemed
possible to think there, as the darkness drew in.
Ahead, across the water, the ice rose, rock hard
and immutable. Walking in the cold air of evening
was like plunging your face into a barrel of dark,
icy water. She felt wide awake. Karina wondered
what had happened to Anders. He was probably
still on Ven. Perhaps Barta had joined him and
that had been enough. Why was it always the
choice of the man? Why couldn't a woman have
her way?

From below, the shadowy figure of a fellow
smoking a cheroot appeared. As he walked
towards her he reminded her of a tugboat, set
upon a mission. Squinting, she realized it was
Pearse and she steeled herself for a conversation
about pastry.

'There you are,' the midshipman said, the burning

tip of his cigar pulsing orange. 'I heard you had a spat with Hooker.'

Karina's heart sank. Perhaps they all knew below decks. Even silence couldn't mask aboard ship.

'Well,' Pearse said. 'That's a turn-up.'

She didn't reply, only turned to look over the side. Far off a seal splashed. The sound carried on the night air. Pearse loitered.

'You know I'd have you.'

She turned back. His teeth seemed almost fluorescent as they held the cheroot in place. 'I think I'd be happy with a wench such as you, Mrs Lande. Why you can't be more than five and twenty and fair too. I like yellow hair. It is more feminine. If matters haven't worked out with the doctor, I'm sure you and I could come to an accommodation. You might be wise to consider it. My family has a lot of money.'

Karina wished she had never baked the boy's damn custard tarts. Pearse puffed loudly. 'I knew that you were a woman. I had my suspicions all along.'

'That is the trouble with a ship such as this,' she rounded on him. 'Proximity.'

She started to walk away but he followed, pulling her arm.

'Come on,' he said. 'Be reasonable, won't you?'

'Let me go.'

'It'll feel warmer with two of us together.' He steered her off course, pushing her against a barrel. Quickly he tossed the cigar overboard and moved in to kiss her. His breath was thick with tobacco. Karina struck out, but he was strong and

107

held her in place. She felt his mouth closing in and she pursed her lips tightly.

'Oh, for heaven's sake,' he pulled back, fumbling his fingers inside her greatcoat and pawing her breasts through her dress.

'Stop it!' she shouted. 'Help!'

He slapped a hand over her mouth as if he was trying to smother her. He was breathing heavily now, nuzzling into her neck. Biting. Licking. Gathering all her might, Karina stamped on his foot and brought up her knee. It winded him just long enough for her to struggle free.

'I should have thrown you overboard, the day I found you,' he spat, his eyes alight with fury.

As she kept going, running to get below, he called after her. 'That's what the men say. It's unlucky to have a woman aboard.'

Almost at the hatch, Karina let out a yelp of fury. She rounded. 'Go to hell,' she said. 'Lucky or unlucky, what the hell does that mean?'

The midshipman laughed. 'You'll come round.'

She ducked inside, leaving him in the freezing air. It was, she realized, the assumption that angered her. Not only Pearse's assumption, for he was a fool, but Hooker's too. These men took it for granted that she was not good enough for them. That she should be grateful. It was a very British kind of insult.

Furious, she stormed towards the galley. Behind her, she heard Pearse fumble down the stairs, following at a distance. Back at the stove, she armed herself at the rack of knives, scrambling to pick out a sharp paring blade. She grasped it, ready to turn on him, but as he rounded the entrance, he smacked into Si Bevan, just arriving back from a visit to the mess. 'Sir?' Si asked, placid as a Jersey cow.

'That woman,' Pearse spluttered. 'She struck an officer. She struck me . . .'

Karina stuck the blade in her pocket. She'd keep it with her from now on, she decided. Si smiled.

'Well, if she struck you, sir, a strong chap like you must hardly have felt it. I'll have her scald you some brandy, shall I, and Hepworth will fetch it to you.'

Pearse deflated. He dusted down the arm of his greatcoat. 'I'd have her flogged if she were a man.'

'Too late for that, sir. Now she's uncovered, eh?' Si's laugh was throaty and dismissive.

Pearse glared but he stalked away.

'I won't scald him brandy,' Karina growled from the corner, pulling off her coat.

'Won't you now?'

'He tried to hurt me . . . He offered me his attentions.'

'I'm surprised you ain't been offered more, madam. Maybe if you're out from under Doctor Hooker's protection you should stay here where I can keep an eye on you.'

Karina sank onto the stool in the corner. She had a sudden longing to be alone. To stay here in the south and somehow survive the bitter winter that was coming.

Si poured a draught of brandy and heated a poker in the oven till it glowed. He plunged the tip into the liquid, which hissed violently. Then he stirred in sugar. 'Hepworth,' he called. When the negro appeared the cook handed him the tankard. 'For Mr Pearse,' he ordered, and Hepworth disappeared down the corridor. 'I'm retiring for the night,' Si announced, rather formally. 'And tomorrow I want no more nonsense.'

Nine

Thebo never liked the English. 'You can't trust them,' he swore. This assessment was based on his acquaintance with sailors who hailed from the south coast. Men from Southampton and Portsmouth with whom he had crewed packets and merchant ships over the years. That and the war, in which he had not fought, but was legend among his father's generation. 'They are, to a man, obsessed with their flag,' he swore. 'They love it above everything.'

Karina could not help think that he had proved right about the flag. The *Erebus* and the *Terror* would not leave the far south without claiming the place for the queen. Ross announced an expedition to be mounted to plant the jack ashore. The flag the ships had left there the year before had long since blown to tatters but that did not mean it should not be replaced.

Karina could not help wonder if every ship in Her Majesty's navy kept a store of flags to leave behind – territories claimed across the globe, colouring the charts that men like Ross were mapping as they went.

That night her dreams were troubled and she woke feeling panicked as if she had lost something important and could not find it again. She lay on the floor and stretched her limbs. The hard surface stiffened them. For a moment she thought she might cry, but she controlled herself. He ought to be beside her, she realized. And there was the rub. She loved Hooker. She had come to love it here, aboard the *Terror* too. She loved the unrelenting white landscape beyond the porthole. Many years ago, she thought it was Thebo who had been her love match. But it was travel she craved – the glamour of the world's most exciting cities, and when it came to it she had found something good here in the middle of nowhere – a place it was impossible to survive.

Si lumbered in and they prepared the breakfast. The crew was excited and the meal finished quickly. The flag ceremony would mark the end of the Antarctic leg of the trip and there was the prospect of setting off northwards, over open water. Heading for home. Each man had a spring in his step. On deck two able seamen whittled dice out of whalebone and whistled cheerfully. Karina stirred a pot of brose and listened to them. She peered periodically towards the ice. The weather was exceptionally fine, as if the sky was on its best behaviour. From the corner of her eye she caught sight of a shoal of elephant seals that swam between the *Erebus* and the *Terror*. The spray from the animals sparkled like a scatter of diamonds above the silky water. She knew, above, many of the sailors would take it as a sign.

In the middle of the morning, he knocked on the door frame. Si was on deck, taking a turn. Hooker stepped sheepishly into the galley. He seemed taller today as if he was held from above, dangling towards the boards, almost out of control.

112

'At home, a chap would bring flowers and here there are none of course,' he said with a shrug. 'I've come to say sorry.'

She laid down the spoon. 'I don't know what I want,' she said.

'Would sorry be a start?'

'From a man who values me so low, he'd shut me up in his house and make a whore of me?'

'Not a whore, Karina. That is harsh.'

'What then?'

Hooker hesitated. 'What we have is outside of normal life. Whatever it is between us, it is not in the run of things. That is why it thrived here, perhaps.'

She felt herself flush and was glad of the galley's darkness, which meant Hooker might not notice. Out of the porthole she caught a snatch of the ice cliffs. She wished she could be as majestic. As distant.

'We could make what we have grow a different way in England,' he suggested.

'By keeping me separate to everything? Housing me close enough to visit. What would I do, Joseph? In this house, while I waited for you? Tell me about my days?'

'There is something of the wild thing about you. I like it.' His smile was endearing.

'I will miss it here in the end. That is what I have been thinking.'

There was a clatter in the corridor and Si appeared in the doorway. 'Apologies, sir,' he said, and began to back away.

'No. Come in.' Hooker waved him through. Karina cursed the old man's timing. 'Well,' the doctor's tone changed. 'I will join the shore party.'

Karina turned back to the pot on the range.

'I'm looking forward to some heat in my bones,' Si chipped in amiably.

'I wondered if you might join us?' Hooker ignored him. 'Would you like to step onto the ice, Karina? Just once before we go.'

This captured her attention. She felt a thrill at the idea. She had not been off the ship for months. It seemed a shame to leave without going ashore, if the chance was offered.

'May I?' It felt forbidden, though nobody had expressly said so. 'What about the men . . .'

'You will be with me,' Hooker said firmly. 'I have spoken to Ross. He will allow me to manage it.'

At the ropes, the shore crew assembled above. Karina held back from Pearse, who acted as if she was below his notice. He chivvied the men, who were loading a jute sack, two pickaxes and a wooden box.

'I don't know,' she said to Hooker.

'I thought you'd like to come. It is my way of saying sorry. And a good way to say goodbye to this place. You said you would miss it.'

The water looked inviting today, she thought, as the sea lions frolicked. If she was ever to try out the ice, she couldn't ask for milder weather.

'All right,' she said.

The boat was small so they huddled together. Two able seamen manned the oars – Farmer one of them. Pearse, Hooker and Karina sat for the ride. Karina's skirt ballooned around her legs and she could not settle it. She was swaddled in a woollen blanket with the old greatcoat on top. Hooker looked resplendent in his fur hat. She avoided Pearse's eyes. The sound of the wooden oars cutting through the water was soothing and she found she could scarcely take her gaze from the shore as it drew closer. The *Erebus* had sent a rowboat to join them – the planting of the flag being a business with which everyone wished to be involved. The English loved ceremony.

Farmer was first on the ice. He sprang from the bow and efficiently hammered in a peg to tether the rope. Hooker turned to help Karina ashore, offering his gloved hand. The ice was rougher than she expected, running in frozen waves as if someone had thrown it like a piece of cloth across a wide table and had left it wrinkled. The grains were thick. *Saltis*, she thought. Sea ice. As she stepped ashore it crunched underfoot. Pearse saw the kit unloaded – the box and the sack and some rope to hoist the flag.

Karina didn't help. Her head swam as she regarded the vista before her, relishing the steadiness of her first land in months. Beyond the mooring, the glacier stretched to a range of low hills that fell away to sheer ice cliffs. She felt as if she was flying without the dark, heavy ship to moor her. Thebo's old boots afforded a good grip and she stretched her hands wide and walked away from the party, which was now welcoming the men from the second boat. When Hooker called her back, she felt like a boat being pulled in by the tide. The first time she did not heed him.

115

'Karina!' His second call was more insistent.

Reluctantly, she rejoined the party. The men from the *Erebus* nodded in her direction, their eyes still with interest as they took her in.

'Madam,' one of them mumbled.

They haven't seen a woman in months, she thought.

They set off inland, Pearse ahead leading the seamen. Behind, Hooker and one of the officers from the *Erebus* drew out a compass each and took readings. There was some talk of magnetism as they trudged towards the lee of the hill, which it had been decided was the best place to raise the flag.

'It will never last the winter,' Hooker said.

'It might,' the other officer chimed in. 'You never know. It will be protected by the slope.'

'Well, we must raise it inland a way at least. Closer to the shoreline would be uncertain. At any time the ice could sheer off and we can't have the jack adrift.'

'No. We can't have that.'

It felt good to be moving unrestricted. She was reminded of walking for miles when she had hunted for eggs on Deception Island, scouring the cliffs for nests to raid. It felt a long time since she had been that hungry. It would be odd to see Deception Island again – the ragged line of shacks on the dock and the stink of the smelting vats. She wondered if, waiting for her, was the letter from Marijke at last. It felt alien to hope for news from Amsterdam and perhaps even some money. She wondered if Van Kleek

116

might have opened it to retrieve what she owed him. How might he manage here, she wondered. Of anyone, she thought, the grizzled old company man would suit this kind of isolation.

They stopped and two men set to the ice with the pickaxes. It was heavy work. At sea, there was always an element of blue between the water and the sky but here if you turned away from the shore, the whiteness could overtake you, like stepping through a curtain. Like wrapping yourself in a frozen shroud.

In the other direction, the ships looked like children's toys – tiny, dark vessels floating on an icy pond. One of the officers from the *Erebus* pulled a hipflask from his pocket and offered it to Hooker, who took a gulp and smacked his lips. One of them said something Karina didn't catch and they all laughed. Hooker looked as if he belonged here, in this company. His green eyes stood out against the snow. He was smiling. She liked that he was taller than the other men – only a shade, but still.

She lingered uncomfortably on the fringes of the group. Pearse eyed her and turned away. The officers laughed again and Karina decided she might head a little further along the hillside. She could see a small fissure framed by icicles. There was something intriguing about it. Behind her, the laughing continued. A little way off now, one of the men scooped up a handful of snow and formed it into a loose ball, which he threw at Pearse, who retaliated in kind. They were, she thought, like children.

Looking down at her boots, she stamped hard,

testing out her land legs. Then she peered into the crack. It was like a sculpture. Snow made everything beautiful, she thought. It covered both mud and decay. As a child, the morning the first snow came was always an occasion of excitement.

The fissure opened into a small ice cave. She turned in the entrance, staring at the vivid blue sea framed by the walls. A smile played on her lips. Back at the flag, the men were missing this. They simply brought their world with them, she thought. She stamped her foot, enjoying making a deep footprint in the rough surface and stretched up to reach an icicle, which she broke off and held in her hand like a dagger. Then, in only a second, there was a tearing sound and a crack.

Behind her, the fissure in the ice opened and over at the group, the laughing stopped and there was a shout. 'Karina!' Hooker's voice sounded. She swung round. The men were still planting the flagpole but Hooker, Farmer and the officer from the *Erebus* were running towards her. Pearse held back and gestured to the men to keep working. She hadn't realized she had come so far. It was only watching them running, she realized the distance. She started to move, but before she could take a step, she tipped as the ice gave way beneath her, just as Farmer appeared in the frame. He sprang, missing her outstretched fingers by an inch. Karina heard herself scream. Time slowed.

Farmer was above her now, the light from the sky formed a slash between shady, sheer walls

118

of ice. His face was pink. He looked like a raspberry, she thought and then wondered why this had come into her mind, as he tumbled towards her, overbalancing. Then someone caught him and hauled him back over the edge. Karina reached upwards but there was no such help and she kept falling, falling, falling. Before it went dark, Hooker's face appeared in the light like a flash. He seemed as far away as the boats had been.

Her cry was cut off as she landed, the last of the air leaving her body so that in the end, it was only a sigh.

'Karina,' he called into the silence. And again, 'Karina.' The officers and men talked so quickly that the sound formed a knot. Above, where she couldn't see him any more, Pearse was the only one still tending the flag. Closest to the shore, he hoisted it carefully as the others crowded around the crack, terrified by what had happened – the woman disappearing into the earth, so far down they couldn't see her body. And then, real-izing that this spot was dangerous and that the ice might open to swallow them, the officer from the *Erebus* pulled Hooker away. On the boats, as the men turned, they caught sight of the glint of an eyeglass in the sun. The officer waved, to signal his distress. Over the side a fellow waved back. 'It isn't even snowing,' Hooker said, in shock. 'There is no sign of a storm. There was nothing to harm her.'

'Karina!' he called, but she could no longer hear him. The silence stretched.

'Come on, doctor, we must leave,' the officer

said. Hooker tarried and the man raised his voice. 'Come on!' he repeated. As if in response, the ice shifted once more. The crack was like a groan.

They hesitated only an instant and then took off for their lives. Running hell for leather, Hooker turned only slightly to look back at the shattered cave. Pearse joined them as they flew past. At once, the air felt colder. The sun became unaccountably low and, after that one shift, which seemed a kind of warning, the land lay still, as if it was waiting. Throwing the pickaxes into place, the men scrambled onto the open boat and cast off. The seamen rowed like billy-o. 'Come on!' the officer from the *Erebus* encouraged them, his voice carrying across the water. They half expected the ice to answer.

Hooker could not take his eyes from the receding crack at the foot of the hill, which from a distance looked only part of the landscape, not even particularly dramatic compared to the ice cliffs to the south. He stayed on the rowing boat as the others climbed on deck. 'Sir?' Pearse called over the side and only then did the doctor turn towards the *Terror* and put his hand onto the rope ladder.

At the top, Ross was waiting.

'Where is she?' the captain asked.

'There was a crack in the ice. She fell,' was all the doctor could get out.

Ross ordered someone to fetch tincture of opium. 'I shall prescribe for you sir, today,' he said.

'She might not be dead, James. She fell but she

might not be dead. What if she is down there?' Hooker wailed.

Pearse shook his head in the captain's direction. A solid judgement. As the news spread, the men on board whispered in a rush that sounded like the tide. The horror of it.

'We must fetch ropes.' Hooker thrashed his arms in a windmill of grief. 'My God,' he declared. 'She could regain consciousness. And even if she's gone, we cannot leave her there without even a prayer. It's not Christian.'

In the end Ross gave Hooker leave to return ashore with three volunteers. Archie stepped forward, Farmer, despite his shock, and the young lad whose brother sailed aboard the *Erebus*. Together the unlikely rescue mission rowed solemnly ashore. They disembarked carefully and then trudged across the ice as if it was only a thin sheet over a frozen lake. At the fissure, Hooker lay flat on his belly and called, low, into the heart of the earth, as if he was attending a birth.

'Hello!' his voice disappeared as if the continent had swallowed it. 'Hello.'

Silence.

He waited and tried again. Archie took off his hat despite the cold and recited the Lord's Prayer. Farmer hid his hands, for they were shaking. Still, he readied the rope in case it was needed. 'Karina.' Hooker sounded as if he was pleading. 'Karina. Can you hear me?' he squinted downwards. 'Sweetheart.' The crack appeared to dwindle into the heart of the world. Down. Down. Down. She was gone. 'Karina.' This time his voice raised too high. There was a disquieting shift at the echo.

Above the mouth of the ice cave, a shard fell into the endless gap. The boy jumped backwards. Farmer called 'Look out!' A shower of ice started, slowly at first but then fine as flour, it poured down. Hooker sprang to his feet, not noticing his journal, wrapped in a scrap of paulin, as it tipped from his pocket into the deadly chasm. He turned and as one, the men abandoned the rope and ran for the boat moored a mere three hundred yards away. It felt further.

Archie fell behind quickly, too fat and old to sprint like the others. The ice heaved and cracked behind him but it missed the old man as it fell away. 'Come on!' Hooker shouted, stopping at the water's edge to usher the others aboard as the crevice filled. Archie jumped as he hadn't jumped in twenty years, Hooker springing in behind him. As they cast off there was an almighty creak and an island of ice sheered off the edge of the land like a piece of bread being torn from a loaf. It launched into the water buoying the boat on a wave, as Farmer and the boy rowed for their lives.

Further offshore, the crew of both ships were hanging over the sides, shouting. 'You can make it, lads! You can make it!' When they reached the portside, the men were hauled on board. The boy was heaving for breath and laughing. Archie hugged Si like a long-lost brother. Farmer turned with the doctor and stared back at the view. The Antarctic looked as beautiful as ever. If you saw it for the first time, you'd never guess that part was missing, floating on the swell now, off into the distance.

'Well, the flag stayed in place,' Ross said, as he joined the party. And there it was, fluttering only slightly for there was hardly a breeze. Ross saluted and the men around him did the same. Hooker stared. 'We will have a service, Doctor Hooker,' the captain said, as if Hooker was being in some way unreasonable. 'We shall sing a hymn.'

Ten

Karina felt herself wake almost at once. At first she could remember nothing. It was strange. She seemed to be viewing matters from an odd perspective. Was she behind glass, she wondered. She put out her hand to check. Then, beside her a bright light appeared, as if a door had opened onto it. 'What is this?' she whispered.

There was nobody to say. The light was warm and comforting and she felt drawn towards it, but her mind was clouded. She loitered. A familiar voice started speaking beyond the door. 'Come in,' it said, but the sound was muffled, as if the speaker was far off, or perhaps underwater.

'Thebo?' It sounded like him. It was a man's voice, speaking Danish, in any case. But Karina was too distracted to investigate. Instead she turned her attention to figuring out what had happened. Slowly, the events fell into place. The sound of the crack. The men shouting. Hooker's voice. The sensation of spiralling into the earth. *And yet*, she thought, *I can see the shore. The boats are there.*

As she watched, a callous kind of calm pervaded the frozen scene. Around her, the light faded slowly. She looked up, squinting, and saw the *Terror* in the distance and the shadowy outline of the *Erebus* in its wake. Then she realized that the ships were underway. They were sailing northwards. The voice from the light, still somehow beside her, became so low it almost disappeared as she jumped up, howling.

'Don't leave me. Don't you dare leave. Help me!' She shrieked like a banshee but her words disappeared as they hit the air.

And then as if Captain Ross's telescope was in her hand, she found she could make it out easily – she could pull the receding boats towards her as if they were on castors, or at least, the vision of them. At first, Joseph Hooker was nowhere to be seen but then he emerged, striding onto the bridge.

'Come back!' she screamed.

As he turned, she could see he was wearing her green scarf. Her fingers fumbled at her throat but it was gone. She remembered leaving it in the box in the galley. Folding it and deciding she wouldn't wear it ashore.

She spun round. The tall rectangle of light was still beside her but it had softened at the edges. It looked strange in the dusk. *Where is it coming from?* she wondered. The voice had almost gone now. She felt as if she should walk towards it, that behind the door there might be something warm. Or not exactly that, for she wasn't cold now. Still, behind the door there might be something. But she couldn't concentrate. Her mind could not tear itself away from her confusion and she was nursing fury in her belly. Her eyes were drawn back to the ships. To the sight of them leaving.

On deck, the captain joined his surgeon. The men were singing a hymn. The words floated towards her though they were miles off. 'Praise my soul, the King of Heaven,' they boomed. *Heaven*, she thought, *how foolish*. Hooker was crying. One of the officers passed him a handkerchief.

Then, the strangest sensation started behind Karina's eyes. She could see them, but she could see much more – a street, a house, a woman. A woman in a fine dress the colour of claret, sitting at a cherry wood writing table. Her heart felt suddenly leaden as she took it in the scene. The woman was younger than her. She looked English – her dress had a particular cut. Her features were plain, reflected in the gilt mirror over the leather-topped desk.

My Darling Joseph, the woman formed the words, her pale hands holding an elegant ebony ink-pen and her dark chignon perfectly placed as her head bowed over the letter. *I have every faith you are now on your way home and that our nuptial plans will be soon completed.*

Then she stopped, this other woman. She played a moment with an emerald ring on the betrothal finger of her pale hand and Karina knew at once what had happened. She knew it, though she had not a single inkling all the months they were together. In a rush of anger, she realized she was dead. She had tumbled. And this was his life, she was seeing. Everything she had not known before.

Back in London, the woman in the claret dress resumed writing. It struck Karina she had chosen curious words. She read the phrase again over the woman's silk-clad shoulder *our nuptial plans will be soon completed*. She thought of herself lying on the furs in Hooker's cabin and pondered the idea of a marriage being completed after the ceremony instead of over the course of the many years to come – the ups and downs.

Joseph had never touched this woman. She knew that, but still, he had been promised. Their lovemaking had been an adventure. The lady in London did not admit explorers. She was why Joseph had wanted to hide her away in the country. How dare he? Karina's instinct was to push this hurtful vision away. It felt as if she was red raw and bleeding, as if Joseph, impossibly, had slashed open her heart. She let out a scream of anguish and reached out as if she might touch it – the London study with its ticking clock and its measured decorations. Not too showy. Not too plain.

Then an old man appeared in her line of sight behind the woman's tidy frame. The woman continued writing, oblivious, but he raised a hand in greeting. He looked her in the eye. Karina reeled.

Can he see me?

The man's clothes were out of fashion by a hundred years – he was wearing britches and an old frock coat. Still, both angry and curious, she raised a salute. The man smiled. She looked down, understanding clicking into place like a rusty hinge. Her mind creaked.

If you die, your spirit haunts the place where you fell. And between such places, like taut ropes, sightlines connect people who matter to each other. People like this women and I, unacquainted in life, but loved by the same faithless man. In death, you see everything.

127

Beside the old fellow, a young girl walked into the frame. She pointed at Karina and squinted before turning to say something. The woman in the claret dress continued to write, undisturbed by this whispering of ghosts over her head. It occurred to Karina that no one had ever died on this uninhabited ice shelf, this terminus at the end of the world. No one, that is, except her. She would be alone here. She whirled around. The last of the sun was sinking and the sky was turning slate grey. The door of light had faded. Soon it would be dark for the whole lonely, Antarctic winter and she was the only soul on the continent – the only corpse in a thousand miles.

In London, the man put his arm contentedly around the child and in a flash Karina understood the true irony. She did not have it quite right. You were not trapped where you fell. You were trapped where you were happiest. *The sea is not kind, why should we be?* Thebo's voice echoed and Karina shook her head as if trying to rid herself of it. Perhaps the world was not kind either. And here she was. *Hooker has done for me twice over, the snake.* She gasped. It seemed so unfair. She had truly loved him here of all places and now here she would stay. It was not the ship or the cabin but the sheer cliffs and the isolation that had fired her passion. Had Hooker been genuine, perhaps they would have been reunited in death and this would be their heaven. Instead when his time came the doctor would join the shades in the London morning room and his plain fiancé who had been waiting patiently these four years of his voyage. That was where his true life lay. Despite any momentary tears, that would be his happiness. Karina had been a passion. A distraction. That was all.

From the shore the wind whipped up. Beside Karina the light faded and disappeared. The vision of London dimmed. She stared after it, till it was gone and she was alone. The southerly storm spun her hair into life but she did not feel the slightest chill. She pushed the visions away – the *Erebus* and the *Terror*, the sitting room on the other side of the world. She would have none of it. With the gloom darkening, she made a vow with a clarity of purpose she had not known in all the months she had lived in the cold. The sub-zero temperatures slowed the minds of the living but that was no longer her concern.

I will rise with fire in my eyes. I will rise.

The wastes were shrouded in darkness. The Union Jack fluttered uselessly, no more than a tiny speck. The edges of the flag had ripped already. And as far as she could see, it all belonged to her. She moved like a skater across the plain. She glided up the snowy peaks and rolled down the far side of the glacier. She could see for miles. The darkness meant nothing. The landscape was clear, the vertiginous cliffs as beautiful as any cathedral. The ice was diamond. And inside she was burning.

It does not matter how long it takes me, Joseph. I will wait.

Her fury twisted and as she whirled back towards the shore she swooped like a wheeling gull. She landed on the fresh snow, on top of her make-shift grave. Her feet clasped an indentation in the ice. As she gazed down, the opaque crystals cleared in her vision so she could see her corpse, frozen beneath the ice – her skin like glass, as if she was only sleeping.

The sight was fascinating and Karina settled to watch herself. The skin had tightened over her face. It was darker than in life. Her flesh was frozen rock hard. Then, with her head to one side, like a curious bird that has found something it does not understand, she noticed the notebook that had tumbled on top of her body when Hooker sprang to his feet to get away. She reached through the ice, surprised as her arm stretched down, grabbing the journal. The book had no weight in her hand, and as she brought it up she realized it remained lodged beside her body. *Do books have ghosts?* she wondered.

Laying this matter aside, she opened the first page and settled down to snoop. The story started on the voyage south and unlike any of the other officers' journals she had caught a glimpse of, this one contained less in the way of charts, of latitude and longitude or weather conditions. Instead Joseph wrote that he was excited. He admitted he was afraid. And for the first time he mentioned the other woman – Frances. *Frances.*

Karina repeated the name, lolling it around her mouth. The sting of jealousy was as strong as when she had seen the woman, oblivious, sitting there writing. Fleetingly, she wondered how long it had been since the ship left. Since she had died. She had no way to measure time. Were they home yet or had they only just sailed out of sight? She shrugged and bowed her head to continue reading as Hooker waxed about autumnal walks round a country estate and about a Christmas ball. He wrote about a need. More than one. He kept using the word. Karina tried to understand. *My need is great*, he wrote. A need for sex? For money? For advancement? She could not tell. *The needs are various.* He put down once more. *What needs were these, Joseph, that led you to betray her with me and me with her?* Karina's eyes flashed with sadness peppered with anger, but she kept reading.

By the time his closely packed scribbles arrived at Deception Island, he had sailed for years. He had seen the world – the bustling coastal cities of South America and the deserted wastes of the Antarctic plains. He liked the Australian coast-line and was amused by the variety of birdlife. He loved the weather – the mildness of the Antipodean winter as much as the chill Antarctic summer nights. He was impressed by the majesty of glaciers and pondered whether the Emperor penguins were some primitive, flightless form of life so strange that he doubted they were they among the usual run of God's creatures.

Quite apart from the weather, he noticed a great deal. The customs and the land around each port. The appearance of the people. The frequency of whale sightings. Rum that was distilled in a remote village, spiced and fiery. He listed the artefacts he had found and those he bought – a

131

bundle of topaz and an ancient carving. Animal skins and fossils. And then, at last, she came to his account of the day she was discovered hiding on deck. That very first day. And Joseph wrote of something else entirely, something he was reading – his concerns about a scientific theory.

A glimmer of a smile played around Karina's lips. She did not merit as much as a sentence though she was beaten by the bo'sun. She recalled that for all his medical efforts, Joseph did not doctor her on that occasion. Perhaps he simply didn't know – billeted in his cabin, pondering the ins and outs of one species and another. Did he only hear a boy had been found when he sat down to dinner? Were those twelve lashes so inconsequential that no one told him about them?

One way or another, the notebook was more than two-thirds full before there was any sight of her – its heroine. Even then he only noticed her when it was discovered that she could cook. Karina pictured herself. She looked thin and taut like the boy she was pretending to be. She understood why he did not question her appearance. There was nothing of her but a strange, terse creature, odd to see now in her mind's eye.

Hooker jotted down the details of the menu. Fish stews. Corn breads. An occasional pudding steamed in syrup. On board all sweetness was as treasure and Joseph had a tooth for it. He had been transfixed by her chocolate cream and dedicated half a page to it. *Then he noticed me, only then.*

She sighed, wondering what might have happened

had her luck been different? It had all been so brief. If only the storm hadn't floored her, might Joseph have asked her to cook in his house in Glasgow? From cabin boy she might have been promoted to head chef. She read on, looking for the memories that were important to her, and for the most part not finding them. He did not mention the day he helped her with the dropped slop of food – that moment of connection. He must have been terrified of what he felt. And from then it seemed he could not bring himself to scribble a single word about her or even her food until she was uncovered.

Then – *Karina sets me alight*, he put down. Karina's heart rushed to read it. She stopped and read it again. *See, it was not only me.* She felt a flood of hope. Carefully, she calculated the entry to two days before he first touched her, curling his hand around her waist as she read on the bed. *She is a mesmerizing flame*, he said. She wondered why he held back, then. And why, if he was so mesmerized, would he still marry his Frances; for though he never said it, it was clear he would turn his back on passion for the sake of propriety or money or society. Whatever it was. All his needs. *Now*, she thought, *I can see every shabby intention. We had a fire that was to be fed as long as it suited him and then abandoned to burn out or locked away to burn in secret. Which was worse?*

She dropped the pages and in temper she took off and soared. She flew up and down the glacier greedy for revenge until she had run herself out.

133

Then she sat on a bank of snow and wished for redemption. It amused her that she had never believed in ghosts. And neither had he, for that matter. It seemed foolish now. All at once, she wanted to repent, but there were no sins to speak of. Foolishness, certainly. Poor decisions too. She had not been a good wife to Thebo, perhaps. But sin – that was another matter. They said there was redemption in death. She had heard that. But nothing changed, here on the other side. She missed not home exactly. She missed the living. She missed being alive. The privilege of knowing so little. Of taking some kind of revenge on Joseph or at least being able to tell him that she knew he'd betrayed her. *It is a kind of torture to see inside your lover's heart.*

Inland, the Emperor penguins huddled, nesting. They sang to each other. When the light came it surprised her. The sky opened and suddenly the world was bright blue. Karina perched on her vantage point, as the birds fussed around their eggs. Then she spotted one little fellow – fully grown, on his own. At first, she thought he was lost, heading inland, away from the rookery and any hope of food. Karina stood up. Her body stretched and she felt a cloud brush through her hair. She could swear that she creaked like a tree. Inland, the penguin continued walking away from the shore.

Determined to direct him to safety, she swooped, waving her arms. But he showed no sign of knowing she was there. She landed in his path but he walked straight through her. *I am no longer part of the world*, she thought. In the ghost stories of her childhood, spectres touched the living, but not her, not now.

In the end, she followed. The little bird waddled ten miles, advancing to his doom. She rose to look back at the colony, but the others made not even a call in his direction. After days, the poor creature could only crawl, determined, still pulling himself on his belly away from redemption and then, a tiny pinprick on the dazzling white, he gave a shallow pant. Fascinated, she watched as his life slipped away. When he was gone, she shed an unexpected tear, cursing her foolishness as she lingered, waiting to see if he appeared in death, but there was nothing – only the ice shelf – a sheer void in the world.

On the light nights, the eternal days, she visited the penguin colony often. The seals and whales swam close to scoop what they could out of the water. From time to time, she realized, a penguin simply slipped across the surf towards them voluntarily. Perhaps they were stranger creatures than the crew had realized. Perhaps some of them simply wished to die. She wondered if Joseph had presented his penguin skeleton to the Society, as he had planned. She wondered what the gentlemen of London might have made of it. She wondered if he thought of her. *Poor Karina*, he might say. The way he'd talk of a dead lapdog. A happy but inconsequential memory. It was clear that those nights in his cabin had an entirely different meaning for the doctor. She gritted her teeth when she thought of it and nursed her fury.

Eleven

It would not be true to say that she did not see the men, though she did not see them clearly. Like interlopers in a dream, they were indistinct both to the eye and the ear. Once she heard Swedish, she could have sworn it. A snippet of conversation about a recipe, that caught her attention, but she could not make it out. The men camped on the ice and brought dogs. Karina watched, thinking of Hooker, who had never quizzed her about dog sleds in the end. She squinted at vague shapes as they fumbled through the snowstorms, but she could not tell one fellow from another. They were too swaddled – not only in wool and gabardine but almost as if the edges of them had melted into the air. She wondered, momentarily, if they could see her. And then they were gone.

Time meant nothing any more. She drifted in and out. A day. A week. A year. A decade might pass overnight. Then a snatch of Italian, perhaps, from a fuzzy shadow. Or was it Latin? She tried to bring the man into focus, but she couldn't concentrate. The stars were too beautiful. The snow twinkled like a kaleidoscope in the moonlight. Then she closed her eyes and a few more months simply disappeared. Sometimes she heard the empty days as they whizzed by, just missing her. She was a bright star. She was a frozen outcrop. Eternal in spirit, spread thinly over the plains.

She was lying on the glacier one day (or was it night?) when a buzzing started behind her eyes and even if she closed the lids she couldn't stop it. She waved a hand in front of her as if she was batting off a fly. Then, she scented *Braunschweiger* on the air. Karina had not smelled anything for a long time, long before she had passed over. The sensation stopped her dead and all at once she felt the satin edge of the quilted cover her sister and she had slept beneath as children. *This is the final consequence*, she thought, *the last sad vestige of my earthly feelings. My love for Marijke. It takes a long time to leave it all behind. In death, it is life that haunts you. Its limits dictate the edges of everything.* Now, too late, Karina knew the importance of her passions, for she was carrying them into eternity. It was her love for Hooker that had trapped her here. It was her lack of interest in the indistinct shapes of other men as they passed that meant she had become so long, so thin, so alone. *Where are the ships?* she wondered, and then, hauled back by the sensation, she felt the sun on her face, as if she was lying on the pantiled roof once more, watching sightseers come off the ferry.

Karina leaned forward. Marijke drew into focus, a vision on the snow. She was the first person Karina had seen clearly in a long time. Thousands of miles away, her figure was absolutely distinct. She was an old woman now. Her face was lined and her hair was a wisp of white, though Karina would know her anywhere for she could see the freckled eight-year-old blonde girl inside the fragile, elderly frame. *How many years have I been here? When she sees me, am I still twenty-four years old?* Karina wondered and reached down the edge of a sheer ice cliff.

Marijke's eyes were cloudy. They had buried her with black cloth swaddled tightly around her tiny body. There was an amethyst brooch at her neck and she still wore her wedding ring. She was not smiling. This old lady, Karina's sister, perched alone upon the crest of the pantiled roof like some strange raven. Exactly where she had sat all those years ago. Called by the same buzzing noise as her sister, she looked around and waved, examining Karina's ghost. The two women smiled at each other. *Ah, you died. That's why you did not come home. I wondered for years. I waited.* The old woman's blue eyes were sad. *Yes, I died young and beautiful and it is no consolation*, Karina said. Marijke shrugged as if to say, *And you are not here? You never came home?*

It crossed Karina's mind that, as a child, her sister had been wrong in her appetite for the world. She should have stayed in Ven. She felt desperately sorry that Marijke was never happier than her childhood days. What kind of life was that? Karina wished she could see her now in death, perched in her wedding bed or in a ballroom or some fine hostelry. Or in the grand dining room where she must have eaten

138

every day with friends and family, mistress of her husband's house. Marijke's life had seemed so much more settled. Now it was clear that she had not been happiest with her wealthy husband in her luxurious home. *I always thought you loved him.* Karina said. *Love?* The old woman laughed. *Never love.*

She had sent the money. Karina could see that now, her story unfolding. And Van Kleek had sent it back, deducting her debts and a carefully calculated interest payment before doing so. He had proved a studious accountant. The letter had not arrived on Deception till the spring after Karina's departure. Trafficking news across the world's oceans was an inexact science and Marijke's kindness languished a long time in Chile before a vessel was heading in the right direction. *Would I have survived till spring?* Karina wondered. She might. She might not. She had been so thin. So frail in the face of Deception's hardship. Perhaps it would have been better for her to remain there and take her chances, for it was clear now that there was a different life to be had with a different death at its crossroads. *You don't think that way when you have breath in your lungs.* She waved again at her sister and turned her eyes to the little village beyond the roof tiles.

Ven looked the same. The same wooden houses. The same main street. The little village was so ordinary and so very far away. To one side, beyond the roof, there was a shocking slash of yellow beach and rising behind it hills of misty green. *They look so soft.* After years of jagged outcrops, the green was mystifying. She strained, trying to see her mother, but even as children it had been clear their mother hated life in the backwater where she was born and where she would die. Together the women wondered momentarily where their mother had gone but they did not know her well enough. They did not know what she wanted. *Perhaps there is another place*, Marijke ventured. *And you?*

I loved a man here, Karina replied. *A faithless man who was promised to another. And now I must stay here at the end of the world.*

I'm sorry, Marijke said. *What fools we have been.*

Below her, a scatter of children ran up and down the beaten earth of the walkway. Two boys threw a leather ball back and forth where the boats weighed anchor. *Are they Sverre's sons or his grandsons?* There was no way to know. A sullen carthorse tethered outside the village shop watched them. Karina drank in this little vignette. She ached for it. She thought of the ghost stories they used to tell over the winter. Her mother baked rosy red apples in the embers and her uncle tried to scare them with tales of the dead returning or worse, the dead who never left. The creak of a floorboard left the other children squealing. These boys no doubt did the same.

Now we are the dead.

And did you never have children? Karina examined her sister's face for an explanation.

No. Not that. Children, indeed. And you had three men?

140

Three? Karina shook her head. *Two. Thebo and the other one. The faithless English doctor.*

Marijke shrugged. *No, I'm sure it was three*, she repeated, before moving off. Death did not allow you to feign interest.

She disappeared across the village roofscape, trailing a length of black cloth in her wake and carefully picking her way towards a ship docking at the jetty. Doubtless, she would name the people who disembarked. She would know every one of them, every story now. Karina cried out, knowing the vision was fading. She wished she were there. She wished so hard, she believed that it would move her, but her heart had made the choice long ago and there was no leaving. She blew a single kiss and the light faded. Then she cried out and fell dejected, onto her knees. Was Marijke the last living soul who held her dear? Could the wrong choice really leave her stranded forever? Could ghosts not cling to each other? Could they not be held? She wished she could cry but there was not even enough warmth for that any more. Instead she hardened, impenetrable as the ice.

Slowly, she stepped off the edge of the hillside and onto the air. She flew past the penguin colony and out to sea. From above, the coastline looked like Ross's map – white ice against blue ocean. 'Marijke!' she called, as if her sister was walking ahead and might wait for her. Karina kept going. She felt the breeze in her hair. To one side the sky turned vermillion as the sun sank. And then, it was like hitting a wall. The world disappeared into total blackness and all

141

she could think was, *Is this a second kind of death?*

When she woke again she was laid out on the ice, back where she had started. There would be, she realized, no going home. She kicked the snow but it did not shatter. She blew in the face of the wind, but it made no difference to the Antarctic storm. She screamed at the seals, bathing in the cool sunlight but they were as nonchalant as deaf old men.

Utterly alone, she sat on the edge of the ice shelf, dangling her feet in the glacial water, as if she was lazing in the tropics. How long she sat there it was impossible to say but it got light. *A man might run mad, waiting for the first polar dawn after the interminable darkness,* she thought. She continued to splash her toes in the water but could not displace a drop. *Christ,* she thought, wondering where that word had come from, *who on earth can possibly save me?*

Part Two
Fingers Like Ice

'Playing the game means treating your dogs like gentlemen and your gentlemen like dogs.'

Ted Tally

Twelve

8 February 1902

There was no telling how much later it was but Marijke had long faded. The sky lightened and darkened so many times Karina lost count. When she first spotted it, it was only a pinprick on the horizon. It was difficult to focus on something so small and yet, like an itch in an awkward spot, she could not leave it alone. It was moving slowly – not fluid like a whale but too large to be anything else. She waited and then as her vision cleared, she gasped.

'A ship.'

The hull was black, the rigging hoisted like an old maid's tangled knitting and she could read the name on the side – *Discovery*. Compared to the clean majesty of the ice shelf, the ship looked grubby as it sailed into the bay – a mass of wooden planks and thick rope sprouting what looked like old man's whiskers. Fluttering behind she saw the colours – that unmistakeable interlacing of red, white and blue. That pirate's flag. *Yes*, she thought, *it's real*. There was a ship. And aboard it, scuttling like mice, she realized there must be men.

With her mind racing, she stood on tiptoe. She had grown in death – thinned and elongated. When she was alive, her hands were pale, and aboard the *Terror*, her nails were carefully trimmed for work in the galley. Now she was no longer contained by flesh and blood, she had talons like a wise Chinee. When did they grow, she wondered. When did she become a creature that could swoop like a gull?

She looked down half expecting both feathers and scales but mostly she was made of light. Then she stretched one white alien finger and was mesmerized as it reached the mountain a mile away. *That will never do*, she thought. *I want to look inside.* So she squirmed as if she was drawing on a bodice. For a vivid moment, she was reminded of vanity – of what it was to be alive. Then she contracted and pounced inside.

After all this time and so many indistinct figures, it was difficult to focus on the living. And then, slowly, the figures stepped from the shadows. They moved in a scatter and with fascination she named them. She took no less delight in that old game. And all at once, in a rush that almost knocked her over, she saw every-thing – their home towns, their dingy kitchens, their small discomforts. The delight of leaving port. A snatched kiss with a loved one. A hearty meal. It all crowded in. Every man aboard carried a sitting room in his memory, populated by a woman wearing peculiar clothes.

Karina's nails dug into the floorboards as she tried to steady herself. She squinted at these mothers and wives as they went about their busi-ness – darning or reading. Making their toilette with a spray of lavender or rose or violet. Dressing their hair. Choosing what would be served for dinner. Balancing the household accounts. A thousand tiny dramas played out on a hundred small stages. With her head to one side, bemused, Karina watched them pin their hats in place and set off for a walk in the park or a trip to the haberdashery. They bathed. They read a while.

As the ship edged steadily closer she was overwhelmed by the freshness of the memories. She struggled to see the world again with all its scents and colours. And slowly she realized that she could control the visions, walking around them as she pleased. A stroll in Islington. A swim in Strangford Lough.

In one, the ship itself was being built in Scotland on the Tay – only half completed. There in her mind's eye was the commander inspecting it. He strained to understand the engineer, whose accent was as thick as Keiller's marmalade. The smell of freshly cut timber swept the Antarctic air and then, before she knew it, she was on an Australian road in some kind of machine that threw up clouds of dust. She attended a formal dinner raising funds for this expedition. There was music, which was a riot of sound – not like anything she had heard before and course upon course of fancy food with ices and jellies and glossy butter sauce. And then, in a blink, she found herself standing in the shadows of a bedroom as a man made love to his wife tenderly and afterwards kissed her goodbye. Later, she loitered in the background when he paid for the attention of a different dark-haired woman, somewhere the sun was blazing.

147

Karina silently dallied in the recesses, inspecting these secrets and feeling the prickle of a hundred shabby lies. *Are all men the same?* One fellow was in love with a seaman from another vessel – a desperate, grasping ache snatched behind a public house. A kiss full of longing. Another stationed himself outside the house of a pale, blonde woman, watching her from a distance, every hour he could spare. *He has never spoken to her*, she realized. And between all this, the intimacy of life on board, the knowing of each other, as far as it is possible. And like flashes of lightening, images of the women at home. The Franceses of the world, hopeful and proud, telling tales to young children of the exploits of their menfolk. Confiding their pride to their friends. As if these sailors were heroes.

Has he regretted his decision? Has Hooker returned? She could not help think on it. She searched the scatter of men on deck. She dived into the wooden cabins, the galley and the heads. She made a full survey, but he was not on board. Disappointed, she was surprised by the strength of her feeling. She had not thought of him for years now. Decades maybe.

The ship weighed anchor in the bay as if it was a painting. On deck, the crew was full of energy, but to Karina they played out as a mime, silent as the snowy wastes. Then suddenly her ears popped and the ruckus of voices chimed a familiar echo. It brought back the *Terror* tenfold – the twang of English – the difference between an upper-class accent and the rounded vowels of the men. At first she could not distinguish a

148

single word. Only the tone. *How long has it been? How long?* She wanted to shout. *I am here. I am here.* She felt as if she could run again, up the mountain and down the lee of the slope. As if she could touch the world and make a difference. As if she might fit into a small, frail, pink body after all.

The men collected on deck. The sight of the lapidary, diamond-white mountains was a glory. Karina joined them. Usually she only looked outwards, but now, her perspective reversed. It was strange to see the vast plains of her prison from beyond the shore. The crew had been waiting in anticipation of this arrival for months, no matter the storms or the hardships of the journey (for this ship, she saw, had already battled its share of icy waters). These men were driven. They wanted to prove their mettle – that was why they had come. They wanted to be the heroes their womenfolk dreamed of. Unlike Ross's weary Antarctic band, they were eager. In their eyes the vista was fresh. It was larger and brighter than their imaginings. Out of the babble, the words began to chime clearly.

'Commander Scott, sir,' one man said, 'Isn't it magnificent? We must unload our provisions at once, sir? We must set up camp.'

My God, Karina thought, *they think they can attempt the interior. They have come for the pole.* She laughed. It was unbelievable. These would-be heroes with their pink skin and their fragile heartbeats reckoned they could travel inland. *Have they no idea how small they are? This place will eat them. It will squeeze their lives raw onto the ice shelf.*

She circled the ship and wove between them, intrigued. Their clothes were different from Ross's crew. The style had changed. Each man wore almost the same as the other, like soldiers, though no soldier she knew would be so devoid of feathers and brocade. In the main, they had been trained in the senior service or by the merchant navy. Each had spent most of his life at sea but this trip, they reckoned, was the highlight. *They think will make their names. They think they have a shot at history.*

Weighed heavy in expectation and swaddled in two knitted sweaters and a blue hat, Robert Falcon Scott, for so she had named the fellow in charge, stood at the prow, delighted by the sight of the bay. His eyes burned with determination and Karina could see that though every one of the crew wanted to prove themselves, their commander had the greatest need. It was with difficulty that he turned into his cabin, away from the view.

News flooded towards her. Poor Queen Victoria was dead, she realized. It happened only a year ago and yet it seemed no time at all since her marriage. Captain Ross had disparaged a woman's ability to rule, and he had proved wrong. Like a magic lantern, she witnessed the old queen's funeral. A million black armbands over England. And now the country had a king once more. She thought how relieved Ross would be.

Curious, she settled high above the vessel and

150

soaked it in. She had had no news, for decades. None at all. And now each image arrived like a fiesta – a titbit. Bit by bit it came to her – the indistinct shadows that had passed her by. The men who had come to the ice shelf. Their names were known here. They had written journals. They had reported. Never mind Victoria's sainted death and the coronation they were planning for her son. Never mind the news of the day or the crew's tawdry personal lives. This was interesting.

She leaned in, like a woman hard of hearing and scooped up the memories with more than a modicum of greed. There had been a Swede and an Italian. There had been men who had survived the winter. There had been progress. *Others have come*, she intoned. *Others have come.* And once there was a party that had landed to the south, beyond her boundary. Still, she wondered how could she have missed something so momentous? Surely she would have heard a heartbeat? The animals must have known men were there. The sea lions must have skirted the ship. The penguins, curious, must have eyed the sailors and looked away with disdain. Did the whales sing to them? She couldn't believe all that had passed her by.

As a result, the men of the *Discovery* had charts with them. One of their number was an officer on an earlier mission. He had been here, on the continent, only two years before – a Belgian. Karina spoke a little Belgian. She thought fondly of a chocolate exporter she had met in Venezuela who had greasy hair and yellow eyes. *That must be ten years ago. Twenty. Fifty.* On board the

Discovery, the Belgian sailor was dapper. They called him Bunny – a nickname only the British upper classes could pull off. The man's mind worked in numbers and in patterns. He hardly noticed the panoramic view. It made him hard for her to read, though he was glad to be back, heading for the ice sheet where he intended to calculate the secrets of the continent until he was sick of them. Until he understood.

She curled around the hatch leading downwards. Below decks, this ship was not so very different to the *Terror* – dark wood and rope. Iron stoves peppered the geography. Karina wondered about the galley and was rewarded with sight of a smaller space than that which she and Si Bevan had occupied. She shrugged and moved on to the storerooms. *Bisto powder*, *Colman's Mustard*; she read the names, rolling them around her tongue as if she was tasting the contents of the tins and jute sacks.

Beyond the mess, inside his cabin, Robert Falcon Scott unravelled his charts. She peered over his shoulder, and saw clearly both Swedish and Norwegian written on Ross's map. *My own people.* Scott's interest turned to the fact these northern men had dogs. *Nothing changes. Why could I not see them?* To hear words in her own language would have been like bathing in warm water, she thought. And yet not a single memory had floated towards her. Not a single emotion. Why could she see the Belgian now when only a few hundred days before, he had been indistinguishable? Why, clear as day, could she see into the hearts of some and not others?

152

Above, as if to illustrate the point, the Belgian hung over the side.

'Glad to be back, Bunny, old chap?' a fellow officer slapped him on the shoulder.

'Yes indeed,' the man replied, and remembered boiling ice to make some kind of porridge.

Karina settled in the commander's cabin. She wound round the legs of his desk. It seemed to her that there had been nothing but weather for decades. Wide open spaces. Grand high mountains. The scale had been huge and the cadence slow. And now this mass of humankind cut into it. If she had a heart, it would be beating faster. *They will bring the place to life*, she thought, and then wondered at those words only an instant before being pulled back to Scott as if she was on a leash.

The commander's clear blue eyes were alight. He rolled up the charts, tidying them into place as Karina slipped through his veins, smooth as blood. She moved with him as he made for the door, climbed upwards onto the deck and shouted instructions to disembark at the point. The order had the air of a dramatic performance – where else might the ship dock? What else had they come all this way to do? She could hear the dogs yapping from their quarters below – the animals could sense landfall. Distracted, she abandoned Scott to slide below deck and explore the contents of the hold.

The place was like a museum storeroom – an exploration of the time she had missed. It was not only the fashions that had changed – the bustles and the necklines of the women. In the gloom of the stores, she peered at the fruits of decades of invention, trailing her fingers over the boxes and crates, looming upwards to peer inside. There was a strange machine under waxed tarpaulins. She heard one of the crew call it a *motor.* Beside it, barrels of fuel were freezing at the edges. Her eyes descended further, tunnelling inside the ship towards the spirit lamps and boxes of untried equipment, shining and untouched in their factory wrapping.

They intend to stay for some time. Karina felt glad. Time was the only thing she possessed in surfeit and now she could see them, she was interested. Rising upwards, she burst through the boards on deck. In the light, every man was in his place, crowded together, and all faces turned to their leader. Like all Englishmen, the crew oozed a familiar certainty – confidence in their plans that reminded her of Pearse and Hooker. The sense of entitlement that the world was theirs for the taking.

It was strange that so little had changed. *Why these men? Why now?* Then the answer to her question came in a flash as she fathomed Scott's mind. As blinding as the glacier in full sunshine, Karina reeled. The commander had met Joseph Hooker not a year ago. *Joseph is still alive,* the words dropped from her lips. For a moment she felt nothing and then she almost screamed. Her thoughts raced as she lit on the captain's memory, drawn in as if the ice has given away beneath her once more and she was falling into him.

* * *

It was a cold day for Europe. Scott's coat was taken by a maid and he was shown through a glossy door into Hooker's study. The smell of sealing wax and velum pervaded the dusty air. In the corner, a large green plant grew in a brass bucket. Joseph sat in a velvet chair with ornately carved wooden feet. The doctor was an old man, his fingers thin and his colours faded. The soft pink lips Karina had kissed so passionately had faded to thin grey lines. She stared, her eyes wide. In her memory, he was handsome – eternally young. Now the skin hung in folds from his neck. Still, it was Joseph. Eager to plunge deeper she walked towards him, almost melting into his body. She could see that Hooker's heart still played hide and seek with itself. *He believes his own deception*, she breathed.

Scott shook Joseph's hand – the old man's veins were visible, bulging blue below white skin flecked piebald with great age. Joseph motioned the commander to sit down and the men started with small talk about the journey the commander had made by steam train to get there. The view from the window. *This must be Glasgow*, she thought and looked around the room. Sure enough, there were signs – a book bound in tartan and a mounted stag's head.

'A good journey then?' Joseph checked. His tone had not changed. He might have been enquiring after a healed injury on the deck of the *Terror* all those years ago. Scott nodded and then with a slim smile, Joseph admitted he wished he could have come to London but he was too old to travel. *This is his house and he will not leave*

155

it again. Karina toured the premises as if it was only an architect's plan. She passed through the walls, plastered and painted. The old place he had described to her in such detail was grander than she had imagined. The ceilings were bordered in plaster, like thick swathes of lace. Below them, the skirting boards were a foot high. Behind Joseph's desk there was a penguin, stuffed and mounted – the very fellow he had taken from the shore. On the walls, exquisitely painted plants and flowers were framed in burnished wood hung between tall shelves stacked with books. On the mantle a clock ticked.

Joseph has not thought of me. In his memory, she could see the old man had rewritten the circumstances around their love affair. Karina was a dalliance to be put in its place. *How strange,* it comes into her mind. *You can damn someone and hardly think of them again.* Even as he sat sociably and discussed ice fields and glaciers with Robert Scott there was no image of her in the old man's mind. He did not remember her body, naked under the fur covers, skin as pale as ice and eyes as blue as the azure sky. He could not scent her skin dewed with the musk of their lovemaking. She was nothing. She was gone.

Karina set her jaw. A glimmer of fury cut through her frame. She could not believe that this man had been her whole world and yet, here he was, nonchalant. Hooker was respected – famous even. There were stacks of letters on his desk and articles sent for his comments before publication. Even in his dotage, his view was sought.

In his chair, Scott nodded reverently as Joseph spoke of the dangers of his mission – all those years ago. The commander counted himself lucky to have the old man's advice. He was the last survivor – the only living link. The other Englishmen on Ross's expedition were all dead. Karina wondered where their spirits resided and a reply came to her, from the recesses of Hooker's mind. Ross was buried forty years ago next to his wife in a graveyard in St Albans. Gone now. Gone. Continuing, oblivious, Hooker talked about the fierceness of the cold and Scott told him how he intended to provision the expedition. Joseph listened sagely as the younger man described the motor and nodded at the details of supplies that the crews of the *Erebus* and the *Terror* could only have dreamed of. *What is a tin of ham?* she thought.

Her eyes flitted around the room, landing back on Joseph's wrinkled face. Around his chair there were photographs and childish drawings. She realized that Hooker had children and grandchildren. He was in correspondence with one of the youngest. He watched daily for the child's letters to arrive. This fired her with fresh fury. *He has lived. Just as he went home to do. And I am alone.*

Behind his chair, outside the window a long expanse of green lawn stretched down to a flash of a greenhouse containing exotic plants and a grapevine that showered fruit in season. This man had everything. To see him like this was a final straw. *I could have had children. A boy, blond, with freckles like Marijke. A girl I could teach to cook. A girl with my own blue eyes to see the world with.*

Unable to bear it, Karina burst out of the vision. She flew upwards, rising high over the coast, wheeling above the ship. Looking down on the crew, she hissed.

How dare you?

From this height, the *Discovery* looked tiny and the ice fields beyond the ship stretched eternal. The shelf shifted so slowly that only those beyond life's bounds could see the movement. These men were Joseph's emissaries, engaged upon his continuing mission. Karina eyed the chart in Scott's cabin – the one Ross had completed. She knew the jagged cliffs and shifting snowfields. They were her brothers and her sisters now. All Scott had was mere lines on paper – in life and death the landscape rose differently. You had to traverse the hills to understand them. You had to experience the ice flows. A few marks on paper did not signify.

Beside the chart lay Scott's diary. 1901, she saw. 1902. It had been almost sixty years, she understood at last. Joseph must be eighty years old. *I might have been eighty*, she shrieked into the wind. *I might have had children and a home.* She saw herself in a burgundy dress – the same as Frances had worn all those years ago. She pictured herself flouncing in the lacy Glaswegian mansion, ordering servants about their business and playing in the nursery with her children.

She wanted to tear up the stupid chart with its carefully pencilled calculations. The last time she had seen these curves the map was still being drawn. Now it was printed and the names were horribly familiar, for Ross had called the landmarks after his ships and crew. Mounts Terror and Erebus. The Ross Ice Shelf. Even Victoria merited a mention. In memoriam. And then she read it. *Cape Hooker.* In a snap, it was as if she could feel the cold again. She stared at the chart, listless. There was, needless to say, no mention of her. No Cape Karina. No Lande's Land. *No one knows. No one ever will, for now they are all dead but him.*

She wondered what happened to Archie and Bevan and the crew. She wondered about the cruel-mouthed midshipman, Pearse, and Hepworth, the silent negro with the ring in his ear. They had not figured in Hooker's memory. Maybe he had lost touch, which meant the men were faceless nobodies who had never made a mark on the world. Not his world, anyway.

She swooped low across the bow of the *Discovery* and her mood was black. She wanted to hurt the men on the ship. She wanted to wound Joseph Hooker and his precious reputation. In fury, she pointed at Scott's heart with a single long finger but it passed straight through him. Frustrated, she let out a gasp. Then she turned and whirled over the point and as she did so it dawned on her that the snow flurried with her more than she flurried with it. She had never felt that before. With her newly vengeful heart, she swooped again, and once more the snow shifted slightly, as if she was a whirlwind. She focused her anger and a translucent sliver of ice crumbled and slipped into the sea.

159

From the ship, Scott noticed it with his eyeglass and she glared back at him in triumph. Then she tried again, for ice fell into the sea all the time and it was not unusual for the snow to flurry. But when she blew, the wind picked up and she was at one with it. She smiled.

These men had arrived on her doorstep – all the life a spirit could crave. Enough to make death bearable and give it purpose. *This is my land. And you are encroachers.* She could scent how much this expedition meant to them. Swooping low she could pick individuals from the sea of faces. A squat man whose dark hair peeked from beneath his cap scratched his head and squinted into the cloudless blue. Turning, she soared back over the ship and as she did so another man stared upwards, as if he could sense her too. Sailors believed their superstitions. She wondered whether it was still unlucky to have a woman aboard. The fellow shuddered. Slowly it came to her that the dead not only needed the living but that perhaps, somehow, the living also needed the dead.

This was a connection that had been denied her in her isolation – a contract that she had not yet experienced. Something the old ghost in Frances's study knew, but she had been denied. *When a ghost wakes to their death, if they are among men – can they feed from them?* Perhaps the presence of the *Discovery* was her way back into the world. For the first time in a long time she could vent her feelings. Slowly, she pointed a long, white finger at the blue-eyed sailor. As it passed through him, she could see he felt it. *You will be among the first*, she said.

The man knotted a tatty scarf around his neck. He had the pale skin of northern shores and the certain gait of the English when he moved. He turned his attention to the glacier ahead. The bo'sun was discussing how to unload quickly while the weather held. The men were leaning over the prow. One, his name was Shackleton, Karina pronounced the word in her mind as if Marijke had asked her to – yes, that one stretched so far she wondered if he might tumble. Slowly, like a cat toppling a vase, she swiped at him and the man laughed and pulled himself back on deck. *Give me time*, she snarled.

Sixty years were nothing and these men were Hooker's emissaries. As the ship reached the glacier, she whipped upwards into the clear blue sky. *Hallelujah!* she shouted as she wheeled and they dropped the anchor. *Hallelujah! They are returned.*

Thirteen

The ships were unloaded promptly. The crew could not wait to get onto the ice. Huts would be built. Expeditions into the interior attempted. But first they must unload. Karina peered as they brought off the living cargo. The men and the dogs before anything else.

The men did not trust their instincts when they sensed her, but the animals did. The dogs had been kept in cages the whole voyage. As the boat docked, they were leashed and led onto the ice amid a veritable opera of barking. Karina taunted them, joining in and howling at the white moon in the blue sky as if she was part of the pack. Weller, the dog handler, justified their excited response. 'They need a run. There are no polar bears down here. The closest penguin colony is miles away. They will have to come back for food,' he commented to Shackleton, the officer she had almost tumbled. Ernest.

Excited and tormented at once, the animals ran in circles and snapped at Karina's spectre as she swooped among them. The men, unaware of the drama, offloaded the first of the supplies. Even the largest crates seemed tiny next to the majesty of the mountains. The hold had been stowed so that the things the expedition needed immediately were nearest the openings. The crew set to bringing them off with vigour, working in teams scooping out the saws and nails, sledges and skis, lamps and rucksacks as the animals snapped at Karina's heels.

'Careful,' Wilson, the surgeon, hovered over the men, and Karina halted to watch him from her place high above the pack. Hooker used to bear over the crew in the same way, nervous that if they got injured, they would not heal because of the cold. Karina inspected the new doctor carefully. It didn't comfort her to find that he was married and that he had no lover. Or that he was godly and his memories were peppered with church visits. He liked hymns.

Unaware of the ghost high above making her cursory inspection, the doctor's attention was taken up by one of the dogs, which had stopped halfway across the ice field. The animal cocked his head to one side and snarled, sending a thick stream of hot breath clouding onto the air. Then he barked like a guard dog seeing off an intruder. The other animals skipped around him, jumping up at nothing at all. Wilson looked bemused. There was nothing to be seen a mile in any direction. What on earth were the animals doing?

The doctor looked around but everyone was bent to their work. The dogs continued to bark at the icy air. The doctor squinted and decided they must simply be confused after the long voyage. This was a strange place and it would take the men and the dogs alike, a while to settle.

Close to the ship and under Wilson's steady eye, the men raised the first tent. As she lost interest, Karina abandoned taunting the dogs. They quietened as one and settled to a steady pace, moving off to explore the ice. One of the younger pups stopped to eat mouthfuls of snow, crunching crystals between sharp teeth. Back at the point on the map Scott had christened Winter Quarters Bay, Wilson marked out a plot by scoring the white surface with a pickaxe. He directed the men to raise a tarpaulin over it. As they started, it felt as if the very ice itself rejected the tent, turning its hard white back on the expeditionary force from the off. One man began to hammer in the first peg but it snapped in two. As it did so, a biting wind picked up from nowhere and the seamen's eyes narrowed as the hair on the back of their necks rose. *It's too empty here,* she heard one think as Wilson spotted what had happened to the peg.

'Bad show,' he said. 'Come on, man, let's try again.' The doctor's tone was encouraging. He couldn't have the men giving up. The seaman picked up his hammer and fetched another peg. He positioned it at a different angle and was about to strike when from somewhere among the pile of kit, a rope broke free and skittered across the ice on a rogue squall. Karina laughed. She shrugged in time with the movement pushing the scatter of rope further away from the party, seeing how far she could go with it. One seaman ran in pursuit for 100 yards before flinging himself onto the end as if it was a tiger's tail and he was wresting a wild beast to the ground. Laughter ensued and Karina glared at them. This was her joke, not theirs.

'Good man,' the doctor raised a hand. Then he turned back to the tent team. 'Chop, chop,' he directed them.

Slowly they raised their hammers and the pegs penetrated the surface. They put their backs into the job. This time only one peg snapped. The unfortunate man reached for another without comment or complaint, sneaking a glance sideways at the doctor. As he did so he caught a glimpse of something moving like a long white snake in the distance. He squinted momentarily into the blinding sunlight and then turned away. What good would come of knowing, he thought as he banged the peg into place.

Over the next few days, with the first tent successfully raised, a small village began to grow on the ice. Karina stalked around it, kicking ropes and placing hammers out of reach. She honed her skills, learning to double her growing strength by tapping into the movement of the breeze. When harsh winds whipped up the snow, she made sure to direct them to topple carelessly placed crates. She slipped catches on doors and burrowed holes into tarpaulin. She eavesdropped.

The officers were concerned to keep up the men's spirits. Behind closed doors, on the ship, Ross divided the duties. Shackleton was put in charge of entertainment.

'Keep 'em busy,' Scott instructed him. 'Mark their time, eh?'

Popular, Shackleton found it easy to rally everyone, no matter the day-to-day difficulties of missing tools and unlucky breaks. No matter that there was something unsettling in the silence – an undercurrent that he feared would carry him off. More than once he heard a voice say his name and when he turned there was no one. Shackleton was ashamed of his imagination. He thought of it as his Irish side. He'd always had a facility for stories and had believed in fairies as a child.

Unaware that his understanding surpassed any of the others, Shackleton ignored the female voice cooing, *Ernest*, as if she was trying out the word for the first time. *Ernest*. He responded by biting his lip and ticking himself off for daydreaming.

Karina watched him carefully. He was a big man with startling blue eyes. This meant that though he wore the same polar kit as the others, he was easy to pick out. He had an easy gait and the men looked to him. She noticed Scott jealously watching the sub-lieutenant from the deck of the *Discovery* as he went about his business on the ice and she realized that the commander did not trust this tall, bluff Irishman. Scott was keeping his enemies close. *As if the expedition did not have enough stacked against it.*

Still, the skipper had chosen well when it came to the charge of the entertainment schedule. Ross's men had made their own entertainment, dicing with cubes of whalebone and singing below decks all those years ago. These men would shoulder an Antarctic winter but they'd have help to keep up their spirits. Shackleton understood instinctively the importance of occupation. The usual comings and goings – light and dark, high tide and low – did not exist on the Antarctic plane. At the extreme of summer, there was no balance of darkness to match the light and the water barely showed a tidemark. In winter, in the dark, it would be worse.

Karina now had the crew to mark her time. These days she would not lose her way among the minutes and hours and days and weeks. That was Shackleton's skill, she realized, giving the men something to grasp.

First off, a football pitch was laid out on the ice. Two of the able seamen laboriously marked the lines with pickaxes.

'Come on, lads,' Shackleton encouraged the men. 'Who's for a kick-about?'

Bruised from the voyage, tired and aching after the long days of work, two teams of eleven men formed surprisingly quickly and Karina settled to watch them play.

In their enthusiasm, the able seamen slapped each other on the shoulders and chattered about their favourite teams. Hotspur and Aston Villa. 'Come on, Skelton,' Shackleton called to a fellow Karina had seen wrangling a camera on a tripod during the afternoons. Once she had tripped him up and he had spent half an hour reassembling his kit, humming a music hall song under his breath. A ripple now went around. Skelton, it transpired, had played for the Royal Navy, upholding the Senior Service's good name against those johnny-come-latelies, the British Army.

Those not playing stood on the sidelines as Shackleton tossed a sixpence in the air and Petty Officer Taffy Evans (at a shade over six feet, the tallest man on the expedition) called heads. From the newly constructed kennels, the dogs sensed the excitement and a burst of barking echoed on the empty air as Evans chose his end and Shackleton took his place as referee. He cast a glance at Scott and wondered if the skipper ever heard a woman's voice say his name out of nowhere. Then the match kicked off.

With the mountains in the distance the men could not help but feel tiny when they stopped to notice. Karina noticed too. The match was a contrast – an affirmation of life – a statement that men could achieve their aims in this empty, wide, white place if only for ninety minutes. Shackleton had chosen well. The act of playing football made it clear that the southern continent was there to be conquered.

At half-time, the teams changed ends even if in such calm weather there was no advantage in doing so. The second half saw all the action at the goalmouth. Extra time was played. It turned out Skelton was a stickler for the rules and objected when Shackleton allowed a penalty.

'No quibbling,' Shackleton retorted. He was enjoying himself. 'I'm the final word.'

Karina noticed Scott flinching. *He is jealous*, she thought. *He is afraid.* On the pitch the men were too busy to pay any mind.

'Sir,' Skelton insisted, his voice rising, the closest an officer might get to questioning what was, in effect, an order. The objection went no further as Shackleton stared the man down, his blue eyes dancing. He loved a challenge and taken up with this he quite forgot the niggling worry that perhaps he was going mad.

'It'll not be the end of you, Skelton,' he promised. 'Not the way you're playing.'

And that was the truth. Skelton scored two

more goals for the officers' team. It was only that when the whistle sounded, the men had scored three. And they felt good, she could see, to have completed the game and to have won.

As they came off, ready for dinner, the teams shook hands, all flesh still obscured by finnesko mittens or knitted gloves, scarves and furs and felted hats. 'Frostnip can set in as quickly as a snakebite,' Doctor Wilson kept saying. 'Be careful now. Mind yourself.' *Like him. Just like him.* And yet Karina liked the doctor for the first time after the match. The camaraderie had changed something. She looked at Scott and did not think of James Ross. She looked at Wilson and knew that he wasn't Joseph Hooker. Having given their all, the men seemed somehow endearing.

'I'm ravenous,' one of the young seaman let his natural reserve drop.

There was a murmur of general agreement among the others. The cold affected them all that way and their stomachs were growling.

'It feels like I'm starving, I tell you, boy,' the Welsh stoker chimed in.

'Great goal, Frankie!' one of the officers exclaimed, slapping the fellow on the back and distracting attention from the seaman's outburst and the subsequent chatter.

Two–three was a respectable enough score. Frankie, the hero of the hour, beamed. Everyone was satisfied – even Skelton who complained to Evans about hogging the ball.

'Tomorrow you must do better, Taffy. Pass for heaven's sakes and we'll have them.'

169

As they trooped aboard, it was easy to imagine Scott's men forming some kind of club. They knew this expedition would distinguish them. They already talked about how they'd meet for dinner in London at some swanky restaurant on a grand boulevard or in a local pub, somewhere near the port, where sailors were most at home. There would be reunions and a friendly remembrance of unpacking these tons of equipment and finding out here at the end of everything, piece by piece what would operate in the biting cold and what would not. They'd share memories of kicking a ball around on the ice. Of gathering on the mess deck and listening as Bunny Bernacchi, the Belgian, gave a long and abstract lecture about meteorology that sent Karina out, into the night sky, to play among the stars with new knowledge.

Inside Shackleton hung up his coat. The voice whispered so low he had to strain to make it out. *Ernest. What will you remember of this when you go home? What will you leave behind?* Shackleton shook his head as if he was dislodging a drop of water that had become caught in his ear.

'Good game,' Scott said on his way into the meal.

It is the promise of fame that fires him, she thought. The captain. It was not an attractive quality. But then, what else might bring a man here to the end of everything? Hooker had wanted his day at the Royal Society. Ross wanted to be known as the man who mapped Antarctica. Perhaps men always cared what other men thought of them. Karina bristled. Then, distracted by the hot dishes laid on the table, she smiled quietly.

170

For all their tinned supplies, Scott's cook could not manage a chocolate cream.

Scott said grace and as he did so, she settled on his shoulder. The men, heads bowed respectfully, found it difficult not to lash into the food. They were young, or at least there was hardly a grey hair among them for polar exploration was a young man's game. Ferrar, the youngest of the scientists, was barely twenty-three. Such expeditions were the proving of a man and there it was again – these fellows longed to be proven. Scott most of all.

He had already written the headlines that would announce the *Discovery*'s homecoming. He had practised giving interviews in which the incredible spirit of his men would feature heavily. He had decided what he would wear to make the announcement. Before Karina knew it she had strayed from these idle intentions and came face to face with Hooker again. There, inside the commander's head. He was dispensing advice. This time, she turned tail.

'Amen,' Scott intoned and the men sat down. Shackleton's eyes darted. *Ernest*, she cooed and found herself laughing at him. *Perhaps*, the poor man thought, *I am hallucinating because I am so hungry. Maybe that's what it is.*

Fourteen

Shackleton was not the only person who was hearing things. Karina dismissed the echo. It came from beyond her world and theirs. Unlike the lieutenant, though, she knew she was not going mad. The noise made her turn to look behind. It made her fly over the camp to see where it might be coming from. It sounded as if it was calling her away, but she was not willing.

Instead of pursuing it, she turned her attention to the men. The crew was truly diverting. Scott's expedition was different from Ross's in several ways. Karina was not sure if this was simply the nature of the men involved or if it was due to advances. One way or another, there was catching up to do. The doctor, Wilson, had set himself several tasks. The first was to find out how to nourish a man in the deep cold. All knowledge was up for grabs and when the surgeon declared he wanted to find the best diet, Scott had deemed the idea useful. So from the start it had been on the expedition's rota of scientific endeavour.

Tonight and every night, Clarke, the ship's cook, had everything ready. The fellows could not be kept waiting. Each of them qualified for different rations, their diets restricted in either starch or meat.

'What is it tonight?' Shackleton chimed as he took his seat at the mess table.

172

'For you, sir? Well, you know you can't have what you'd like! What with all this business of having to find out about nourishment,' Clarke replied, lingering over the last word, as if it had nothing to do with the cooking of food.

The cook left a boy to serve. The sound of the officers' clanking cutlery drowned out everything. Achettes of bread were passed around and pots of stew appeared from the galley. 'Come on then, Shackle. We must have our rations, such as they are. You're on the experiment, aren't you?'

Shackleton nodded. Eager to eat, he lifted his fork. Wilson, the surgeon, chimed a piece of cutlery on a plate to attract the officers' attention.

'Have you all got the hang of it?' he checked.

There was a murmur of general agreement and only the merest glance of longing at the food some were allowed and others were not.

Karina found herself interested in the doctor. Wilson had red hair. He came from Cheltenham and his memories were peppered with recollections of punting on the English river that ran past the bottom of the garden of his parents' home. As a child he performed experiments on earthworms and frogs. He fished tadpoles out of the water and watched them darting like animated flickers in glass jam jars that he kept beside his bed. He was a lifelong experimenter. In England, he once drove himself to the brink of chronic anaemia by using himself as a control in an experiment. Science was not for the faint-hearted and the officers and the men of the *Discovery* could not be accused of any such indisposition. It was admirable, she thought.

Hooker had reserved his experimentation for the penguins, in the main.

Wilson's counterpart, Koettlitz, Karina sounded his name, was not a doctor, but some other kind of medical man. They had set up this experiment together. But it wasn't only Wilson and Koettlitz who were interested. Everyone had eagerly signed up, and most of the party were now eating extraordinary rations – those that is, who weren't in the control group. At the start, it had been easy – in the cold, men mostly craved fat. The crew shovelled in bread and dripping as if it was nectar in an attempt to sate their hunger pains. They'd eat blubber on its own. They'd eat anything.

At night, she'd noticed, with their appetites piqued, the men dreamed of even huger feasts than Clarke prepared – and he was not one to stint. Their desires surprised them. Shackleton found he missed Dover sole and cabbage. Able Seaman George Vince lusted after sausage and mash. The favoured recipes of wives and mothers were doted on as if they were memories of lost loves, more cherished than the images of half-naked women the men hid among their things. Jam roly-poly. Spotted dick. Barley broth. Even when Clarke produced these dishes, they weren't the same. The whole team was committed to this expedition but their bodies were tethered to civilization. To food.

'We'll enjoy a dinner out on The Strand,' one whispered to another. Or 'Fish and chips at Sarti's. With mushy peas.' The differences between officers and men were easy to spot.

Shackleton had agreed to forgo meat. He would

not have said it was his favourite food – a predilection for cheese or even fresh fruit (which was not available either) would both have ranked higher, in normal circumstances. Karina noted that Clarke's rhubarb tart was excellent and Shackleton had to admit, it would come somewhere near the top of his list. Still, he eyed the stewed seal flesh on offer tonight and realized his mouth was watering.

'You all right, old chap?' Wilson checked.

Even at this early stage, the fellows banned from meat seemed to show different behaviour to the ones banned from consuming starches. Forward thinking, Wilson had not only been looking for physical changes in his subjects but also mental ones. So far he had seen little of either. It was still early days.

'I'm fine,' Shackleton assured the surgeon, the odd stray vowel not entirely masked by years of stolid service with largely English crews. His brogue sometimes broke through at mealtimes. As he bit with relish into a slice of bread and dripping an idea was forming – something to take his mind off sirloin steaks and liver and bacon.

Later, after dinner, Shackleton bided his time before making the suggestion. The voice in his head had stopped its throaty whisper. Skelton and Ferrar were playing cards for piles of pennies they could not spend.

'I say,' the sub-lieutenant looked up from his book. His tone was creamy. 'Why don't we write a newsletter? I miss *The Times*, don't you?'

The idea was greeted enthusiastically by everyone except Scott, who scanned it for any whiff of dissent or ego. The officers and men alike had taken to Shackleton. He was a natural leader and if he burned too brightly the captain would certainly douse his fires. However, Shackleton's idea took hold. One man pulled out his sketchpad and offered a drawing. 'How about this, old man? Your first submission.'

Another fellow mumbled something about poetry and Skelton said he'd sort out some photographs.

'Capital! Leave it to me,' Shackleton said, adding soberly, 'If you don't mind, that is.'

'Well of course you shall be the editor, Shackle,' it was generally agreed. 'Why, it was your idea.'

Shackleton could swear he heard a soft tut.

That night, fifteen journals recounted the founding of the paper and a full forty mentioned the football match but not one gave voice to the fear that they were learning to live with. They knew the rules. When bad weather set in you must call the storm a *frolic. It is nippy today and I found myself peckish*, one man scribbled in a letter that he would not be able to send for a year. Then he assured his wife that he was safe. Now they were here, there was not a man among them who had not wondered, *Dear God, what will it be like in winter?*

Still, those first few weeks, the polar summer prevailed. Karina continued to stalk them, enjoying their discovery of the eternal sunlight. To a man, they were unsettled by it. Here, after all, nothing was as it seemed – the sea turned to ice, the ice was land and the night was bright

176

as a summer day. It was a place out of time and nature.

At night, she watched the ship as she sat on the edge of the glacier, swirling her legs in the icy water under the white ghost of the moon. Aboard the men who could sleep were dreaming.

She shifted as she felt a presence in the silent night. Behind her, on the ship, Skelton, the footballing hero emerged on deck. He was swaddled in material – padded like an Esquimaux. He walked down the gangplank onto the ice and cut through the huts and tents, past the football pitch and towards her. Karina sighed as he stopped at the edge of the water and took in the view.

He couldn't sleep. It was too light and he was hungry. Lazily, she considered batting him over the edge, but then, he had done so well for the team. Perhaps, she thought, the earthly concerns of men were engaging enough to save his life. Skelton, oblivious to the danger he was in, settled into the silence. Karina let her foot splash and Skelton smiled as he looked on, thinking that there must be some kind of sea creature beneath the swell. Later he would note in his journal that the glacier was the most beautiful place on earth.

Such encounters felt domestic. She was like a little girl with a doll's house, following the men across the plane, hiding screws and opening doors. At night, she prowled the corridors and watched them dreaming or sat on the lee of the hill, looking down on her grave. There was a seriousness about Scott's crew with their endless experiments and earnest plans. As time wore on, she found that she no longer wanted to hurt them. She mined Scott's memory gently, in her own time, for every scrap of information about Hooker until there was nothing left.

And then he came. He appeared in front of her. It was deep in the light night and the air was thick and calm. At first, she couldn't see him properly. The vision was blurred. 'Joseph,' she said, and felt a tear trickle. A single, human tear the like of which she hadn't felt in a generation. But it wasn't Hooker who appeared out of the mist. It wasn't his voice.

'Karina?' the man sounded bemused. '*Hej*,' he said. *Hello.*

He smiled and then she knew him. One old man was like another. But not that smile.

'Thebo?' the name dropped from her lips. 'How did you get to be so old?'

He lowered his eyes. 'Oh, Karina,' he said.

And behind him, like a light show, there was a vision of Maine. *How could that be Thebo's happiest place?* she thought. And then she saw a picture of two children – a faded callotype of them, playing in the yard. He had it in his pocket. And she knew. She stood and glared at him and he couldn't meet her eyes.

'You didn't die,' she said.

Thebo shrugged. 'I knew you would make it back to Europe. That's what you wanted. I knew Marijke would bring you home. I was so lonely.'

If there had been air in her lungs, the shock would have knocked it out. 'Didn't you find love?' he asked, breathless as if he was apologizing. 'What is this place?'

178

'I died here,' she said. 'I found love and I died. I stowed away on a British ship after you left me.'

Thebo glanced over his shoulder. Maine was clearly calling.

'You abandoned me,' she said, 'you lied,' understanding dawning and it was then that Karina screamed. It was a sound like no other she had ever made. Aboard the *Discovery*, Shackleton got out of bed. He felt a vein of ice in his blood. Outside, Karina lashed out but Thebo was insubstantial. 'How could you run away? How could you? I almost starved.'

'The mate,' Thebo said simply. 'He wanted to be captain. We arranged it so you'd get the captain's share to see you through till Marijke sent your passage.' Thebo peered at her. 'You still look so young,' he said. 'You did not mourn me, did you?'

She couldn't bear it. She took off. Below her, Thebo faded into the street scene and the air closed over his balding head. He hadn't apologized. There was no lying in death. There was no point in that. Karina reeled. A faithless, lying husband. That swindler of a mate. Where was the justice? She raged. Frustrated, she flew up to the snow clouds and pulled down a blizzard. She sailed with the northerly winds, far out to sea until, like crashing into a wall, it all went dark. In the end, she found herself back on the ice shelf with the *Discovery* moored alongside. *Thebo didn't die and it was all for nothing. Nothing at all.* The sound of her crying was mistaken for wind whistling aboard ship. A freakish summer storm, the men said. And in the end, all she could think of was those children in the garden. His children. His grandchildren. The little ones she never bore. Her wasted spinster's life.

Fifteen

She left. The *South Polar Times* and the football matches seemed senseless now and she did not require entertainment. *There is nothing to do*, she thought, as she laid herself on the side of the ice mountain and disappeared into it as if she had melted away. But she could not settle. She thought of Ven and her childhood summers. She thought of Thebo living in Maine, happy for years. The waste of it. And Joseph too. The thoughts tormented her and from the ship, the men's voices niggled, like a fly buzzing against a pane. She turned away, but she still had the vision of Scott's crew, trudging across the ice. *They are haunting me*, it occurred to her, and half annoyed and half intrigued, she returned to Winter Quarters Bay, deciding there was more to see. She could not sleep anyway.

Last out of the hold, the motor was winched into the light.

'Call me when it's ready to fire up,' Scott instructed.

'Yes, sir.' Evans nodded curtly.

Taffy, as the men called him, set himself the task of checking the spark plugs and oiling the axle while, with a heavy heart, Karina sought information about this strange machine. She saw Scott with Hooker again, outside the house in

Glasgow as they shook hands in front of a motor just like this one. *Joseph, what does it do?* she asked, but he did not answer.

In Scott's memory, there was a good deal of enthusiasm for the idea of flying across the ice at a steady five miles an hour. *It is a carriage that does not need horses*, she realized and it occurred to her she had seen these in Maine, behind her good-for-nothing husband.

When Taffy's work was done, almost the entire crew gathered. Skelton set his camera on a tripod as Evans opened an oil can and peered inside.

'Well?' said Wilson.

'It's frozen, sir.'

Wilson shook the can in the hope that Evans was mistaken. The group slumped. The cold had yet again outfoxed them. Karina's heart sank further. Nothing worked here and Thebo hadn't even died.

Wilson checked the remaining cans. The attaining of the motor had been considered something of a coup in London.

'It's no good. Get back to work,' he waved off the men, who were still gathered hopefully around Evans.

One of the able seamen, George Vince, stumbled clumsily as he turned. Invisible, Karina removed her foot from his path. Vince had cheated on his wife, she saw. And in doing so, had lied to his mistress. Wilson rolled his eyes. The last thing he needed was an ankle injury. As the men disappeared, he turned to Evans. 'I'll tell the skipper.'

Inside, the doctor knocked on Scott's door.

'I'm afraid it's become apparent that the motor is not going to be reliable, sir,' Wilson announced. 'It's the fuel. It's frozen.'

Scott sat back in his chair. 'We did not think of that.' Like Karina, his mood plummeted. The uselessness of the vehicle represented poor planning and as such was an affront to the expedition.

Outside, Karina sat regally in the upholstered leather seat of the carriage like a sculpture on the ice. There was no staying and no going for her, she realized. Like the motor-sled, she was defunct. There was no point in being here but she couldn't leave – couldn't even disappear. It had all been the most monstrous mistake. What was the point?

In the end, the captain had the men winch the thing back into the hold. There was a small chance if the temperature heightened that the fuel would thaw. *Such seekers after glory*, Karina snarled and the idea angered her, adding to all her other anger – Thebo's lie, her mistakes, Hooker's faithlessness. Ross had come to the Antarctic to do one thing – he wanted to make a map. By contrast, Scott's dreams were peppered with a hundred wants and needs. He longed to be loved, to be known, to be admired. He was greedy. And she had had enough.

Once more, she tried to leave. The day-to-day watching of the crew's efforts felt like a bruise now and it ached. Hooker had sent them. The very names the men used as they pointed out landmarks were redolent of her life aboard the *Terror*. And their quest was pointless in any case. How could such frailty ever reach the pole? It was impossible. Still, their presence continued to niggle and the fact she could not ignore them made another, smaller cage of her world – trapped by one man after another and until now, always believing she had been free, though even in death it seemed, that wasn't true.

Not far from the village of huts and tents at Winter Quarters Bay, her body still lay packed below the ice. Decades of storms had blown over it. When the *Erebus* and *Terror* had sailed off, the grave was quite near the shore, but the sea had frozen fresh ice beyond it and now it lay further inland. The ice had thickened slowly, year by year but Karina could still see her body, deep under the thick white crust, her skin waxy, her flesh shrunk, Hooker's old journal splayed to one side and her greatcoat now a rag slung around brittle frozen bones.

Like Si Bevan, Charles Clarke, the *Discovery*'s cook, baked bread in the galley. He had a mate, Henry Brett, who in an hotel would be called a sous chef, but here was only cookie's mate. Karina watched them. The galley at least was a good memory. Once she thought to season the stew differently and knocked over some salt so that Clarke did so.

She lingered there as the men got to work early. They were usually the first on board to wake. As the rest of the crew fixed their attire ready for the sub-zero temperatures and made for the mess. In the last throws of summer, it was not yet cold enough for the men to long for another ten minutes in their bunks more than they longed to fill their bellies.

Clarke was thin for a cook. Years in the galley had had little effect on his frame. If he had a vice it was for tropical fruit developed during the years he was stationed in India. He indulged himself daily in the fantasy of eating mango. That fresh orange rush was an impossibility here, for what little fruit there was in the *Discovery*'s store was drowned in syrup, preserved in tins, not jars, like all modern food.

There was no question where the cook would go on his death. He missed India as if she were his mistress. The Antarctic seemed dispassionate compared to the wild monsoons and scorching summer heat of Bombay. He'd be teased for saying it, but it wasn't only the temperature that was cold now they had arrived – the landscape had a kind of coldness too. Charles was a passionate man and he realized immediately he sailed into Winter Quarters Bay that he'd made a mistake. This place did not suit him and he did not get on well with Henry, a dour northerner with an appalling lack of knife skills and a propensity for simply heating ingredients rather than cooking them.

Still, Clarke reminded himself, being on the expedition was an honour. Each man had competed for his place with a hundred others. The truth was, he had been curious to see the frozen wastes or what little of them would be afforded a man of his station. It never occurred to him that those afternoons gorging on mangoes would seem such a luxury or that things at Scott's polar destination would be quite so hard. He regularly promised himself that his next ship would be a spice vessel of the merchant class. He swore that he'd gobble all life's sweetness as soon as it was on offer and, for that matter, relish the prospect of a small bonus payment, which with expeditionary funds as they were, would not be forthcoming on the *Discovery. He is no Si Bevan*, she thought. *Not a quarter of him.*

Clarke finished the breakfast service and left Brett to clear the decks. The thick smell of baking still discernable on the air, he decided to take a walk. With his movements only partially restricted by layers of woollen clothes, he stepped onto the ice and started away from the tents.

He was the first to set his foot over her. The cook's snow boots were standard issue, made from thick leather. He had pulled on only one pair of socks. As his sole slapped over Karina's grave, he felt the cold run through him like a spike, while below a shudder rushed through her spirit, setting her on edge and summoning her to the spot in an instant, like an elastic snapping her away from the mountaintop where she had been observing the camp from a distance. *You!* she hissed, as if he had betrayed her, fury seeping out. Unaware, Charles Clarke continued. He measured his progress by his memory of Nottingham High Street, which ran for a mile. Today, he decided, he wouldn't go further than the old haberdashery.

But he had called her. The footfall echoed a drumbeat played on what was left of Karina's heart. She looked around as she reeled from being brought here with such violence and scanned the vista to see if more men might follow Clarke in desecrating her grave but the work parties were about their business yards off, facing the other way. Her teeth bared, and seeming sharper than in life, she sucked in cold air from the thin cook's direction. She focused on the receding figure, as if she might swallow him whole. *How dare he? How dare all these men?*

Clarke's leg gave way under him in the sudden rush. He stumbled but regained his balance and looked accusingly at the ground. There was nothing on which it was possible to trip. He stamped his foot as if there might be a fault with his boots. Karina, glaring now, spat the air back at him and the cook, eyes blazing, stumbled again. This time, he lost his balance and fell over. *I'll be lucky if that doesn't bruise my knee*, he thought as he scrambled to his feet, looking round. There was nothing for miles and only the camp behind him. The sudden icy breeze had come from nowhere. The bruises were already blooming up his thigh. A way off now, Karina crouched low, ready to pounce should he return and she didn't look away till he disappeared back on board.

'God,' he mumbled under his breath.

Why won't they go? she snarled. Never had she been so unwilling. Not since Pearce.

But the truth was, the life she drew from the men had given her connection to the snow and ice, the light and the wind and the clouds. And it was growing. She could manoeuvre a stream of air. She could scare them. She wondered if she had turned into Loki, the Norse god of Mischief. But to do so she would have to not care. *Surely no eternal being should care.* Whereas she was drawn back again and again, to the camp. To Hooker. To Thebo. To her death. To the sad futility of her life. To the sense she had wasted it.

For long hours after the cook's excursion, Karina prowled her grave, keeping watch over the icy image of a woman betrayed, shrunken under the surface. Something animal kept her close to her corpse and suddenly, after decades of wishing to flee, all the resentment over a life half lived, after wanting to know what had happened to Marijke and to Joseph, after all that time wishing that she could go back to Ven or Copenhagen or Amsterdam, she realized she couldn't leave. She never would. Her body was here and maybe that was what she needed. She was done with the world. It had all been a mistake and she could never go back. This was where she was now. Awake and ready.

Keeping the expeditionary force and their preparations in her sights, she settled like a mythical creature on a comfortable cushion. She had nothing to be afraid of, she mused, her teeth were as white as the cleanest ice and as sharp, too, should she need them. Thebo had hardened her. *The sea is not kind, why should we be?* These men were interlopers. One icy finger might point at any one of them and a sharp exhalation might blow them over. Who cared what happened to Joseph Hooker? Or who came off the next boat on Ven? She was here now, at one with this place. Her bones were the very bones of it. Her flesh was the frozen sheet that ran over the icy sea.

Sixteen

The commander's next hope was that the dogs would prove useful. A date was set to test the pack. Weller, the dog handler, had some experience and when consulted he was upbeat about the possibilities of putting the animals to good use. Wilson supervised the kennels – he was an amateur zoologist among his other expertise. At home he loved riding. There was little opportunity to discuss this at the mess table, but he was a stalwart of his local hunt. He realized quickly that the huskies chosen for the expedition were a far cry from the beagles at home. More wolf than dog, he concluded, though this was perhaps a positive trait. The beagles would struggle to last even the summer snows.

When one of the dogs fell sick, it was Wilson who was called to the kennel. It was late afternoon. Weller crouched with one hand on the animal's neck. Of all the crew, Weller had the most trouble reading and writing. He was not qualified in anything but he was expert with the dogs. Brought up on a country estate, his father had been Head Groom so he had doctored sick horses, ponies, dogs and cows since he was too young to be working. He had always had a way with them.

'It's Blossom, sir,' he said. 'I think she's lost heart. She won't eat.'

189

It was never discussed where the dogs got their names but it was certainly not from Wilson. Among the monikers chosen for the pack, Blossom, Peaches, Luna and Bosco would not have been Wilson's first choices. Still, Weller was an excellent hand and the kennel was well run.

'Let's have a look, shall we?'

The doctor was not an expert in veterinary science, but after five minutes he had to conclude that Weller might be right. There was nothing physically wrong with the animal. Perhaps Blossom was simply not tough enough. Perhaps she had lost heart because she didn't like her name.

'If we leave her with the others, they'll sense it, sir,' Weller said.

'And what do you think they'll do?'

Weller looked bleak. 'They'll eat her, sir, if she ain't got no fight left. That's the pack's way. Maybe not tonight, but sometime. She'll fall behind.'

'We better hope she perks up then,' Wilson said without a touch of irony. 'With these dry runs on the sledges at the end of the week we need the dogs in good condition. Have you ever known the like?'

An icy finger passed over the kennel as if it was stroking the air. Weller shuddered. When he joined the Merchant Navy he was part of a crew that transported Arabian purebreds from the desert Peninsula for sale at Newmarket and Cheltenham. There were a certain amount of those animals that lost heart because England was so alien. It happened on every shipment. You'd

190

think they'd have been glad to go from the desert into England's lush fields but it didn't always work that way.

'Animals ain't as tough as everyone reckons,' Weller said sagely, 'They've got feelings. Maybe she just don't like the change.'

Wilson passed a rubber ball under Blossom's nose. He made to throw it but the husky didn't stir. He was frustrated that there wasn't something scientific to which he could attribute the animal's malaise. It didn't make sense – these dogs were supposed to like the wide open snowscape. He didn't blame Blossom. Like many of the crew he was finding the polar extremes difficult, although the sense of being on a groundbreaking mission had kept him going so far, and intelligent though they were, none of the dogs had a sense of that.

The atmosphere in the officers' mess had been strained the last few nights. Scott had picked his favourites and everybody knew it. Still, whatever the difficulties, Wilson would sign up again in a heartbeat to serve under the skipper. And it wasn't Scott's fault that the weather was difficult or their appetites were high. Some of the men were sickening, though no one as yet as bad as this dog. His train of thought was disturbed by the sound of howling from the other side of the kennel.

'Are you sleeping all right?' Wilson asked Weller. Karina heard this as if the question was an echo. Lately, it was in sleep she was closest to the men. She had taken to prowling their dreams. Wilson elicited only a half-nod from the dog handler.

191

'It's bright, isn't it?' Weller replied. 'Though the darkness has started to creep in.'

'We should enjoy the light while we can. Winter's coming. It won't be long.'

Weller nodded. The temperature had dropped in the last week. Below decks the stories told round the brazier had taken a turn towards the Gothic. Somehow the summer sun had staved off the sharing of such horrors.

'Yes, sir.'

'Well you better keep an eye on this little lass for now. Poor Blossom. We'll try to tempt her again tomorrow.'

That evening as the men played football Weller found himself distracted. He let in a goal and straight after that he fell foul of the offside rule.

'You've got your mind on the dogs not on the pitch, Willie,' the centre forward glared. 'You've got to concentrate, man.'

'At least you know what the dogs are going to do,' Weller retorted smartly.

'Sometimes I think you care about those bloody animals more than you care about us.'

Weller stayed silent. There was no reply to that. As far as he was concerned, dogs were preferable to people – no doubt about it.

After dinner he dropped onto the ice. Flicking up the collar of his coat against the chill, he perused the half-light of dusk and ignored the feeling that something was out there. The dogs needed him and he'd stay up all night if he had to. Weller slept below decks in his hammock just like the rest of them – but he had discovered it was just as easy to get some shut-eye settling down inside the kennel with the dogs for warmth. Truth be told the dogs were more comfortable than canvas. The huskies had a reputation for being pitiless but Weller knew poodles that would rip out your throat – as far as he was concerned these wolves are no better or worse than domesticated pets. With Blossom poorly, though, the pack remained restless. They kept jostling for position. Blitzen had snapped at him after he'd fed her today and he had had to bring out his whip. Weller checked the kennel, closed the door and decided to bed down below decks.

It was late as he trudged back aboard. Like most of the crew, he didn't own a watch and prayers and mealtimes weren't enough to keep track. Perhaps when the darkness came properly, it would help. Meantime, it wasn't like being at sea, he thought as he slipped down to snatch a couple of hours in his hammock.

Outside, Karina curled around the kennel. The dogs barked into the half-light, their howls echoing on the freezing air. On the *Discovery*, Scott turned and Shackleton woke. For some reason he could not stop thinking about the men who had gone before. Ross. Hooker. And the expeditions since. He shook his head. He was here now, that's what he should focus on. His stomach growled and he wondered whether the ice or Scott's favour was the more unstable. He worried that the skipper disliked him. Then he turned over and fell asleep again, cascading into his dreams as if a trapdoor had given way under him.

The next morning Weller was first on the ice. Blossom was still poorly. He left her aside and got on with the rest of the dogs. Exercising the pack was a brutal business. Weller used his whip and he didn't stint. If he was going to be top dog, they had to understand it. He was looking forward to the first sledge run. It would be a stretch but the pack was ready. With the exercise over, he half melted some ice for the animals to drink and looked in on Blossom in her isolated stall. She turned away her head and with a shrug he decided he'd try again after breakfast.

Just making it on deck on time, he joined the rest of the crew, heads bowed, as Scott intoned the morning prayer and the men uttered a low 'Amen' before they shuffled into the mess.

'Where did you get to?' Duncan asked.

Weller shrugged. 'One of the dogs is sick.'

A sense, if not a smell, of hot porridge and stewed tea lingered round the doorway. Clarke was a shady figure, dodging in and out, pushing Brett to the service. Weller took his usual seat as the men tucked in. A jar of jam did the rounds of the table. The sweetness melted in the mouth but the full flavour of the red summer berries was only a memory. Their mothers, wives and sweethearts picked blackberries from the hedgerows.

A burst of laughter emanated from the other end of the table, Vince, the joker, was pretending mail had arrived. He got to his feet and started to dole out imaginary envelopes.

'Mr Crean, one from Mrs Crean,' he mimed handing over an envelope. 'She hopes you're wearing that vest she made you.

'And for you, Weller, there's one here from a chihuahua that's missing you . . . .'

Weller grinned and accepted the correspondence with good grace.

It must have been a rogue blast of wind that opened the stall door. Weller would swear later that he had bolted the catch. There was no way a dog could have managed to get in or out, but there it was. Several of the men privately put down what happened to a spirit. The notion was whispered between them.

'I don't understand,' Weller insisted.

He couldn't hold with the rumours among the men. He only believed what he could see and touch.

One way or another, that morning as he strolled back towards the kennels with his stomach freshly sated, he noticed a long streak of red and a ragged line of fur lying where it had been ripped to shreds on the snow. Pieces of bloodied bone peppered the path leading to the football pitch and one bitch, Dasher, let out a low growl as she crouched over what must have been part of Blossom's leg. The bitch's mouth was bloodied and her teeth were pink. Weller knew better than to show any distress. He stared down Dasher and whipped the rest of the dogs back to their quarters. Something had badly unsettled them.

'Poor Blossom,' he said under his breath. 'My poor girl.'

Still, with a machete normally used for butchery, Weller cut up what remained of Blossom's body and fed the rest of her to the dog pack. Wilson was not consulted, but then, what else might he have suggested? Weller wondered momentarily, if it came to it, would this happen with the men? One of them was bound to die, sooner or later. There was talk of preliminary expeditions setting out but if they went wrong, what would be done with the casualties? Weller tried not to think of it but the sight of Blossom's body prompted ghoulish imaginings. If a man died on the ice, it would be the only time they'd see the poor soul's flesh, Weller thought. It prompted a memory of the journey south – saltwater showers on the deck and a discussion with Lashly about his array of tattoos. Everyone was so swaddled down here. For a second, to his shame, Weller let an unaccustomed frisson of raw sexual excitement pulse through him. Stoically, he decided not to dwell on it but he promised himself when the ship got back to Auckland he'd treat himself to a boy. Firm flesh made carefree for an hour or two. If he made it through the winter he'd deserve that at least.

And far off, Karina watched him. And she smiled.

Seventeen

Over the next few days, there were other disquieting incidents. Skelton had a system in place to conserve the materials he needed to develop his negatives. He waited until he had taken enough photographs for the optimum process and then he printed them all at once. He lost some plates to overexposure. The light was impossible to gauge accurately, but the images he had were proving promising. He was pleased with his pictures of the *Discovery* – the rigging formed a pleasing frame for the ship, surrounded by whiteness as if it was floating in midair.

Developing the prints was a long process but he was dedicated. When the darkness of winter finally fell, his activities would be curtailed and Skelton was keen to capture as much as he could before the lights went out. As he sorted through the plates, his attention was drawn to his most recent photograph – a carefully chosen team of men before they set out on a short practice run across the ice. If Scott intended to make the pole, the men needed to trial different conditions.

The lieutenant's eyesight was keen. He had taken photographs everywhere he had ever been stationed. It was a hobby as well as a duty. Skelton had spent the last few years in China where he had photographed a number of floating bridges and the spider's web of bamboo scaffolding over buildings under construction. After that he over-saw the building of the *Discovery* in Dundee where his exacting nature proved itself. Scott swore there wasn't a rivet out of place due to Skelton's diligence. He had taken photographs of the huge ship as it grew and took pride that he knew it inside out. Now, as the negative emerged from the chemical bath, Skelton blinked. He held up the paper. Something surely had gone wrong with the process. He did not understand.

He stepped back, trying to be logical. There were a plethora of photographic hoaxes that had been perpetrated ever since the first cameras became available – fairies and spirits and so on. Skelton, however, was a man of science. He knew how he had taken this shot and that it should not have resulted in what he could see. He squinted at the image in disbelief and confirmed that coiled between one man's legs and curled around anoth-er's skis there was a thin, white spectre. It seemed too solid to be a cloud and he could swear it looked female. The ghostly woman was smiling.

'How very odd,' he said out loud.

He laid the negative aside. There must be an explanation – something to do with the cold. Something that did not immediately spring to mind but was, nonetheless, logical. Something to make sense of it. He stroked his beard as he considered the negative and decided to destroy it. An image like that could terrify the men.

The expeditions continued. Like all the equip-ment, the snow skis, snowshoes and the husky sledges were untried and little by little they tested them. Scott was not sure the best way to traverse the snowy wastes but he had until next summer to figure it out, for he would not attempt the pole till then. Shackleton, when it was discussed, always made the case for mimicking the Esquimaux with their snowshoes or the Norwegians with their skis. Both these hardy nations used dogs on the ice. Despite this, Scott wondered whether modern technology or, indeed, the iron will of a British explorer might not find a better way. Karina kept an eye on the commander's journal. She slid around his shoulders and whispered in his ear.

At dinner Scott spoke to his officers. 'This is not a landscape that indulges sentiment or cossets weakness,' he said. 'It is time for action, gentlemen.'

Around the table everyone sat a little taller. This was the speech for which they had all been waiting. The equipment had been checked and some fledgling outings tried around the camp. Now it was time to hazard a proper expedition. One that went out of sight.

'It is time for our first foray into the interior, be it not very far,' was how he put it.

The officers called out three cheers.

The commander had the charts before him and although the shifting shoreline was well recorded, the interior remained uncharted and where there was information, it was patchy. The truth was that the territory shifted according to the season and the weather. A mile that was easily traversed one day might not be navigable the next. Scott regarded the blank stretches of paper. Somewhere, miles to the south, lay the pole – a shining pinnacle. He laid his finger on it.

'Gentlemen, we have begun and when we succeed we shall claim the pole for England.'

There had been much debate both in London and aboard ship about how this conquest should be made, but it seemed to Scott that using a motor (which it appeared would not work anyway) or dog teams would bely an Englishman's glory. A man should be able to cross the wastes under his own steam, man-hauling his kit across the icy desolation – like a true Arthurian hero. Of late it became clear that Scott even considered skis something of a cheat and as his main aim was not only to conquer the Antarctic but to do so with honour. He bristled at the thought of taking a single shortcut.

'You would not consider you had climbed the Alps if you did so in an airplane,' he said, steely willed. *Such foolishness.*

Some of the officers questioned this wisdom privately. You would not climb the Alps without a guide. You would not consider it cheating to have bearers, which, in effect, was the role the dogs played. You would also carry specialist equipment just like the skis that Scott considered somehow *foreign.* Karina laughed at this silly little man with his ideas. The living could only do what the ice allowed here, not what they wanted. Scott's position, however, was born of a skipper's need to be inviolable. He would not have anyone question his achievement. He would not be thought second-rate. The recent foreign expeditions may have used dogs and skis but at heart he believed that a real man should tackle his challenges unaided. Still, he must test the equipment. He had to be sure. As it stood, the officers had more sense than to challenge the commander's absolute authority. Certainly not today when he was about to pick who would be first out of the hatches. They would rise to whatever Scott deemed the challenge of 'doing it honestly'.

'On skis,' Scott declared. 'We will start that way.'

There was a ripple of surprise around the table like a little burst of energy.

'Royds,' the commander said, 'do you think you're up to the job?'

Royds blushed.

'Yes, sir,' he saluted. 'Thank you, sir.'

'Tomorrow,' Scott confirmed. 'And you'll take Bernacchi.'

The physicist grinned.

'On skis, you said, Skipper?' he checked, his accent stronger because he was excited.

'You're straining at the leash, eh?' Scott was satisfied. 'You may only be travelling a short distance but you'll go down in the history books. Our first expedition out of sight of the ship. I think we should raise a toast.'

Shackleton fetched a bottle.

'Good man,' Scott said, and they raised their cups.

That night it got colder and the wind dropped, the sun sank and a long flash of darkness overtook the sky. Karina checked below decks. Over the weeks, the crew had made their wills, or at least those who had anything to leave, which mostly meant the officers and the scientists. The men

201

simply arranged things between themselves with a handshake and a wink, their generosity tempered by late-night drink. Sailors carried all their worldly possessions with them – it had always been that way. Weller regarded the light poplin trews stowed in his trunk (what use would they ever be here?) He picked up the Bible his mother gave him when he first joined the service. It remained all but pristine. It was a wonder that he had not sold it.

'Anything happens to me you can have what you like, Jamie,' he said.

Able Seaman Walker nodded.

'Don't be daft,' he brushed off the complement. 'You ain't going nowhere, Willie. Nowhere but back home.'

Although naval men faced danger wherever they were posted, not a man among them hadn't recognized that they might die here. Karina wondered, if one of them did, would he stay? She lingered over their thoughts of death, their strange expectations of angels and heavenly hosts. As if their resting place would be something separate to their lives. Awake in the long, silent nights it couldn't help but cross a man's mind.

'We'd be buried at sea, I suppose,' Clarke chimed.

A small group of the more experienced men clustered together around the brazier.

'That's good enough for me,' replied Lashly, the stoker.

Clarke had never expected anything else. Though he always thought his body would be slipped into warmer seas when the time came.

The piercing southern light was too white and not a patch on a tropical afternoon in Bombay, sitting in the shade beneath a palm and gulping down the scent of turmeric. He shuddered at the thought of being subsumed into the ice-ridden chill of McMurdo Sound. *You will go back to your mango tree.*

'Makes no difference,' one of the men mumbled, 'not a difference in the world. Not once you're gone.'

Fool.

The timbers creaked a clarion call to send the men to their hammocks. All would dream and tonight their dreams were frantic. Crean was startled by a blonde child on a roof shouting his name. Shackleton imagined he was on a whaling ship and that somehow he fell from the rigging and the skipper dreamed he was so hungry he strangled the life out of a gull and grilled the bird's stringy, stinking flesh over a low fire. In their dreams each man was alone and they woke with relief, glad of their fellows around them. *Not me.*

'The day of our first expedition,' Scott whispered like a child, and put the flapping blade-billed gull out of his mind.

The team was made up of four more – Royds was allowed to choose, after Scott had briefed him privately. The men thus honoured were excited. There were virgin footprints to be made. Scott held back. He had to test the men and that included the officers. He couldn't do everything himself, no matter how much he'd like to.

Skelton checked his camera meticulously before

he took the photograph this time. He set up the shot from three different angles as they stood there with wooden skis balanced on one shoulder and goggles propped on their foreheads, staring past the camera, forming an untidy cluster in front of the wide whiteness they were hoping to conquer. 'You are becoming a regular Valentine Blanchard, Reggie,' Shackleton teased.

Skelton waved him off.

'I just want to be sure,' he said, staring at the men as if he was examining the air around them.

Too busy to be troubled by such eccentricity, not one of them showed his excitement until the shot was taken. Then Royds cried, 'Three cheers for Commander Scott and the crew of the *Discovery*.'

The men concurred enthusiastically.

'Have fun, lads,' Scott smiled.

Bernacchi said a silent prayer and wondered where it came from. And they set off. The entire crew watched from the prow of the ship, Scott with his binoculars in hand, as the party receded. The strange dreams of the night before were superseded by this dream, his great ambition.

After five minutes, the men dispersed but Scott stayed on deck, muffled head to toe. At first, Clarke thought he would bring a mug of Bovril to keep the skipper warm but then he realized it might freeze before he could drink it. As the crew went about their business, they dawdled, trying to make out the movement on the ice.

Fixed on this dry run and immoveable as the centuries, Scott, didn't acknowledge anyone as they passed him. His eyes were focused on the moving figures, who had now donned skis. From a distance he watched. No one but Bernacchi was expert in this mode of travel. Like everything else the long planks of Norwegian wood had arrived untested. The bindings were tricky and though at first a couple of men took a tumble, they seem to get the hang of it. Still, the surface of the snow was not even enough to make it easy. In addition, the party was hauling two sleds, weighed down with ballast. On an overnight expedition, there would be tents, sleeping bags and food under the tarpaulins.

Coming on board from a morning spent in one of the laboratory tents, Scott's second-in-command, Armitage, joined the commander.

'It's a start, sir,' he said.

Scott nodded in the direction of the ice party. 'Skis,' he murmured.

Armitage was privy to more than most but what the commander meant by this, he couldn't be sure. The route of between three and four miles would take almost two hours and the party had dipped out of view after not more than twenty minutes ago. Scott hung on the last of their movements, like a spectator at a rugby match upon which the nation's honour depended. He just stood there.

'Yes, sir. Skis,' Armitage said, clapping his hands around his frame to keep warm. Even swaddled in sheepskin the cold was biting.

Scott was still there when they returned. A small party gathered to welcome them. When they removed their goggles, their eyes were shining. Royds saw that they put away their kit with precision. Then inside, hot Bovril was served with slabs of bread and dripping. Scott, standing still, was colder than any of them. He placed himself by the stove, to debrief the group.

'Well,' he said, 'how were the skis?'

Unpractised, two had taken well to gliding across the ice, while the others said clearly they'd have preferred simply to walk alongside the sled.

'I'm not sure it's not just as quick to walk, sir,' Royds confirmed. 'By the time you've got the bindings on and off again, and accounting for falls.'

Scott was certain in any case that he could improve on the pace of a little more than a mile an hour.

'I like the skis,' Bernacchi disagreed. 'But I am accustomed to them.'

Karina watched the Belgian. As a child she had skied now and then. Neither she nor Marijke had taken to it. They had wanted to cross the water. They had wanted to go south to places where skis were alien and the food was exotic. Places people drank wine instead of beer. Who cared where the magnetic pole was?

One way or another, that night the crew ate like kings. Clarke excelled himself and three bottles of champagne were opened at the officers' table to accompany one of the cook's now famous rhubarb pies.

'We have made our start,' Scott toasted, and the officers raised their glasses as if they had just eaten ten courses at the Ritz. 'Next we shall hazard a day trip, I think. The weather being settled.'

There was a murmur of general agreement

around the table. Shackleton piped up to volunteer for the mission. He had been disappointed not to be chosen before and now he could hardly contain himself. The commander smiled indulgently.

'With dogs this time,' Scott said.

'Yes, sir,' Shackleton tried not to gush. 'And I'd like to try the skis. Just to get the hang of them. The Swedes and Norwegians swear by them.'

Scott held Shackleton in his eye a moment too long as he lifted the champagne to his lips and drained the last of it. Without further briefing, he asked the sub-lieutenant to choose his men. Shackleton smiled, not realizing that in giving him this freedom, Scott was indulging in some kind of irony. Armitage who knew the commander better, marked Shackleton's card. The skipper didn't trust this young Irishman. It was a shame, he thought, he had proved himself capable and the men liked him. Shackleton paused before he spoke.

'I think Weller for the dogs. Blissett perhaps – it would be good to have one of the marines, and Ferrar.'

Scott nodded. 'No time like the present, old chap. You'll go the day after tomorrow. Hike for half the day out and half the day back.'

'You don't think we should make camp?' Shackleton pushed.

Armitage was not the only officer to notice Scott taking only a moment too long to reply.

'You're to make ten miles if you can, Shackleton. Take the kit but don't make camp unless you have to. I want to see how far a team can make in a day.'

'Better safe than sorry, I suppose,' Shackleton grinned, and Armitage noted that the strange and disturbing dreams that have peppered his sleep the last few nights were not nearly as threatening as the look in Scott's eye when he silently made a decision. Shackleton eyed the last of the cocoa in front of him in the jug, and thought that he could not have it. None of them could. To take it would be greedy.

It was late when the knock came on Wilson's door.

'Reg,' he smiled, surprised when Koettlitz appeared.

Koettlitz and Wilson were both medical men but there the similarity ended. Koettlitz was dark-haired and wiry to Wilson's solid red-haired, pale skinned Englishness. He was a man for graphs, while Wilson liked to experiment on living flesh.

'I want to talk about the diet.'

'Now?'

Koettlitz pulled his flask from his pocket. He was of Dutch origin and had brought a personal supply of genever. 'Meat,' he said, 'the three men without meat.'

As well as Shackleton, Vince and Buckridge, the laboratory assistant, continued to forgo the stewed seal and flambéed penguin breast. Clarke cooked them fish and they got extra bread rations.

Koettlitz allowed his gaze to linger momentarily on the sketches tacked to the doctor's shelf.

Wilson smiled. 'It was difficult at first to draw in white but I think I'm getting the hang of it.'

Koettlitz sat down and opened his notebook at a graph.

'They have all lost weight. Buckridge's gums

208

are inflamed and Vince's nails are shattered. Shackleton is suffering, I think, though he won't admit it. We might conclude . . .'

'That meat is the most important part of our diet – in the south?'

Koettlitz raised his flask. 'We must have meat. The chaps forgoing starch are faring far better. And that is my concern. Shackleton will lead a party onto the ice tomorrow. My question is, should we notify the captain?'

Wilson blanched. In the terms of the expedition, this would be to pronounce Shackleton weak.

'I should say no. He's a fine, strong fellow, though his gums are shot. We can hardly excuse him his duties and besides, to quit early would leave the study short of vital data. I'll wager old Shackle is the strongest of all of us.'

Koettlitz put away his flask. 'Well, if you're sure,' he said.

'Absolutely.'

That night the crew slept soundly. Karina slipped along the boards and watched their dreams rather than planting fragments of her own story in their sleeping minds. She let them dream of wheeling over the snow. Of flying.

She had to concede that the men were brave. Braver than Ross or Hooker – neither of whom would have attempted the interior. Had time changed the English? Were these better men than Hooker or Thebo had ever been, she wondered. She was not ready to concede that. Tonight they had been in high spirits. If one of their number was to fall into a crevasse, she wondered, who would try to rescue him? Would these men have rescued her? Would Shackleton have broken her fall? Would Blissett? Would any of these men abandon their wives on a bleak island simply because they felt lonely and wanted to get away? In such circumstances, would they come to some kind of a gentlemen's agreement with an untrustworthy second-in-command? Would they never think to enquire as to what had happened?

She flickered behind their eyelids. Shackleton was not married but he had high hopes that if he distinguished himself on this mission, he might win the heart of the woman he had longed for. Her name was Emily. Karina sounded it out. Tonight, however, the great explorer was dreaming of tournados of steak, flamed before his eyes at a mahogany table by a white-coated waiter. Karina turned away. There were no women here, so it was difficult to decide how the men might behave towards one in need. She had come to the south by mistake, she conceded. Perhaps she would be the only one. Why would any woman want to follow? What kind of woman would be tempted to try?

Like shadows, memories of the expedition's far off womanfolk revolved around her. One or two carried plump babies on their hip. Others were smiling and laughing. There was a profusion of bustles and lacy necklines. One girl marched in the street surrounded by others and chanted something about having the vote. In his cabin, Scott dreamed of his wife, Kathleen. 'You will reach the pole,' she said. Silently the

210

commander worried that he might let her down and if he did, that she might not love him. Karina saw it all. Being here and doing this was the uppermost thing in their hearts. Scott was not alone, she realized. There was not one member of the crew who would rather conquer a lady than conquer the south and for the skipper, and, for that matter, Shackleton, these things were synonymous. Shackleton turned in his sleep and she noticed a pale blue light emanating around him. She could not be bothered either to tease or torture this evening. With a shrug she moved away as, in his dream, he ordered an English pudding, steamed and served with custard.

The next morning Shackleton woke knowing that out of sight of Winter Quarters Bay he would be free. He was brought up one of ten children so the feeling of being one of too many jammed together was one he had been trying to break free of all his life. He hoped the mantle of his childhood would slip from his shoulders as soon as he was out of sight of the ship, and he would fly.

Scott had plotted a route on his chart. He was obsessed with planning. If anything went wrong, he did not want it to be his fault. List after list, he tried to cover every eventuality. These trial runs would allow him to do so more effectively. In time, he would set up supply hubs on the ice. If his expeditions were to go further they would have to be provisioned and in this the Antarctic weather would help rather than hinder his operation. Food here didn't spoil.

Outside, Skelton checked his camera meticulously before he photographed Shackleton, Weller, Blissett and Ferrar with the dogs.

'For heaven's sake, Reggie.'

Shackleton was impatient today. Skelton waved him off. He seemed strangely taken up with the shadows on the rough white ground, as if he had to be sure that each one was attached to a person. From further away, Karina wondered if he would ever get over that photograph.

Too busy to be troubled by his friend's eccentricity, Shackleton checked the fastenings on the sled. Weller geed up the dogs. The men waved as the team set off. There were no three cheers for Scott and the *Discovery* this time. Armitage shook his head. The lieutenant was making mistakes that would cost him dear in the long run.

Shackleton did not even think of it. The exhilaration of being free was apparent already. At first, it was easy going. Skiing alongside the pack, he thought the Swedes and Norwegians were right about it being the best way to travel. He couldn't understand why Royds had dismissed skis so easily. Ahead, Weller sat like king of the ice on the sled as Karina ran ahead of the animals, a barefoot nymph on the snow, leading the way.

'We'll make more than ten miles, surely,' Shackleton told himself.

As the camp disappeared behind them Blissett whooped into the empty brightness. His voice echoed and Shackleton found he was laughing.

Then, two miles out, the terrain became more difficult. The sledge got caught in fissures on the ice and went over. Weller admitted, clinging on tightly, that it had been travelling at too great a speed.

'Sorry, sir,' he apologized. 'We should slow down.'

Coming to a sudden halt, Shackleton understood that the pace they'd set was too dangerous. On skis it meant the men were also subject to the risk of breaking a limb if they fell. Weller and Ferrar righted the sledge and they set off again, this time more slowly. Karina hung back.

Shackleton wondered why the ice had set in frozen waves here, many of which were too steep to ski across. At such times dealing with the skis, the sledges and the dogs took longer than manhauling the supplies would ever do. Getting down to business he, Blissett and Ferrar stopped and removed their bindings, loading the skis on their backs. The truth was, you still had to walk at least some of the way.

Even going slow, the dogs loved the exercise. *They were bred for this*, Weller realized and for the first time he was unreservedly glad he was here. This was an extraordinary experience. He wouldn't swap it. Behind Weller, Shackleton took his turn riding on the sledge like some kind of pagan king and he felt as if he belonged. After four hours of what felt like more or less plain sailing, they pulled up and Weller fed the pack seal blubber.

'Best I'm in charge of the food, sir. It keeps me top dog,' he said.

Shackleton grinned, his skin was almost translucent beneath the scarf wound round his face. He enjoyed sledging almost as much as the animals

213

did. It seemed logical to him to have dogs on a polar expedition, if for no other reason than to keep a fellow warm at night. Blissett's face was concealed behind a thin woollen scarf. Ferrar's eyes were just visible behind thick goggles. With Winter Quarters Bay long gone, it felt as if they were the only men on the continent. As if they were alone.

Waiting for the dogs to finish their meal Ferrar lit a cigarette and poked it between the folds covering his face. None of them wanted to admit it, but the trip was already evoking the almost forgotten excitement of childhood. Each one was the plucky boy who went to the bottom of the wood, climbed down the well or dived into the village pond – it was, in the main, what had landed them here.

As they set off, Blissett took pole position on the sledge and Shackleton put his skis back on and started out side by side with Ferrar. Ferrar struck up a hymn. He had a strong voice and although he kept it low Shackleton caught the tune.

'And did those feet in ancient time, walk upon England's mountain green?'

He smiled. He was not sure he had the breath to join in. Ferrar must be fit.

'And was the holy lamb of God on England's pleasant pastures seen?'

Ferrar cast a glance in the officer's direction and all at once they sang together. Blissett and Weller too.

'And did the countenance divine shine forth upon our clouded hills?

And was Jerusalem builded here among those dark satanic mills?'

A cloud passed overhead. It was a strange shape, Shackleton thought as he squinted upwards. It looked like some kind of wraith – an ancient Nordic goddess or a banshee perhaps. He wondered if it was carrying snow. *So much more.* Karina smiled as she noted that there was part of Shackleton that wanted to travel against the weather. They would have to turn back soon if they were to make the round trip in one day, she thought and then, on queue the sub-lieutenant let fly a wish that he could set up camp. Still, he knew he must stick to Scott's instructions. Perhaps if there was a blizzard he could get away with it. The cloud paused as if it was looking at him and then passed overhead. *It must be windy up there*, he thought. At ground level there was scarcely a breath of air. A little further, he decided. And then we'll turn.

Blissett was aware they were pushing time to its limits, but Shackleton was the senior officer.

'We don't want to be late,' he said. 'They'll get worried.'

'Just to that hillock,' Shackleton motioned towards an incline ten minutes' ahead. 'I want to see what's over the crest.'

Blissett put his back into it. They would chart the terrain they'd covered and Shackleton was right. If they could get a forward view of the landscape – the valleys and hills and the potential danger, the next expedition might be glad of it.

Hours after they finally turned, and far later

215

than they were expected to be away, the camp came into view – a tiny black dot. A stream of smoke snaked upwards from the hut. It was late though the sky was as bright as ever, the darkness yet to cover it. And on the deck of the *Discovery*, Commander Scott stood still as a statue, looking for the party's return. The weather had been stable all day and each passing minute he found himself increasingly angry. There was no need to be so late. Shackleton would always push things to the limit. As the sleds appeared on the horizon, he pulled in his stomach, as if this would contain his temper.

Oblivious, the men waved enthusiastically as the team pulled up at the kennels. The football match was over for the evening. The officers had had their meal. Some of the crew were already sleeping. Scott descended.

'Well?' He couldn't wait for the news. 'What took you so long?'

Shackleton explained how choppy the ice fields had been as Weller and Blissett removed the harnesses, the sledges were unpacked and the dogs returned to their kennels.

'We kept dinner for you,' the words escaped Scott's lips unwillingly.

It had been hungry work and, full of adrenalin, the sledge team boarded the *Discovery* hoping there might be second portions despite the late hour. The officers had stayed up to hear their news and the team were greeted like heroes. Over soup and pie, Shackleton and Blissett pointed out how far they got, using Scott's charts. As the crow flew they had made more than the ten miles allotted.

'I'm sure we could man-haul further in the same time,' Wilson commented.

'Perhaps,' Shackleton granted him. 'Though we might get better on the skis with practice. And the dogs are a comfort.'

'A comfort?'

The notion was not one that the skipper allowed himself. Everything on the ship had been loaded for practical reasons. The idea of having *comfort* was somehow most feminine. He knew the dogs were somehow namby-pamby. Shackleton persisted. It was an Irish choice of word and he wanted to explain it.

'Yes. For warmth and if it comes to it, for food in dire circumstances. It's safer too. If one of us got injured we'd be better able to get him back more easily.'

'That's true,' Wilson nodded. Scott didn't reveal his thoughts, one way or another. The sub-lieutenant was too keen by far and such unbridled enthusiasm was not going down well with him. The Irishman lacked the requisite respect. He was some kind of show-off to go further than ten miles. There was no reason to be late. None at all. Scott valued obedience, not flair. He encouraged the men to think for themselves only if it fell in with his plans.

'We'll see,' he said.

Later that night Karina taunted him. After dark, in his dreams, she showed the commander a vision of the men singing on the ice. Of Shackleton lauded in London. Of Hooker shaking the Irishman's hand. Scott twisted in his sleeping bag. An impossible bead of sweat broke out on his brow, despite the chill. *My, he is like a child*, she thought. And she wondered what she might do.

Eighteen

As the nights drew in and the temperature plummeted, the commander became restless. About a week later, he bided his time waiting to speak to the officers after dinner. The plates had been cleared and the men were lingering at the end of the meal. Clarke had excelled himself, braising seal meat with spices to produce a curry, which he served with a flourish. The second edition of the *South Polar Times* was being compiled and the officers were running with a joke about it having a restaurant column.

'I'll be your food critic, Shackle,' Ferrar, the young geologist, offered. 'The finest cuisine south of, well, everywhere.'

Laughter peppered the air.

'We'll need illustrations,' Shackleton insisted. 'Wilson?'

Wilson watched Shackleton, who had lost another pound or two in the last few days. He wondered if the encroaching darkness had accelerated matters. If he didn't know better, he'd say Shackle was getting scurvy.

'Would you draw us something, Billy-boy?' Shackleton teased.

The doctor liked his nickname, never having been fond of his Christian name, Edward or its diminutive, Teddy.

219

'All right,' he agreed. 'But I have a more serious piece of art for you first. Look.'

He rustled a piece of paper from his sketchbook. On it there was a more than passable drawing of the *Discovery* in its mooring. The likeness was much admired as it was passed round.

'I will draw her again when we weigh anchor for the winter,' Wilson announced, finishing the last of his brandy.

Scott shifted. He toyed momentarily with his cup. On polar missions, ships docked where they could be sailed. This meant, should the winter prove too awful or should there be an emergency, they could always make for safety.

Inside Scott's mind, Karina watched his discomfort. *He has not told them*, she realized. *Another liar.* Now she followed the story of Franklin's disastrous Arctic expedition decades ago as Scott brought it into the forefront of his memory. This story haunted modern polar explorers as much as Ross's Antarctic expedition inspired them. Iced in over two Arctic winters, Franklin's men starved to death. Debate still raged over whether they had resorted to cannibalism. Scarred by the very idea, successive generations of men at the extremes adopted the wise watchwords – always make sure you can get away.

Scott caught Bertie Armitage's eye. His second-in-command knew full well the *Discovery* was moored where she would stay. The knowledge had been a burden. The matter was decided months before the *Discovery* had even left British waters. In the grand drawing rooms of London's private clubs, tables had been banged and voices raised. The truth was, alone, the *Discovery* could not carry enough supplies to make the mission possible any other way. She had to remain in use as quarters. Financing one ship was a gargantuan task, never mind financing two. The matter had been finally agreed over cigars at Admiralty High Command. At the time, it hadn't seemed the slightest awkward that the officers and men would not be told in advance. The ship would be released in the Antarctic summer, after all, when the sea finally thawed. If she was not, there would be a relief vessel.

'We always get our men out,' the chairman of the Royal Geographical Society pronounced, though that wasn't true. Men died all the time on British expeditions. It was considered regrettable.

Now Scott weighed the necessity of telling the officers against the possible response. Already there were banks of slushy seawater forming in the bay. Under the tabletop, his finger beat a pulse onto his knee. He knew he had to make the announcement. The commander's nod was almost imperceptible – a signal that he expected Armitage to back him up.

'We're not going to move her, Wilson,' he said casually. 'Your sketch will stand.'

It took a moment for this to sink in. Wilson closed his sketchbook. Skelton took a drink, only because it was something to do. His cup clattered as he replaced it on the table. Ferrar cleared his throat.

'You mean . . .' he started, 'that we will be iced in?'

The naval men stayed silent. It took a scientist to dare speak.

'Those are my orders,' Scott replied. 'There will be no shifting from Winter Quarters Bay. That's why I named it.'

It felt as if the commander had been laughing at them, hinting at this unusual and unpopular plan without revealing it. Winter Quarters Bay indeed. As the idea settled, none of the officers wanted to show his shock. Come what may, every man intended to last the weather but they would all prefer there was an option to leave. Polar exploration was an uncertain business.

Royds's hands were shaking. He glanced down as if his own flesh had betrayed him and folded his traitorous fingers out of sight. Shackleton's skin prickled. How dare Scott agree such a thing and not tell anyone? The rest of the officers fixed their eyes on a distant point, as if they were trying to work out a tricky crossword clue.

Below decks the news travelled. Karina could feel a wave of anger roll over the evening air. There was little that was not overheard at the commander's table. Unguarded, the crew were not silent as the story broke, delivered by young Buckridge, the laboratory attendant, who had been passing the mess after taking a turn on deck. He told the petty officers who informed the men. Tall Taffy Evans crossed his arms and refused to join the conversation, which to his mind was tantamount to mutiny. The rest of them felt cheated and said so in whispers, knowing that none of the officers around the commander's table could hear them. One or two of the pluckier fellows reacted with bluster like pigeons puffing their breasts to make themselves look larger.

'He shouldn't have,' one man objected and around him the others nodded agreement.

Above, in the mess, the officers remained stunned.

'Thing is,' Scott continued, 'we didn't want to disquiet the men. There will be a relief ship, of course, come the spring and we are well supplied, so the risk is negligible. The Admiral himself issued the command.'

Armitage cleared his throat.

'Well, we weren't for turning, were we, chaps?' He dutifully backed up his senior officer. 'And I for one am happy to be quartered on the *Discovery*. No changing cabins, eh?'

Shackleton swallowed his anger and raised his cup. There was nothing else but to make the best of it.

'To a winter on the ice,' he said and after only the briefest pause, the men toasted. For a second, Scott forgot his reservations about the Irishman and allowed himself a moment of relief.

That evening, settling to sleep in their quarters, more than half of the officers were so angry they could not commit Scott's announcement to their journals. The idea was to write a genuine account, but every man was aware should anything happen to him, the commander might peruse the pages and they did not want the slightest suggestion of mutiny to be found.

Karina stalked the ship. In Scott's cabin, she

223

leaned over and whispered in his ear. *They hate you*, she hissed. *And they are right.* Then she flew up into the rigging and watched as darkness took over the sky and the sea hardened.

Nineteen

As time passed the prow became fixed. The hammocks hung unmoving and the seagoing equipment stayed rooted to its spot. The steadiness of the *Discovery* was not as strange as the men expected. Some said they missed the slow rhythm of the tide that used to lull them to sleep but as time wore on, it was generally acknowledged that they were sleeping better in the darkness.

'It is hibernation,' Koettlitz joked.

Wilson considered whether this was possible. He could not quite decide.

On the downside, the air became cold beyond imagining, as if the whole bay had plummeted into a bright frozen cave. The men realized that what they had thought was chill was only high summer, and autumn now was bad enough. The encroaching cold slowed everyone. Every movement. Every thought. On one particularly chill day, a poor fellow took the knife from a jar of red berry jam and licked it clean in the mess. The cold metal fused to his tongue and he sustained an ice burn that would scar him for the rest of his life. His screams were heard across the deck – an animal squeal that no one would ever forget. Wilson blamed himself that he had not given adequate warning. He simply had not thought of it. Like all wounds this one would heal slowly in the low temperatures.

225

'Be more careful,' Wilson dismissed the fellow. It would do no good to cosset the men. Not with winter almost upon them.

As the weather worsened, harsh winds whipped up the snow.

'At least there's still a little light,' Royds said.

Not for long. The coming darkness was like a sinister character waiting offstage. Rumours abounded that when the sun set for the last time it would damn them twice. There would be no light again until the Antarctic summer dawned. The storms became more frequent.

'At least we're not at sea,' Clarke said, inspecting the riot of wind and snow from the safety of the *Discovery*'s deck.

The seamen nodded, unable to take their eyes off the last of the brightness. In this weather the waves on open water would be titanic. The vicious winds were running at several knots an hour. And then out of nowhere, a mild day would dawn and it would seem as if that was normal.

'Even the dogs want to stay in the kennel,' Weller said.

'The *hounds* you mean,' Clarke teased him. 'If not the *wolves*. They are practically feral.'

Weller cast a glance that belied the very idea. 'I've got them trained all right.'

'So far,' Clarke quipped, 'until one of them is poorly or we run out of supplies.'

Upon occasion, the snow became so thick that it was almost fog. From the ship, the men looked towards the little village they had built on the ice, unable to make out even the hut.

'You'd lose your way in a minute,' Clarke

said. 'Why, I can hardly see my way back to the galley.'

One or two of the men looked sideways at Able Seaman Vince. If anyone was likely to get lost, trip over or make a mistake, it was he. The rest of them, especially the team that built the hut, peered warily across the bay but there was no hope of them making out whether their hard work would survive the storm.

'We did our best,' Duncan concluded, 'but it's filthy weather. If the hut comes asunder we'll just have to fix it.'

In his day, Ross would have stuck to the shifting outline where the ice met the sea, but despite the weather, it was Scott's plan to explore the interior. Storms or not. He had made his lists and he felt ready. There were scientific soundings to take and much to learn. Conditions had to be tried. He was undaunted by the downturn in the weather. They must make the best use of the light, that was the thing. There were only a few weeks left until the darkness became total.

It was the 8th of March – the very tail end of the summer. The snow had abated and it was a crisp morning. The final party comprised twelve men – more than any other yet to date, but they intended to go further and Scott wanted to give as many of the crew a chance as he could. He decided the expedition was to be led by Royds again. As the officer who was mostly responsible for the construction of Winter Quarters Bay, Royds had the physique of a gym teacher and the personality to match. He was strict but fair. 'You choose your men,' Scott said, having briefed the lieutenant on the route.

When George Vince volunteered, the lieutenant chose him for the team. Vince was a willing soul. With a free reign Royds continued. As it was his job to oversee the men's work, he knew them better than most. He picked a fellow officer – Barne, Evans from the Mess Deck (at which a ripple goes through the men for Evans had already had a turn), Quartly, Clarence Hare, the ship's domestic, of all people, and Wild. With Scott's eyes on him, Royds paused. The commander did not betray his feelings about the team and the lieutenant returned to the job of choosing six more. He had sense of fair play and wanted to give some of the weaker men a chance. It would be heavy work. But there were enough of them.

Karina watched. She licked her lips. The cold thickened the air. You could cut the sub-zero temperatures like a hot knife through a penny lick. Skelton was nervous when he took the now customary photograph as the group assembled. As usual he placed the men carefully, checking the area for rogue shadows. Scott watched him – was the fool trying to clean the ice? Skelton paused before he pressed the button. He could swear he heard a laugh.

Then the commander moved forward to shake hands with the team. Royds checked the supplies were strapped in place and the sledges were in good order. They gave three cheers and set out. Content that despite the biting cold the clouds had snowed themselves out, Royds thought that there were no words to adequately describe the feeling of moving through such coldness. England, that land of rainy summers and bright crisp winters, had not spawned vocabulary worthy of Antarctic excess.

Scott watched with satisfaction. The lieutenant was a serious fellow. Unlike Shackleton, there would be no freewheeling or undue high spirits on this trip. Doggedly, with the territory beyond McMurdo Sound awaiting them, the chosen men set to man-hauling the sledges as Scott had instructed. They carried enough supplies for the last days of light – though they would be away for less than that. Best to be safe. There was pemmican and biscuit to make a thick, hot soup, or, as Clarke had christened the mixture, hoosh. After a day on the ice, it was delicious though not a man among them truly preferred it to roasted duck, not least Vince who recently had been fantasizing about all kinds of meat – roasted pork with a veneer of crisp crackling, soft, stewed beef and game sausages. His father was a fishmonger and if he'd had to guess back in England, he'd have hazarded that he'd miss a nice fillet of cod or perhaps some haddock – the taste of home. But no. Only three days after he started the doctor's diet, he began to dream of steak-and-kidney pie and he had not stopped since. Last week he lost a tooth, though he has not told anyone.

Commander Scott watched from his place under the mizzen boom until the twelve figures disappeared, black dots into the blinding white.

The round trip was calculated at thirty miles. At home, a man might walk that in a day but here, across the wastes, it would take longer. The pole, by their calculations, lay far more than 100 miles to the south. But that was for later.

'The waiting will be the tricky bit.' Armitage appeared at Scott's elbow.

The camp seemed suddenly too quiet with so many men absent. Scott thought that after this trip he would collate the differences between leather footwear and finnesko though already he was of the view that fur got soaked too easily. He smiled at Armitage.

'Perhaps tonight we shall have Shackleton give us a lecture about his seawater samples,' he suggested.

'Yes, sir.' Shackleton's voice cut in.

The skipper stiffened. Armitage ducked below.

Shackleton squinted into the distance but he could not make out Royds's party. Dark circles had appeared under his eyes. He had caught sight of himself in the shaving mirror that morning and thought that he looked like a man who could not sleep, when the truth was quite the reverse. When the doctor had asked if he felt well, he had insisted that he did. Nonetheless, he could not tell if it was the disquiet or simply the onset of winter, but his limbs ached. He had longed to be part of Royds' party, though he knew it wouldn't have been fair to choose him. Everyone should have their shot.

'Sir,' he said, deciding that he should tell Scott what was on his mind. 'This man-hauling. The

230

sledges I mean. If the native people elsewhere use dogs, then should we not—'

'Should we what?' Scott snapped. 'I am the skipper.'

'Yes, sir.'

'I won't have you making choices, Shackle. It's not your place.'

'Yes, sir. It's only I'm not sure we should discount the dogs. Or the skis. When the men become accustomed to the skis, for example, they find them most useful. It's faster than man-hauling.'

'And more dangerous. Leave this to me. I am responsible for everyone.'

'But, sir—'

'You are dismissed, lieutenant.'

Shackleton lingered.

'Dismissed,' Scott repeated.

Shackleton blinked. He had served under several naval captains but none had been so obviously wrong about something so important. Scott's jaw set and Shackleton decided he'd best leave it for now. He turned smartly and disappeared below. If Scott wanted him to talk about seawater he'd need to prepare, but perhaps he could catch an hour's sleep. He could certainly use it.

Miles off now, the snow was fresh and that made it heavy going, like walking across sand. The route Scott had plotted took the party south. Royds navigated carefully. The other pilot expeditions had not covered such rough terrain, but they had given Scott confidence in how far the men could make in a day. A new challenge, there

231

was a peak over 1,000 feet high ahead. At home, all the men, outdoor types, would have climbed higher, but a mountain in England was easier than a gentle hill in the Far South.

Royds was a fellow for whom the phrase slow but sure might have been personally coined. Taffy Evans was at the front – a beacon for the others to follow. For George Vince and Clarence Hare, close behind him, the sensation of crossing this icy wilderness was beyond what both men had expected. Vince was wearing a pair of fur boots. There was no grip on them and the burn on his hand was starting to ache in the biting cold. Clarence cracked a smile to encourage his friend and then realized with his face covered, Vince couldn't see it. He raised a hand instead. Vince nodded and lost his footing. He had no energy for such niceties and as he regained his balance he turned his gaze to the small patch of ground in front of him. He must simply keep going, eyes down.

Karina danced her way along the route but today there would be no singing of hymns. No joyful flying across the ice. The men were tethered to heavy sledges, packed with supplies.

After four hours of hiking, Royds stopped to rally the party.

'We've covered a good three miles,' he said. 'Another one and we'll have made it to the foot of the mountain. We'll camp there and rest.'

He could see that some of the men were already finding it tougher than others. Hauling the sledges was exhausting. The lieutenant was fit but even his limbs were aching. If you exposed your skin to the air it became painful in seconds. Evans moved the scarf from his mouth and cracked a grin.

'Not long till supper, then, lads,' he said, putting an arm on Clarence's shoulder. 'That's your job, if I'm not mistaken?'

Clarence nodded. Between his other domestic duties on board he sometimes helped Clarke in the galley. You brought your expertise with you on such missions. Clarence didn't mind.

The great hill, as yet unnamed on British maps, came into view almost as soon as the party got going again. It was at least something for which to aim though the men quickly realized it looked closer than it was. Perhaps something to do with the curve of the earth. Perhaps it was simply that they were naturally optimistic. At the talks Shackleton had organized in the evenings, there had been much vaunting of the mission's contribution to science and how Britain would be proud. Hauling their equipment, it didn't feel that way.

The hill didn't seem close until they were almost upon it. At the base, Royds stopped. He did not want to push the party too hard on the first day. He chose a spot and rallied them to raise the tents as Clarence Hare got the hoosh pot underway. Once the tarpaulin and canvas was up, they huddled inside in an uneven circle and gulped down the food. Able Seaman Frank Wild, piped up.

'It seems even more silent once you're away from the ship. Doesn't it, sir?' he said.

233

There was a murmur of general agreement. Bored, Karina played with the tent ropes but they held tight.

'Peace and quiet for us, eh, Wild?' Royds tried.

The idea of normal society – people passing each other on the street – had seemed alien for months now.

After the meal one or two lit up a smoke – the last diehards who had decided they didn't care if they couldn't taste the tobacco. Vince was the first to turn in. He didn't say anything but his hand had gone an alarming colour of white and he could no longer feel his left foot. There was no point in making a fuss, he thought. Perhaps sleep would help.

Outside, Royds checked the tent and made sure the sledges were secure. When he came back, Barne was playing cards with Quartly. The men were not supposed to bring personal items. 'It's only a pack of cards,' Royds told himself as he slipped into his sleeping bag.

In the morning, he woke first. Ninth of March, he noted in his journal and then with a flourish *On The Ice*. As the men opened their eyes a rumble of good-mornings rolled around and catching a glimpse of the mountains with fresh eyes, it occurred to more than one of them that sorting out their kit seemed mundane in the face of such majesty.

'We'll get some view up there, Royds,' Barne said.

Royds had not considered this. He was there to take measurements and, if he was lucky, have a landmark named in his honour. However, he nodded and gave the thumbs up, ordering Clarence to get on with breakfast.

Many hours later, when the party had conquered the summit, Barne was proved correct. From 1,000 feet you could see the sea in one direction and an astonishing vista of ice and snow in the other. The truth was that from here the camp to Winter Quarters Bay was hardly any distance – at home it would scarcely take an afternoon.

Watching the men after their climb, Royds realised some were suffering. He had not chosen wisely. He wished Wilson or Koettlitz was with him. He could do with medical advice. He did not want to curtail the journey – to do so would see him disgraced in the commander's eyes and he was positive he could make it as far as Scott had marked on the chart. None of the men had actually complained. But still, he could see them.

With the tent in place Clarence melted fresh snow and brewed tea adding copious amounts of sugar. Then he got started on the hoosh. Evans dried out by the stove. His finnesko boots had almost fused to his woollen socks. The fur got damp too easily. Still, he enjoyed the warmth. No one had enough energy for cards or for writing their journals.

'We should sing,' Royds said. He was not musical but he knew that singing was said to keep the spirits high. He started a shaky chorus of 'The Lord is My Shepherd' and the men joined in. Then Quartly and Evans broke into a round of 'Tararaboomdiay'. The others laughed. Royds shrugged off his discomfort. He was not one for the music hall but they had started now. Hare

235

told a story about a theatre in Hull where a woman fell off the stage and later married the man who caught her.

'They'll try anything to snag a fellow – those showgirls,' he grinned.

There was silence as the men in the tent daydreamed about catching music hall actresses, should they fall from a stage.

Quartly woke in the night. The others lay on the groundsheet in their sleeping bags. There was not a spare inch of space. Towards the tent flap someone was snoring gently. He turned over as the tarpaulin shuddered suddenly, as if something was pressed against it – someone trying to find a way in. Perhaps the weather was rising, he thought, as he closed his eyes and listened to the wind making the sound of a woman sighing. Curious, he thought, as he drifted to sleep.

On the third day no sooner had they started than Royds noticed Vince was limping. He gave it twenty minutes but the able seaman was falling behind. The lieutenant stopped the party.

'What is it, Vince?' he asked, motioning towards the man's leg.

'I'm all right, sir,' Vince squared up.

'Good man,' Royds replied. 'Is it an injury?'

'It's the cold, sir. These boots.'

Royds insisted he showed them. Unwillingly Vince bent down to remove his footwear. Wild offered his arm and Vince took it. The finnesko was sodden already.

'Quickly, man,' Royds said.

Exposed flesh had only a matter of seconds. It was too late to save Vince from that, though. As he uncovered his foot it was clear that he already had frostnip. That was bad enough. But what really horrified Royds was Vince's hand. Where his cuff rode up he saw the skin had been singed and there was a patch of frostbite that, when he inspected it, ran down to Vince's thumb. The skin was blackened and the thumb was dead. Why didn't he say something? Royds thought and tried not to panic. 'We'd best take you on the sled,' he said.

There was no argument though this made the load heavier for the others. After an hour, Vince felt so uncomfortable that he got off and limped alongside. No one stopped him but it was one of the reasons that this third day they covered two miles less than Royds intended.

The lieutenant made a decision as they pitched camp. Scott couldn't have known but twelve men were too many – especially with one man injured and, if Royds was frank, at least three more who were not up to the pace. Giving the weaker men the opportunity had not been a kindness, he realized now. As far as he could see there was only one thing for it. Tomorrow morning he'd split the party and forge ahead with the more able. The rest would be sent back to the *Discovery* with Barne in command. It was the best way to complete his mission.

After dinner Royds took Barne aside.

'Help me with this map, would you? I need to take another measurement.'

Barne jumped to his feet and the officers left the tent. Outside there was no measurement to be taken. Royds motioned Barne to accompany him further away so they would not be overheard.

'We have more than a day to go. And with Vince injured . . . I think you should take half of the party back to Winter Quarters Bay under your command, Michael,' Royds said. 'The stronger men can come with me. Vince is a liability. Wilson might need to take off that thumb of his. I just hope it's not the whole hand.'

'His whole hand?' Barne sounded shocked.

Royds nodded. 'Frostbite,' he said. 'Didn't you see?'

From the tent there was a background noise of indistinguishable chatter as Barne tried not to think of what it must be like to lose a hand. Wilson's surgeon's saw kept coming into his mind's eye and he kept dismissing it. Instead he sized up what he was being told to do in terms of his career. He was the junior officer. Royds was in charge. He'd like to complete the mission with the stronger party but this was an opportunity to lead. A quiet personality and with less experience than any of the others, Barne knew if he wanted to shine he would have to take any chance that came his way.

'I'll get them back to base,' he said. 'You can rely on me, sir. Shall we inform them?'

Royds shook his head. 'I'll tell them in the morning. It'll take you two days, I reckon. Going down should be quicker than climbing. You can take Wild and Evans – they're both experienced and pretty tough. Apart from that it'll be the lame goat, Vince – Hare and Quartly.' *And that*, Royds thought, *is what comes of playing cards when you shouldn't.*

Barne nodded. 'We'll get Vince home,' he promised. 'Do you think the others will be disappointed?'

Royds shrugged. He vowed to be tougher next time and stick to a smaller team. If there was anything Scott would want to learn from this expedition, it was the extent to which incompetent and injured men could slow you down.

They never tell the men the truth, she thought and drew the darkness around the tent as if it was a cloak.

The next morning Royds announced the plan. There was no time to object. Barne stepped in efficiently to take command of the returning party. The supplies were split and the teams parted, shaking hands.

'The expedition is the thing,' Royds said solemnly. 'We must achieve what we came to do.'

Ice picks at the ready, there was a sense of relief in the ongoing men – the job would be easier now they could pick up their pace. Each one of them thanked his stars that he wasn't being sent back early.

Barne watched as they set off. Then they loaded Vince onto the sledge.

'Well chaps,' Barne said. 'Let's get to it. Homeward bound.'

Evans and Wild put their shoulders into hauling. Vince objected twice and tried to get off and walk, but Barne overruled him. Now and then the lieutenant glanced over his shoulder. He could still see the others as they continued up the slope until at last they were so small it was like watching spiders climb a pipe. He knew his team would move more slowly and it crossed his mind as long as he got back first it wouldn't be too shaming.

Karina decided to follow the weaker party. She might as well see them back to the ship. Besides, Royds was boring. She wheeled ahead of the sledge for a while, stopping every so often so they could catch up.

Then, just as she got into her stride, there was a sudden flash of light ahead, as if the world was making an announcement. The sky tore open. She whirled round but the men couldn't see what was happening. A buzzing started behind her eyes and she peered through a rip in the clouds onto a picturesque scene.

It was a sunny garden with roses trailing across latticework and flower beds strewn with flaming yellow and orange petals. Through the bushes she saw a swing strung from the branch of an oak tree. *Is this England?* she thought. Without pondering more, she left the ice and entered, following the path and crouching in the shade beneath the oak's heavy boughs. Scott's men seemed a million miles away. Above her the sky was bright and blue and beneath her feet the grass was lush. There was no darkness. No cold. No ice anywhere.

Then she spotted her – an old lady on the other side of the oak. She was sitting alone. Karina peered. The woman was wearing a

240

high-necked dress of pale peach silk. Her fingers fumbled in the long grass around the base of the tree. Her expression was mournful. She started when she saw Karina as if she hadn't expected anyone, but she didn't acknowledge her. *You are a ghost, aren't you?* Karina asked. Nothing. Was this old lady blind, Karina wondered. Was this her heaven?

Then she glanced beyond the tree and recognized the red sandstone building and the greenhouses further up the slope, and what was happening fell into place. It had nothing to do with George Vince's injury or Scott's expedition. This was Hooker's house. This was Glasgow. And this woman – was she Frances? Frances who cut a trim figure in her claret dress all those years ago? Karina peered at her. *Perhaps.* She was so old now and, it occurred to Karina, she seemed old-fashioned. *She has died.* Karina realized. *She has seen the story of what happened. She has only now understood his lies.* The old lady lifted an arm and pointed, furious straight at Karina.

He is my husband, she said. Then she winced. She had seen the connection between them. She knew now.

But he went back to you. You had him, Karina objected. A tear rolled down the woman's cheek.

So young, she said vaguely, and ran a palm over the stiff fabric of her dress. *He loved the money I brought. All the money. How could I have been happy here?* she wailed. *I should have married Stanley.* The regret was palpable, it glowed from the woman's frame like firelight.

241

I'm sorry, Karina managed. *It was wrong for both of us, then.*

And the woman began to fade, an image made out of light alone, freckled with flashes of what looked like certificates and cheques and stocks and shares.

Karina knew she didn't have long. These visions faded quickly and when they did, they were over for ever. She ran across the lawn and looking down realized that she was not a wraith any more. Pink-skinned she was in her twenties again and she could feel the grass beneath her feet and the sun on her back. This is where she should have ended up – here in his house.

At a stretch she made it to the long windows of Hooker's study. Inside, he sat in a leather chair, dressed in mourning clothes. He seemed so frail. So ancient. He was comforting a younger man. *Is that his son?* Raising her fist she banged on the window, her nails cleanly cut again, the hem of her skirt flitting around her ankles in the breeze.

'Joseph,' she shouted. 'Joseph. Let me in.'

Hooker passed his son a well-laundered handkerchief. The mirror behind him was draped in dark cloth. A maid entered the room and poured brandy from a decanter. The men took a glass each and the girl bobbed a curtsey.

'Joseph,' Karina howled. 'I'm here! Joseph! I'm here.'

Finally, as he looked up he squinted through the window. He put his head to one side as if he was confused. 'Joseph,' she shouted. But it was as if he didn't recognize her. *Did I mean so little? Did you ruin me for nothing at all?*

She was about to shout louder and bang harder but before she could the lights dimmed. Her heart sank in her chest and she was lassoed backwards, past Frances who was standing now, a collage of paper and coin, looking bemused at what had just transpired in her lush Glasgow garden. *He didn't even know me. He didn't even remember.* The last thing she saw was the old woman smiling. And howling, Karina was pulled upwards, through the rip in the sky and along a thin, cold tunnel until the pinprick of bright yellow light that was Hooker's home was extinguished.

With what felt like a slap in the face she landed once more only a mile from where she started. Barne and his party were ahead. She lay still a moment, defeated and all she kept thinking was, *How could he forget?* Snow whipped around her. A blizzard had started and the men could not see further than ten yards in front of them. It was protocol to pitch a tent and wait it out but they were freezing cold and starving and the *Discovery* was only two miles away by Barne's calculation and they all wanted to continue as far as they could.

Vince had been taken off the sledge but he needed help walking. Barne and Wild hauled while Evans took on the duty of guiding Vince, step by step. He did so without complaint though it made the going hard.

'Shall we pitch, sir?' Evans asked, though it was not really a question.

Barne looked to Hare for inspiration.

'Your view, Hare?'

Clarence, lowest of the low, paused nervously. It was difficult to know if Barne was asking for his opinion because he wanted to foster team spirit or if the lieutenant had become somehow confused. Clarence, unlike the more experienced seamen, didn't know what he thought – it was the first time an officer had ever asked him for an assessment of anything.

'Well, sir, we've seen worse, haven't we?' he tried.

That was true. A fortnight ago there was a blizzard that afforded no visibility at all. But they weren't out in it. The spectre of one of Clarke's rhubarb pies, tantalizingly close, coloured Barne's judgement. Besides, Vince needed a doctor.

'We should attempt to make it back,' he said. 'Let's keep trying.'

Evans didn't argue. Barne was an officer and Evans had made his name by taking on the difficult jobs without complaint.

Karina rolled over in the soft snow, heaving for breath. She cursed herself for being stupid. Hooker didn't love her, he never had. She watched the men trudging as the group battled on for another twenty minutes, dragging leaden step after leaden step. None of them could think clearly enough to describe the penetrating cold and how difficult it was to move through. All any man could contemplate was his next footfall. They hardly looked up and when they did there was nothing to see anyway. After another few yards, Barne stopped and wheeling around realized that they were one man short – he could not see Hare, the most junior of the team. A sense of panic rushed through him. He stopped the group and the men shouted into the storm.

'Hare! Clarence!'

Evans gave a piercing whistle that you'd think would carry for miles but the snow muffled it. They waited but the weather had wrapped Hare in its soft white blanket and he was nowhere to be seen.

A few yards away, Karina draped herself round Clarence Hare's shoulders as he stumbled through the blizzard. *The damn English. Damn sailors. Damn men. He left me here. He left me.*

'Damn,' Barne cursed under his breath, surprised at himself because he would never normally swear.

He didn't know what to do. He thought back to Royds' evaluation of Hare. 'He's a tough enough fellow,' he told himself. He was in good fettle when they had stopped only a little while ago. He voted to go on. The priority, surely, was Vince who was injured. They should try to get the poor man home. Hare would fend for himself and if not they'd send a party back later.

'This way,' Barne turned.

No sooner had he done so than he slipped and went down. Evans tried to help him and went over too. One by one the men slid as if someone had pulled a carpet away and before they knew it they were tumbling down the long slope. All Barne could think was that damn fool Royds saying how much easier it was going to be on the way home. This wasn't even the steep part of the hill or at least he didn't think it was.

* * *

245

There was no way to be sure exactly how far they'd come. The men landed like sacks of potatoes piled against each other. Barne got to his feet first and panicked, calling to the others but the wind distorted his words and the men fumbled, following echoes, reaching out to grab each other – an arm here and there as they clustered together. The lieutenant decided once he'd rounded everyone up they'd have to damn well pitch camp till the weather cleared. Enough was enough. He came across Quartly and helped him to his feet. Then there was a scream of desperation on the frantic air. The tone was so frenzied that it carried despite the storm and so high pitched it almost sounded animal, though there was nothing else living. Both men turned, trying to locate it.

'Where are you?' Barne shouted.

'Here, sir,' Evans called. He sounded afraid. It wasn't like him. 'It's sheer. A sheer drop. I can't see properly. Oh God.'

Slowly, measuring step by step, Barne and Quartly headed towards Evans's voice.

'Help me,' Wild shrieked. 'I can't hold on.'

Quartly felt something brush by him but there was nothing there. It was as if the wind was alive. His heart was racing. There was something else in the blizzard. A presence. He could swear it. Something thin and white, darting. *It's the fall*, he thought. *It's shaken me up*. Still, he put his hand on Barne's arm so he would not be alone. Then there was another scream and more shouting.

* * *

Karina hovered at the edge of the cliff. They were so stupid. She thought of the grass beneath her feet and how she had longed for decades to feel it. She thought of Hooker's eyes, blank as he stared at her. The pain of that. Had none of them loved her? No one at all? Unable to bear it, she launched herself onto the icy wind and flurried with the snow. The cliff was white and craggy. It was difficult to make out where it ended and where the drop began. Lazily, as if she didn't know what she was doing, she caught the man in the folds of her dress and tugged.

'Man overboard,' Evans's voice sounded.

These men were Royal Navy – they had no other word for it. Barne stumbled towards him.

'Oh God. Have we lost Wild?' he asked.

But then Wild appeared – short, stocky and still limping. Even through the snow they could see he was in a bad way.

'I couldn't hold him any longer,' he burbled. 'I lost my grip and he went over. It's Vince. He's gone.'

Barne bristled. Vince was the man down – the weakest one they should all have been protecting.

'Where?' he shrieked.

Wild motioned and as Barne made to look over the edge, Evans grabbed him.

'It's a sheer drop, sir. Into the sea,' he warned.

'It's as if the wind snatched him from me,' Wild shouted desperately. 'There was nothing I could do.'

As Barne looked down he saw where the snowy

surface disappeared but he couldn't make out the water below.

'It's sea down there,' Evans insisted.

Barne couldn't take it in.

'Vince!' he shouted over the edge.

There was no reply. The realization settled on his stomach. There was no surviving the Antarctic waters. If the fall hadn't killed Vince the sea would finish the job. He had lost a man.

Karina slid across the choppy waters watching Vince as he struggled. If this was revenge, it was satisfying. As the others scrambled above, realizing what had happened, she hovered watching Vince's terrified eyes as he fought the sea. Then suddenly he stopped struggling and disappeared. She had killed a man.

Momentarily she hoped he might appear in death – a companion at last. There was a second or two when she thought that glimmer of hope might be realized. She swooped low over the water and Vince's pale-faced spirit surfaced only for the merest snatch of time until a bright corridor opened above the whirling sea and in the distance she saw him sucked into a meadow that she knew was called Dorset. *Is it England?* He must have been a country boy at heart. *One down.* She relished the thought, letting her hair stream in the wind. *Faithless creature.*

Above, Barne was crying but the others couldn't see. He was thinking that he should have saved poor Vince. *The living can do so little. Did any of the men really try to save me when I fell?* she wondered. And there it was. She was brought back to it. The day of her fall. The very second. If Hooker had cared for her surely he would have tried harder. He had pulled Farmer back from the edge but why was Farmer the first one there? Karina searched her memory. Hooker and the officer from the *Erebus* had been standing together as Pearce managed the flag being raised. When she had screamed, what had happened? 'Women.' Hooker rolled his eyes. *Women?* she snarled. She had not seen him as she tumbled and she had not heard what he said. But now it was clear, decades later. *Women.* As if women were all the same. As if she was not worth the trouble.

Above, Barne and his men succeeded in raising a tent. Inside, they huddled, trying not to share their guilt and their grief. As they settled to wait out the storm, Karina saw Hooker all those years ago, clear as day, scrambling on board the *Terror*. She saw him beg Ross to go back, to check that she was truly gone. The crew considered him brave for that. Three men stepped forward to volunteer. *But it is show. Just show.* Women? *Is that all he could have said?* His old eyes without a glimmer of recognition flashed in front of her through the study's uneven glass. His son fussing. The maid and the brandy. *Did I mean nothing? Or simply not enough? Someone might have saved me*, it occurred to her. *And what then?*

Above, Barne and Hare fell asleep but Evans couldn't. The wind howled around the tent and Karina considered killing all of them. It would be easy to whip away their shelter and let the weather do its work. No one would ever find the bodies. *No one will ever find mine.* And then she thought of Marijke on the roof of their house in Ven. She thought of what Marijke would say. Karina was always the one with the temper. *But who can blame me?* She realized it was possible that all those years ago Hooker had simply frozen – just as stunned as Barne had been when Vince disappeared over the precipice. Just as clueless.

Evans was crying quietly now. Vince would be missed. When they got back with the news none of them would be able to face unpacking his trunk. It would stand to one side as a monument. Whatever was in there would have to wait. *What has become of me?* she thought. Wild turned in his sleep. He had had George Vince by the hand and he let him go. He was afraid now that George might come to him – some kind of furious ghost. Wild's gut turned as he wished it had been different. If only he'd been stronger. If only the blizzard had eased. If only George had moved to the left instead of to the right and he'd have been able to keep a grip. The poor man was tortured.

Karina hovered. *He's happy where he is*, she cooed.

She could not for the life of her think why she would say such a thing. She had no idea if it was true. Wild started. His eyes opened. He pulled his hand from under his cover, touched the air and crossed himself. Evans pretended not to notice.

'Are you an angel?' he moaned.

250

His fingers quivered and he stared right at her. *Can you see me?*

Wild nodded silently. 'Yes, miss,' he said, hesitating as he searched for the right word. 'Are you an angel?'

And instead of taking her revenge on the men in the tent, she flew upwards, spiralling on the wind. She took off for the stars. She drilled into the heart of the mountain. She spread herself thinly across the ice plain until she was at one with the stretch of McMurdo Sound where George Vince's body lay. This way she would not notice them. This way she need not return to the world of men. Eventually Scott and his crew would either die or they would leave and Karina decided it would be best for her if she did not care greatly which of these things transpired. She would not take any more notice of them. Never again.

'We will never forget him. He was the first of us to give his life, here at the end of the world.' Scott's voice was flat.

The title was a dubious honour. The darkness was coming and the light would not return for months. The men around the table did not catch each other's eyes. For once the mess felt too warm. Shackleton had noticed that his dreams had calmed. He no longer heard voices. Perhaps the darkness would be easier than the light.

'It was a sheer precipice,' Barne mumbled.

He could not bring himself to say more. He was in charge. He should have made camp. Vince died because Barne wanted to get home for dinner.

251

He'd never forgive himself. Scott had already berated him, privately. Royds would do so again when he returned. Now the skipper cut in to forestall any public hand-wringing on the lieutenant's part.

'At least the end must have come quickly. The sea is all but ice,' he said.

Barnacchi looked particularly low. He was the only man who had spent a winter on the ice already and Vince's loss reminded him of the two men who died on that expedition. One was a Norwegian sailor washed overboard in a storm. And then there was Barnacchi's friend, Emile, who fell foul of heart disease, here where there was no help for such trouble. This tragic accident was worse even than that, though. Not one of them can help imagining falling into the sea awash with icy slush and there being no hope of rescue. They only hoped that Vince died when he fell and didn't have to endure the water.

'Poor Vince. We shall always remember him,' Shackleton said, thinking that Vince was wearing those foolish fur boots that had no grip. Kit, he was realizing, was of vital importance. Scott did not seem to have entirely taken it in.

The crew spend the evening reminiscing fondly about Vince's limited abilities. Later the skipper would have to write a letter to the boy's next of kin. Poor Mrs Vince would not know what had happened to her young husband for months, perhaps more than a year. The boy's father, Scott recalled, was dead. His mother too. He had no idea how many brothers or sisters Vince might have had or who might comfort his wife, who could not be more than twenty-three or -four. He tried not to think of it.

'We shall raise a cross to his memory. It will stand where he fell. We shall have a proper service,' he promised.

When Royds returned, the sun disappeared over the *Discovery*'s prow for the last time and the light went out of the sky. The blackness was tempered by snow, falling lightly in the plummeting cold. *Gnasterver*, Karina would have called it. Each kind of snow had a name in Swedish. It was odd that despite the English obsession with weather, they did not name it properly.

The ship was going nowhere and to the men, the darkness felt like a homecoming. Lighting the lamps became a ritual. The little stoves that ran on seal blubber gave off a smell to which they became accustomed. Already the mess looked as if there was a celebration underway with yellow strings of light crossing the table. Outside when the temperature was taken it proved to be an unexpectedly low: minus thirty and dropping fast. At minus fifty there was no question that winter was upon the camp. They merely needed to survive it.

Part Three
Into the Light

'All men are possible heroes: every age,
Heroic in proportions.'
Elizabeth Barrett Browning

Twenty

She tossed and turned like a feverish child, but she did not wake. She lengthened. She hardened. But her dreams were human. Had she guessed, she would have thought it might be Hooker who disturbed her, but in the darkness it was the men of the *Discovery* who appeared in the flashes that cut into the safe silence under the ice.

Scott and Shackleton were high above her, screaming at each other as they travelled across the plain. The sky was light for the beginning of spring. The winter air still lingered. Shackleton was bent, heaving for breath. His skin was patchy as Wilson looked on, trying to break up the argument, about the use of skis. *Skis?* she thought. *What foolishness. Why are they arguing about that?* Wilson sighed. The skipper and Shackle had fought the long journey there and half the way back. They had argued till they were hoarse. They disagreed about the skis. The dogs. The sledges. They bickered about everything except the real problem. That Scott couldn't bear having his authority questioned and that Shackleton thought he could do better.

Shackleton's blood was thin. Karina could feel it coursing through him too quickly. His joints were aching. He was twice as exhausted as the other two men but he wouldn't give up. She shifted.

257

'You aren't fit for this. You will step down,' Scott spat at the sub-lieutenant.

'We could have made the pole. We could still make it if we get the equipment right,' Shackleton insisted.

Scott stamped his foot. They had been hiking over the plain for weeks. The ice was scarred with ski tracks and footprints where they had hauled everything they needed in this first attempt on the magnetic pole. *How pointless.* Eventually Scott had taken the difficult decision to turn back but they'd made it the farthest south of anyone. Heroes. Record-breakers. Pioneers. Still, the skipper cursed the day he'd chosen Shackleton for the expedition. The sub-lieutenant had been sick from the off. From the first night he had been shaky, his gums were raw and some mornings he could scarcely breathe. That notwithstanding, he'd hauled his share or as close as dammit. Together the three men battled the difficult conditions, navigating too slowly for the supplies to last. That was the problem, Scott cursed. As far as he was concerned it wasn't the skis. Or the dogs. Or the sledges. The trouble was the speed at which Shackleton had been able to travel.

Wilson marvelled at Ernest's fighting spirit. Even breathless and so badly run down that his teeth were loose, he still found the strength to raise his voice. It did no good. They had ended up killing the dogs one after the other and feeding them to the rest of the pack just to keep going. *Is it his diet?* Wilson wondered. *Could the experiment be having this much of an effect?* Whatever it was, the invalid was still fighting.

Shackleton's eyes were alight, flecked with yellow. Karina could feel his hatred on the air. He'd kill Scott if he thought he could get away with it. *In the end, you get away with everything*, she thought, and turned over. She knew that murderous feeling. That moment of numbing anger. That need for release.

When she blinked the men were back aboard the *Discovery*. The crew had turned out on the ice to welcome them. Later, fed and after the kind of sleep the living imagine the dead would savour, Scott gave Shackleton a dressing-down – it would be the last time he spoke to him directly.

'You will go home. Medical reasons,' the skipper commanded. 'I'm invaliding you out.'

Shame turned in Shackleton's stomach. He was stronger already. Sleeping in a proper bunk had done wonders. Most men would have died from what he had endured. Karina wondered if Shackleton died, would he linger at the pole? It was all he wanted, after all. But who could say where Shackleton had been happiest. Did death take account of a man's hopes and dreams?

Later, in the doctor's cabin, amid the iodine and rolled bandages, Shackleton tackled Wilson.

'The skipper is too bloody stubborn. He can't accept his mistakes,' he insisted. 'He isn't being fair.'

Wilson did not indulge the grievance. Instead he decided that Shackleton ought to reintroduce meat to his diet.

'The skipper is the skipper,' was all he said. 'You didn't help matters, Shackle, old man.'

* * *

259

When the relief ship, the *Morning*, sailed into view Shackleton's health was improving. He could not bring himself to stand on the ice with the others, cheering and waving the ship to its anchor. Nor did he help to unload the supplies for the second winter – the one he'd miss. That night the officers dined together and with the mess cupboards restocked, Clarke put on a fine show.

'The weather doesn't seem so bad down here,' said the *Morning*'s captain, Colbeck – a decent enough sort.

It was the same kind of Antarctic day as had greeted the *Discovery* when she sailed in. The ice cliffs were still. The sky was blue. It was cold but it wouldn't kill you. No one wanted to enlighten the new boy. It would have sounded like they were complaining. Instead Scott proposed a toast to the *Morning*.

'Well,' Colbeck said afterwards. 'Who's jumping ship and coming back to England?'

A couple of weeks later, below decks, heading northwards for Blighty, the array of hopeless cases banished from any prospect of glory were tortured by nightmares they did not speak about. No one wanted to be branded the man who couldn't cope. They joined the *Morning*'s crew where they fitted in like pieces of a puzzle but their hearts were still aboard the *Discovery*, where the darkness was descending. If their injuries were physical, they sought to overcome them. By the time they docked in Portsmouth, every man had fully regained his health. Shackleton included.

'Sounds like scurvy,' one of the medical chaps back in London at the Royal Society diagnosed when he managed to prise the symptoms from Shackleton's mostly sealed lips. 'I don't understand it. You chaps had lime juice in your rations, didn't you?'

Shackleton nodded. The navy wanted to subject him to a medical examination but he had refused. 'And this is the diet that Dr Wilson prescribed?'

'Several of us were on it.' Shackleton's tone was dismissive.

The man's eyebrow arched but Shackleton wouldn't say any more and there was so much else to discuss. Who could help be enthused? The men on the expedition were heroes – no matter that the sub-lieutenant had been sent home. The doctor leaned forward. 'Do you think the pole is possible to achieve?' he asked, eyes dancing. 'Perhaps it's just too much of a stretch, Ernest. There might be some places on earth that man will never conquer.'

'I can do it,' Shackleton insisted. 'I know I can.'

Karina batted away the visions. She craved darkness and solitude but when the light came and the men with it, she found herself unable to turn away. Between the momentary sightlines, one long winter stretched to two, then three. The *Discovery* was long gone but still the men appeared in front of her eyes. They played around the fringes of her memories alongside the imprint of old sensations. A slap on the wrist in school. The smell of apricots, only a glimmer. Hot jam made by her mother more than a century before.

Nibbled hazelnuts sprinkled through the vibrant orange jelly. And then a vision of Vince, drenched, dead, trickling water onto wooden floorboards. The sum of all her days. Who can tell what will stick? You don't know what will make you turn in your grave. What will rouse you. A puff of anger passed Karina's lips and the darkness descended again. The soft, dark silence.

But there was no getting away. Time and again she came back to them. She could never tell who it might be. Wilson. Scott. Vince. Four years, five, six. This time, it was Shackleton she had the run of. He lit a cigar as he sat back in his chair somewhere smart – in a gentlemen's club. The men reading newspapers pretended they didn't notice him but she could feel the unspoken rustle of English interest behind the headlines. Tall, broad and with his dark hair parted in the centre, Shackleton cut a dashing figure. It had been a long time, she realized. They used to ignore him in this lounge because he had been sent home all those years ago. Now they ignored him because of his notoriety. He had led his own expedition. He was famous and they didn't want to intrude.

Karina sat up. It didn't matter if her eyes were open or closed. What did she need eyes for? The world was playing this inside her head. When had he come back, she wondered. Why didn't she see his second tour on the ice? There was the flash of a tattered flag and the sound of a man crying quietly. He had attempted the pole and he had failed.

'Sir Ernest,' the bartender brought whisky.

The toffs drank brandy but Shackleton had never got used to the taste. The fire crackled and shifted in the grate.

'Lady Shackleton will be joining me for dinner,' he said. 'Will you let me know when she arrives?'

Sir Ernest, was it? And his beloved, Emily had succumbed to his proposal when he got home from the *Discovery* expedition, or as he thought of it now, the *Discovery* fiasco. What had happened still rankled. *Wait till he's dead*, she thought. *If he can't let go of it, Scott will haunt him. All that time on the ice.*

In London, the Shackletons dined together every night, though as Emily occasionally pointed out, the conversation was either about Ernest's last trip or his next one. She frequently wished that she had at least one other interest in common with her husband. The garden perhaps.

'I shall inform the porter of Lady Shackleton's imminent arrival,' the waiter confirmed.

Here, at the centre of the civilized world, where all decisions were taken, ladies were only permitted if they had come to eat. The horror of an unaccompanied woman roaming the club in search of her husband was unthinkable.

London, Karina thought. *I wouldn't have liked it.*

Shackleton did, though. At least, to some degree. He liked the lecture circuit and the adulation but the truth was, once you'd lost yourself in whiteness and frozen your dreams not once but twice on the way to an as yet unreachable pole, they did not thaw the same. He was restless despite his marriage and the title. Despite the polar medal they'd given him.

263

When he first came home he found the myriad colours distracting and the noise unbearable. It was too cluttered. Too easy. Too soft. People didn't understand how the Antarctic had changed him. More importantly, he hadn't planted a flag at what was now the most important destination in the world. No one had. And as a result the endless lectures and dinners and congratulations didn't sit well on Shackleton's conscience. He came up ninety-seven miles short every time. If he was haunted, it was by the inaccessibility of the pole's coordinates, its wide white spaces and empty silence. Its impossibility.

Ernest, Karina cooed. He shook his head. It had been a long time since he'd heard that voice. He associated it with the madness of the *Discovery*, the pain in his joints. A shade of concern twisted. But then luckily, another voice distracted him.

'What ho, Shackle,' it chimed from behind the chair.

Shackleton turned. 'Wilson!'

He put down his drink and puffed his cigar as he got to his feet to shake the surgeon's hand. Over the years they'd run into each other now and then. Wilson sank into a chair and was brought a gin and tonic by a passing waiter. No one who was anyone had to order at the club. That was the point of it being a club.

'I'm having dinner with Emily. Feel free to join us,' Shackleton offered.

'I'm already eating with a couple of other chaps. I arrived from Cheltenham this afternoon.'

Shackleton nodded. 'Visiting your family?'

'We went boating – the weather's been marvellous.

My mother claims it's too cold, but well, you know,' Wilson rolled his eyes.

All of them the same. All of them smitten. She leaned in, reading the doctor. Wilson knew how it had been more than most – he was the doctor after all. The first months after the crew arrived home none of them could bear the mild English weather. The voyage across the equator felt like a baptism of fire. When the *Morning* had anchored in South Africa, Shackleton couldn't sleep for the heat. It felt as if the sunshine had kindled a fire at the centre of his being and his skin was burning from the inside. He roamed the grounds of his hotel like a zombie, fanning himself, unable to bear it. When he got back to Blighty, England's weather seemed somehow indecisive. Here there was no blade of ice hanging over your head, a frozen Damocles' sword to focus the mind. Whoever would have thought the bloody awful sub-zero temperatures would prove an addiction?

Shackleton was not alone among Antarctic veterans in finding himself uncomfortable anywhere above freezing. Many of them dreamed of snowstorms, of the icy breath of the southern wind on their skin and of the clear clean days of Antarctic summer. Unlike Shackleton, though, none of them ever dreamed of the blonde spectre about which he had never uttered a word.

'And you're well?' Wilson enquired.

'Of course.'

'Bad luck. Not making it. I hoped for you, Shackle. I really did.'

He did come back, she thought searching her memory.

265

Wilson's concern was genuine and Shackleton knew it. Still, the words rankled. It had almost been almost a year since he returned to London and he was painfully aware it would be a few more before he got to head to the far south once more.

Such uncomfortable feelings were an ongoing maelstrom. *Perhaps that's what draws me.* Shackleton knew Scott's second attempt was funded now. That's why Wilson had been visiting his family – he had been saying goodbye. If this expedition reached the pole, the aristocracy's latest lord would never forgive himself. The bad blood between him and Scott rendered the business a grudge match.

'Are you . . .?' his voice lingered.

'I'm Chief of Scientific Staff this time,' Wilson admitted. 'Truth is I've missed the old place. The skipper has been on the circuit for months – organizing it all.'

'I wish you'd come with me,' Shackleton allowed himself to say. 'We could have done with you.'

Wilson's eyes were drawn to the floor. 'I couldn't, old man. It would have been terribly disloyal,' he almost whispered. 'I'll have a crack at the pole with the skipper. Sooner or later one of us has to make it.'

Shackleton never knew what to say when anyone mentioned Scott. Drawing up his courage, he smiled at his friend. Still, Shackleton couldn't help be reminded of the sinking instant when he realized the bastard was sending him home and that there was nothing for him to do but take it. Scott had pulled rank when he banished him – like a coward.

'Have you seen any of the others?' Wilson changed the subject as he sipped his gin.

'I took Frank Wild with me,' Shackleton replied.

Wilson smiled. 'Wild's a good man. I read that you saved him. You gave him your last ration.'

Shackleton shifted in his chair. 'The press made a lot of that.'

'Scott amended our supply depot plan on account of it.'

Shackleton's stomach turned again.

'It was brave decision, Shackle. The last thing we'd want is a tent of frozen, half-starved corpses but it's difficult to put someone else ahead of yourself. You can't run an engine without fuel, old man, can you? We learned that first time out.'

Wilson blushed. After all, it was the experiment with diet that had caused the poor fellow's scurvy. He often thought if Shackleton had been in the other group of men, perhaps things might have been different. But he had never said so.

'Tell me, how is the old place?' he ventured.

'We visited George Vince's cross. We laid pebbles. I expect Wild found that particularly hard.'

'Terrible business,' Wilson shook his head.

From the other side of the room a short, stocky fellow with ginger hair caught Wilson's eye. Wilson smiled and Karina felt the focus shift. This was a new face but the man was somehow familiar. She circled as he approached. He was naval – that much was clear from his bearing – she'd seen too many Englishmen at sea not to recognize the signs. He loved swimming. His leg was in pain. He had spent much of the day with his mother, shopping. *So trivial.*

267

'This is Henry Bowers,' Wilson said. 'He's Royal India Marine. Bowers – Ernest Shackleton.'

Shackleton proffered a handshake as he took in the young fellow's appearance. He was an odd-looking stick. It was almost like looking at Wilson in a distorted fairground mirror. Wilson was tall and this fellow was short. Wilson was slim and Bowers had a paunch. Wilson's features were even and Bowers sported an extraordinarily prominent nose. Shackleton put his head to one side. Now he came to think about it he realized the two men were not alike at all – the comparison only arose because both had red hair. When Bowers spoke he had an accent though she couldn't say from where.

'I am a long-time admirer,' he admitted shyly as the waiter approached.

'What can I get you, sir?' the man enquired.

'Some cordial, if you please.'

Bowers, then, is not a member.

'We were just catching up,' Wilson explained cheerily.

'I don't want to intrude,' the lieutenant seemed somehow younger in the presence of these two polar giants. The truth was, he was reeling from being given a place on Captain Scott's expedition. This time there had been eight thousand applicants.

'You're not intruding, old man. Not at all,' Wilson insisted. 'Lieutenant Bowers has been in charge of loading the ship, Shackle. Our *Terra Nova*. He's done an immensely good job.'

Henry brushed a hand over his hair. 'I'm hoping to support the team that will make the pole.'

'We were just discussing the pole,' Wilson said.

'What else is there to talk about?' Shackleton cut in.

Bowers nodded. 'You were ill your first time out, weren't you, sir? Bad luck.'

The boy's cordial danced green in the light from the fire. Shackleton restrained himself from commenting on Scott or his damn expedition. *If he isn't the one to see the pole first, he doesn't know how he'll bear it.* You'd think one piece of snowbound icy ground was much the same as another. But it wasn't.

'Bowers is developing quite a reputation.' Wilson decided the new recruit was probably the easiest topic of conversation. Bowers cracked an easy smile as the surgeon continued. 'He fell into the hold at West India Quay. Landed on a ton of pig iron and got up, dusted himself down, and got back to the job.'

That's the kind of thing Scott would love, Shackleton thought, but he played the game.

'Good man,' he said.

'It was luck,' Bowers shrugged off his heroism and ignored his aching leg. 'I have a bruise, that's all.'

'I'll bet you want to see the pole, don't you?' Shackleton said. 'I bet when you fell you thought, I better get up or I'll never see it.'

'I've read everything I can lay my hand to,' Bowers admitted. 'I can be a bit of a swot. I doubt I'll be lucky enough to go on the ultimate expedition but I can support it. I bought the identical overcoat to you, sir,' he admitted, suddenly shy again.

269

Shackleton warmed to the fellow. He hadn't meant to slight him.

'It's wool you need,' Wilson said sagely. 'Layers upon layers of wool, never mind a gabardine.'

'Finnesko. Fur mittens.' Shackleton held up his hands.

'And boots, maybe? Finnesko boots?' Bowers chimed in. Shackleton didn't demur. It was Scott's job to make sure his men had the right kit. 'The skipper's all set,' Bowers continued cheerfully.

Shackleton shifted in his armchair and the leather creaked. He caught Wilson's eye only momentarily. Questions about Scott's leadership trailed a shaky undercurrent to polar discussions by the experts, the backers and the general public, never mind those among his personal acquaintance. At heart, Wilson knew that though the skipper was brave, different decisions might have produced different results. Certainly some of the *Discovery*'s scientific findings had not proved watertight. Scott had vigorously defended his methods and his stories of derring-do had charmed the nation. Boys' magazines venerated him. Ladies wrote admiring letters. His wife called him a British hero, publicly. But the unanswered questions and doubts formed a gnarling nugget of discomfort that left the way open. Shackleton had stepped eagerly into this gap once and he hoped to do so again.

Shackleton let the taste of malt pervade his mouth. He'd been drinking too much since he quit the *Nimrod*. For a few uneasy months now, both of Great Britain's most famous polar explorers had been in London at the same time.

270

There had been no love lost. The Establishment's approval had fallen neither on one side nor the other. The Navy and the Royal Society were even-handed in their accolades. Scott had been promoted and Shackleton was elevated to the peerage. Neither man had yet congratulated the other.

Scott would never forgive Shackleton his landing on McMurdo Sound. When he got command of the *Nimrod*, Shackleton promised to stay away from the sound, which Scott claimed was his territory. But as he sailed in he realized it wasn't possible to make land anywhere else. Scott could hardly have expected him to turn tail, but he still hadn't forgiven Shackleton. This was only the latest irritant in the open sore of their relationship and while neither had outright bad mouthed the other, they poached each other's men. They tried to catch the march on each other's innovations. They bristled when the other's name was spoken. Shackleton had designed a tent ideal for polar conditions. Scott refused to use it. They were an odd pair – walking in each other's footsteps, taking it in turn to lead.

Karina shifted. She laid an icy finger on Shackleton's shoulder as she realized that last month he had travelled to Scotland to meet Sir Joseph Hooker. Two knights of the realm together. *Ah, so that is what brought me here.* The old man was ancient now – his skin was like paper, his eyesight was failing. In his study, the air smelled of talcum. Shackleton was guided to a chair by a butler. Hooker peered at him with rheumy yellow eyes that were unable to distinguish anything more than light and shade. He reached out and laid his thick fingers on Shackleton's hand.

'Tell me about your adventure,' he said. 'It has been a long time since I saw you.'

Shackleton wasn't sure how to reply. He'd never met Hooker. The old man thought he was Scott. He'd be angry if it wasn't so tragic. He realized that he hoped, most fervently, that he never got to be Britain's oldest explorer. Better the ice should take him.

In the stillness of the old man's study, it was clear that Hooker's memories had faded and his passion for the Ross expedition was no longer fired by any kind of spark. Many of the names on the Antarctic map these days commemorated men with whom Hooker was not acquainted.

'I cannot settle,' Shackleton admitted as if it was a holy confession. 'Once you've been down on the pack . . .'

'Marry.' Hooker grasped his arm. 'You must marry a good woman. A family life is the thing. The right woman will be your greatest conquest, you'll see.'

Karina reeled as she stared at him.

'Emily,' Shackleton said.

'Well, there you are.'

After the meeting, in the first-class waiting room at Glasgow's Central Station, Shackleton waited for the London train. He'd hoped to find a kindred spirit in Hooker – a veteran of the ice. He'd hoped to find someone to whom he could admit that he had felt as if something was with him that first time out and that it had never entirely gone away. A whispering spirit or a

272

deity perhaps. Either way, he'd swear on his mother's grave that someone had been walking alongside him. One minute it was a cloud, then a gust of wind and sometimes a thin ray of sunshine, but it had been there. It had stayed with him, troubling and comforting at once. Shackleton tried to dismiss it. He thought of this sixth sense as his Irish side, but when it came to it, he knew that in this matter, and perhaps this matter alone, his instincts made more sense than his rational mind.

'Are you married?' Shackleton asked Bowers.

'No,' the boy said. He was young – still in his twenties – and, Shackleton noticed, his shoes were worn. Not all the Royal Indian Marine's sons were monied. This one, however, must be talented, at least, and Scott must trust him if he was in charge of loading supplies.

'Where have you served?'

'Ceylon,' Bowers smiled. 'America, Australia, Burma – you know.'

'Those are different waters to where you're going. Positively tropical.'

'I'm from Scotland. Greenock.'

'Still.'

'A chap can only fling himself into an expedition. I've always wanted to see the south. I've thought of it since I was a child.'

'After glory?'

Bowers shook his head. 'Was it glory for you?' he asked.

Shackleton laughed. He no longer believed in heroes. It was the challenge that counted. Proving your mettle.

'There is no glory in it, Bowers. That's the truth,' he said. 'The Antarctic is a hard place and mesmerizing. She'll take your love, your life and your devotion and she'll give nothing back. An attempt on the pole is only unfinished business. That's all it can ever be. Afterwards, when they offer you glory, it doesn't mean anything any more. You can't help yourself. You just want to get back on the ice.'

Wilson was disquieted by such talk.

'Well, it's for the good of Britain. It wouldn't be our glory in any case – it'd belong to his Majesty – to the nation.'

'Strange how countries are female,' Shackleton pondered. 'Both Britain and the South Pole.'

'They just are feminine, don't you think?' Wilson said.

At the next table, a man peered carefully around the corner of his newspaper. It was the most extraordinary conversation. Generally in the members' lounge if you were going to discuss anything it was the cricket.

'It is women who inspire us, though,' Bowers said. 'That's why England is always referred to as *she*.'

Karina laughed. He was a romantic. Women indeed. She saw him with his mother, earlier and his sister too. He had scrimped on his equipment as they had trailed from shop to shop picking up the last things he needed on his ever-decreasing budget. Bowers dreamed of softness. Girls blonde as angels, like she used to be. Frills. Flounces. Accomplishments.

'Well, the Antarctic is definitely not a lady.'

Shackleton's laugh sounded like a bark. 'She's a cold and knowing widow, if anything. An ice maiden. A callous whore.'

'Oh, for heaven's sake. You'll scare the boy with this nonsense,' Wilson objected.

Bowers leaped to his own defence. 'I've wanted to see it since I was a nipper. Whether I'm on the final expedition or not. I want to see it. Her, I mean.'

'And not make the pole? Surely, the pole's the thing. You're chipper, Bowers. That's good. Just make sure you don't die trying whatever Scott sets you to.' Shackleton couldn't help himself. 'Sometimes the skipper makes poor decisions. You're trusting the old man with your life.'

'That's enough!' Wilson raised his voice. 'Your life was never in danger because of Captain Scott, Shackle. You take that back.'

Shackleton waited for a moment. The whisky had gone to his head and the discomfort on the air sobered him.

'Probably not,' he admitted. 'But it could have been. I maintain we might have made it if—'

Wilson put up his hand. 'That's quite enough.'

Bowers shifted. He thought both Scott and Shackleton were marvellous. With so much in common, what could they have to argue about?

Wilson looked relieved when the porter whispered discreetly in Shackleton's ear. Emily was waiting for him in the hallway. He got to his feet with gruff good humour and pulled himself away. Emily made Shackleton happy, but the Antarctic was a formidable mistress.

'I wish both of you the best of luck – Wilson.

Bowers. And my best to Oriana, Wilson,' he half bowed.

Wilson and Bowers remained silent as Shackleton strode away.

'I'm glad to have met him,' Bowers said, his voice low.

As Shackleton turned his wife towards the dining room, he wished fervently that his marriage was his greatest conquest. It would be far simpler.

Karina was surprised at herself. Her mind's eye was not drawn back to Hooker's study. Still, the image of him stayed with her. At least Hooker knew he was alone, she thought. The very old always do. He was separate somehow from his chair and books and papers. From the family photographs and his attentive butler. He was, she realized, ready to die. And yet, she didn't stay there. She couldn't. Her gaze lingered on Wilson and she caught up with him, not that night but some days later.

The doctor had one last mission before the ship left London. He had said his farewells, he had left money in the bank for his wife to draw on, he had prayed privately in the sailor's church in Greenwich – a personal totem for luck – and lastly, he had held Oriana as she wept, which she did every time he departed. Now he made for the west of the city – to Notting Hill Gate where George Vince's widow had settled – as far away from London's ports and their population of sailors as possible.

Scott had written to Mrs Vince upon the occasion of her husband's death, as he had intended.

But it was Wilson who sought her out when he got home. Writing was one thing, he felt, but having the courtesy to look the woman in the eye was quite another. It was a shabby brick-built terrace like thousands of others in the capital. Children played in the dirt on the road. He bided his time on the doorstep of the boarding house Mrs Vince ran, until a shabby-looking serving girl answered the bell and saw him into an unexpectedly bright front room while she went to fetch her mistress.

Mary Vince entered, rolling down her sleeves. She must have been engaged in some kind of household activity.

'Oh, sir,' she said, shocked to see him. 'It's you, Doctor Wilson. The girl said you was a gentleman looking for lodging. Whatever can I do for you?'

Wilson smiled. 'I am returning to the south, Mrs Vince, and I wondered if I might do you the service of taking anything with me. Anything you might like to leave at your husband's memorial?'

Mary hopped onto a comfortable chair by the fireplace. She was a sprightly woman almost thirty years of age now.

'I can get the girl to light the fire, sir, if you would like? It's cold for June,' she offered.

Wilson shook his head.

'The thing is,' Mary Vince continued, 'I got married again. It does no good for a person to be on their own, does it, sir?'

'I am certain George would be glad to know you are settled.' Wilson said.

Mary Vince looked only a little dubious, for she married a man with whom George was acquainted.

277

They once brawled in a bar not half a mile from where she was now sitting and they never made it up before George left.

'Will you sail soon, sir?' she changed the subject.

'Almost at once. Well.' Wilson did not want to linger where surely he was unwelcome. 'I must be getting along.'

Mary Vince jumped to her feet. 'It's kind of you not to forget me. George would have appreciated that.'

Wilson was not sure how to reply. Now and then when a man died in the business of polar exploration, it was generally unavoidable. The Antarctic weather was a trap set to freeze a fellow's blood in his veins. A wave might sweep a sailor overboard into icy waters from which his body would never be recovered. Anything might happen. But George Vince's death was entirely avoidable. Barne should have camped. Mrs Vince was too kind or perhaps the poor woman simply did not realize.

'All good wishes, madam, on your marriage. My congratulations to the lucky man,' Wilson said as he turned to go.

Walking uphill towards the more salubrious area of Holland Park the doctor marvelled at how quickly the world recovered from the death of its heroes. He wondered how quickly it might do so should he succumb to the grim Antarctic weather. The night before Oriana had clung to him but a year or two from now if he fell victim to the pole, might she simply find someone else? *Love is the only thing we have in the end. That and a few scraps of sensation.* The thought surprised him. Wilson was not given to dramatic statements or sentimentality. The idea came out of nowhere, a gift from the heavens, and he decided not to ponder it – the implications were simply too awful, for if love was all he had, then what was he doing boarding the *Terra Nova* and setting out on this difficult mission? He turned into Holland Park Avenue and comforted himself that Mary Vince, after all, was quite a different kind of woman from his wife.

And far off, Karina felt a sting of jealousy that Mrs Vince had taken her husband's death so lightly. That she had loved again. That she had not been abandoned. She turned back towards the pole and she waited. For, it seemed Scott was set to return.

Twenty-One

In no time at all, she could feel him. The cluster of dark wooden huts waited, ready. There was still a crate of whisky in the store, left behind in the rush to leave last time. Out on the ice both Scott and Shackleton had peppered the landscape with provisions they had buried and marked with flags to supply their expeditions. The winter had swallowed the tins and boxes whole, smoothing them over with snow till they were only bumps on the horizon and the flags had disappeared, cut to pieces by the wind.

She curled on the craggy edge of the ice and relished the silence. A shoal of seals stared back at her and then dived casually under the waves. The whales beyond them sang the whole dark winter long. A mother would dote on her calf, even a fully grown one. It was quiet now and the snow sparkled in the low sunlight. It seemed impossible there had ever been a blizzard or a storm. That the weather had ever been any way other than this, here and now. Blue sky. Calm water. *They think they can tame it.*

She thought of the women who had been left behind. Scott's wife, who, she realized, had travelled with him as far as New Zealand, ambitious for her own part in his glory as the muse of a national hero. Oriana Wilson, the doctor's true love. Mary Vince. While their husbands embarked on extraordinary adventures, their lives were day-to-day but also somehow fruitful. Frances Hooker had bequeathed the world her garden, her children and her home. Hooker must have loved her. He must have. *What did I leave behind?*

Karina cast her eyes towards her grave. Her ice mummy stared back, eyes shrunken. *That is my legacy and nothing else*, she thought, and came back to Hooker's blank-eyed stare as he gazed uncomprehending at her spirit through the window. The men would become famous for their sojourn in the south, but nobody would even know she had been here – the first woman to step foot on the ice pack.

Still, she was drawn to them. She tried to sleep but the darkness had not taken her.

Aboard the *Terra Nova*, now, it was late. In the small hours, the mess table was littered with glasses, the empty bottles moved with the ship. The officers had settled. Wilson had retired to his cabin, but a few of the others still sat around the table. Bowers was there and another man called Evans, which was causing problems because what was one to do with two Evanses. And then there were Oates and Cherry – two new recruits, plucked from the eight thousand hopefuls. They pored over the photographs that had been taken by Skelton on Scott's last expedition. Some pictures seemed to be missing – days unrecorded – but they were too drunk to discuss why. Skelton, for his part, had been quizzed by everyone from the Navy to the Royal Society to Scott himself but he would only say that there was a problem with the developing process in the cold.

281

The officers were excited about arriving – the Far South was within reach. They had put out from Christchurch after a final night during which many of them had stayed at Warner's Hotel – a last night of clean, thick sheets, running water and deep, safe sleep.

'This is what it's about,' Evans said pointing at a picture of Winter Quarters Bay, 'this great white nothing.'

'What's it really like?' Bowers sounded wistful.

Evans, the only man among those assembled who had been there, searched for the words.

'I'd hate to know I'd never see it again,' he said. 'It changes your life.'

They knew that already. The difference between the men who had been tested and those who hadn't was obvious. Karina put her head to one side as, Cherry, a good-looking young officer, searched for a bottle that still contained some spirit. He poured four glasses.

'To the south,' he toasted and they all drank.

'And now I suppose we better sleep it off,' Cherry smiled with good nature.

There was a general murmur of agreement.

'It's after two,' Bowers checked his watch.

Then, all of a sudden, there was a loud bang from beyond the mess. It sounded like a door being slammed. Bowers stumbled off to investigate while Evans fumbled, trying to do up the buttons of his jacket – no mean feat after the better part of a bottle. Then Scott's door swung open. There was another crash from inside the captain's cabin. Bowers poked his head through.

'Sir?'

Scott's eyes were alight. 'Bloody lies!' he said, brandishing a piece of paper.

Bowers stood up straight, or tried to. He focused and realized that the piece of paper was a telegram. 'Sir?' he repeated.

'Bloody Amundsen,' Scott hissed. 'Arctic expedition my foot. He's coming for us, Bowers. Sneaky bloody Norwegian.'

Bowers glanced back at the others in the mess. The captain followed the lieutenant's eyes and realized that some of his officers were awake. He pushed past. The skipper offered no explanation, instead striding into the disarray of a night of heavy drinking. The fellows jumped to their feet.

'Gentlemen,' Scott nodded, ignoring the detritus, 'the Norwegians have thrown down the gauntlet.'

Oates stifled a hiccough. The rest merely looked troubled.

'Sir?' Oates enquired.

Scott rustled the telegram.

'Roald Amundsen left Oslo weeks ago. He declared his expedition was for the Arctic but he's a damned liar. He's heading south in direct competition with us. He's got dogs and he's aiming to reach the pole before we do.'

The officers became suddenly startlingly sober.

'*Beg to inform you,* Fram *proceeding Antarctic,*' Scott read from the cable. 'Bastard.'

The men didn't know how to express their shock.

'Well,' Evans rallied, 'we'll give him a run for his money. Bloody cheek!'

Scott's eyes narrowed but Cherry picked up the baton.

283

'Let him try!' he said. 'Just let him try.'

'Interloper!' Oates wholeheartedly banged the table. 'How dare he?'

'Well, he can't get there more quickly than we can,' Bowers pointed out, ever the tactician. 'We have the lead. He'll need to lay supply depots just the same as we do. There's no short cut. We'll have our base at Ross Island, he'll have to establish his own.'

'He'll choose the Bay of Whales.' Scott crumpled the telegram in his hand. He did so loosely because he wanted to keep it. First Shackleton had wanted to take over his camp. Now Amundsen was trying to cut in on his shot at glory.

'We must get there at the double,' he pronounced.

'Yes, sir.' The men stood to attention.

'Well, then, let's get on with it!'

Karina watched. They were heading into a storm though they didn't know it. The wind whipped ahead of them. The forecast from Christchurch had not predicted the weather accurately. It was worse than was usual at this time of year. Behind her, she looked towards their destination. The pole. It had never interested her but now it seemed some kind of drama would play out there with the Norwegian and Scott converging at the same time. She thought for a moment and then turned away from the ship, catching an air current to the south and riding it.

She had never tried to fly that way before. Somehow, it hadn't occurred to her. Behind her figure, there was a school of whales on the horizon. They fell out of sight as she crossed the ice mountain. All the tracks the men left had disappeared, buried long ago. The snow was blinding in the sunlight. And then she realized she was over virgin territory and at once she found herself engulfed in blackness.

When she opened her eyes again she was returned to the shore, to the place her body was buried. It was as if the world had slapped her in the face. *My grave is the centre of everything*, she thought. She got up and rose on the air again, this time more slowly, heading south again. As her eyes began to dim, she stopped, drawing back before the endless white turned instantly to pitch. She hovered there on the edge of her world and felt a kind of fury. If Scott made it to the pole she'd never see him. There were edges to her world. Not only to the north, but southwards. The pole had not tempted her till now. The men and their ambitions had uncovered a new kind of curse. To be able to see it, but not go herself. She'd go no further than Shackleton – not by her own volition anyway. The world might take her other places but she had no control over that.

Far across the sea, the *Fram* headed south long behind the *Terra Nova*, which now was engulfed in the storm. Karina watched from a distance. Scott's ship was taking on water. The wind howled so loudly that the men could neither hear the shouted orders or their prayers. The crew dealt with the crisis calmly. Below, Bowers dived through the incoming water to locate a pump which had ceased to function. His sodden clothes were covered in thick smears of sticky filth so he looked as if he had been rescued from a mining disaster. As he came up, his teeth chattered so hard, Karina wondered if they would chip. Two men rubbed him down and gave him a tin cup of hot tea but the trauma of the icy water was too much and his body rebelled. He vomited the liquid as soon as he drank it.

'The crew are taking it in shifts to save the ship,' Scott wrote in his log book. Karina settled to watch, distracted from her anger at the boundaries of her world. Bowers turned and dived back under the water. His skin screamed with the cold. He could hardly think. An engineer was hammering on the other side of a metal wall and Bowers helped him to clear sludge from the pump. It had been at least an hour or two, she realized. A long time for the living.

Elsewhere on the ship the dogs were howling uselessly into the screaming wind. They were cut off from all hope of rescue by the rising water. On deck, Cherry, Oates and Wilson directed a party of men to throw items overboard to lighten the load – Bowers' carefully packed supplies were tossed away. *If the ship goes down they will all die*, she thought in a rush and realized she would feel let down. After all, then they would never make the pole. But no. Below, as the pump burst into life the small crowd that had gathered cheered. Slowly they waited, expectant as the water began to go down. Bowers' knees were weak but he felt elated – the hero of the hour or one of them.

'Birdie, good on you.' A man slapped him on the back as it became clear that his efforts had paid off. *These naval men and their nicknames.*

Karina regarded Bowers and his beak of a nose. He had been bullied all his life on account of it. This was a fond sort of nickname – better than what had gone before. Scott sent the sodden men to change and rest and she followed them.

She toured the cabins of the *Terra Nova*. In Bowers' naval trunk, marked with his initials, was an embroidered pennant for his sled. His sisters had made it. She remembered Marijke sewing by the fire at home, stitching little flowers into their winter scarves and hats. Carefully placing small blue crosses around the edge of their mother's apron. It was a way of saying that she cared. Later she would be paid by strangers for these efforts – it was her embroidery that had made her famous – among the women of Copenhagen and Amsterdam at least. Tucked beneath the pennant, Bowers had started to write a letter to a girl in Australia – a blonde, pink, warm creature. She was the way he imagined a woman should be. Soft. Gentle. *In death we give no such impression*, Karina thought. She had been soft once, or softer.

Then, as the ship steamed towards her, she turned back to the mountain and lay down under the ice. She'd wake, she supposed, when they got there.

Twenty-Two

She was roused suddenly as if from a nightmare some time later. She seemed to be cutting in and out as if the earth was claiming her – taking her away. The sky was dark as pitch and she was on the ice in another storm. Beyond her, on the mountain, she swung round to see three men sitting in the snow, singing hymns in English. She peered at Wilson, Bowers and Cherry. 'Onward Christian Soldiers.' How had they got there? Their equipment was stacked around them and they were singing into the wind. She mined their minds to find out what had happened and all she came up with was: penguins.

Wilson had been sketching penguin skeletons and examining penguin beaks. They were an ancient species and he wondered if they were some kind of living link to a time when reptiles and birds were more closely related. This seemed a strange, academic concern compared to the madness of the men out here on the hill, in the worst kind of weather, but Karina pursued it. The doctor, she saw, had formed a plan. The emperors nested over the winter. Having laid at the end of the summer, the females abandoned their eggs and it was their mates who congregated to endure the sub-zero winter with their unhatched young slipped under their skirts. Hundreds gathered at Cape Crozier, more than thirty-five miles away from Scott's base. And that is why they had come, these three men, in the dark, to collect penguin eggs. How the birds survived temperatures of minus seventy for months on end was a mystery, she thought, but Wilson, Bowers and Cherry certainly could not pump blood in this temperature without the cold freezing them to death.

Wilson felt guilty, she saw. He considered it his fault they had ended here. He had encouraged the others. When the doctor first mooted the idea of the expedition, privately, in the captain's cabin, Scott had stayed uncharacteristically silent. It was early June – the middle of the worst weather. The idea of a round journey of over seventy miles to Cape Crozier and back in the grip of the cold was too crazy even for the skipper. Conditions were devastating. For a start, the darkness was unrelenting and the men would have to navigate by the stars. Wilson's eyes fell to his leather boots. He examined the laces.

'The penguins are ancient, Skipper,' he said. 'There will be interest from the Royal Society and if we take back an egg, it'll go on display at the Natural History Museum. Who knows what we might learn?'

Scott had a vision of the pale stone museum building next to the Victoria and Albert Museum. In his mind's eye it was spring and doily-thin apple-green leaves were fluttering in the breeze. A crowd formed at the entrance. It was comprised of women in smartly buttoned boots and men with ebony walking sticks. Every one of them had come to see the egg the *Terra Nova* had brought home. The skipper allowed himself a smile. He'd like to have material from his expeditions in all of London's museums, nonetheless he was taken back by Wilson's pluck. Even if he was lucky, the going would be hard as granite.

'It's practically a suicide mission, Teddy,' he said.

'It's the only way to get hold of an egg. A live one. It could advance our understanding exponentially.'

Scott ran a hand over his hair. 'Who would you want to take?'

'Well, they'd need to volunteer.'

The captain considered this. 'But who would you want?'

Wilson hesitated. 'Bowers and Cherry.'

Karina watched from above and felt a frisson of excitement. Over her shoulder, she felt the ice stiffen as if in anticipation. Scott had known it was a suicide mission. He'd said so.

'And you think it's possible to survive? In your medical opinion?'

Wilson grinned. 'Well, I hope so,' he replied.

'How long do you expect it will take?' Scott cast a glance at the chart on his desk.

Wilson's eyes were steady. He had planned everything in its entirety and he knew the answer to any question that Scott might ask, but he did not want to appear presumptuous. He paused as if considering the matter.

'We'd probably want to man-haul the sledges. At a guess it'd take a month. In the dark and the cold I can't see that we'll manage it more quickly. If we make it we'll be back long before you're ready to attempt the pole. Before the light comes, if that's your concern. But the exact timing depends on the weather. There are bound to be blizzards and it's impossible to guess how long they'll last.'

Scott wondered which would be worse – the darkness or the cold. The former would mean the men would have to travel in close proximity, reliant on shouting over the weather to pin down their location, otherwise they'd risk losing each other. That's why Wilson didn't want the party to consist of more than three. The darkness was bad enough, but, on top of that, the cold would be painful. Their lips would turn to aching iron knives and their ears would howl. The ice would sculpt itself over their bodies. No one had ever survived a week, never mind a month out on the ice in the dead of winter. It was almost July and the going beyond the *Terra Nova*, on the hospitable part of the plain, was like a sheet of corrugated iron.

'You better ask them privately,' he said. 'You need to be sure it's not only a matter of bravado.'

She followed Wilson. She trailed him down the dark wooden corridor, not an all-seeing spirit from above but right behind him. Birdie and Cherry were playing chess at the mess table and Cherry had the advantage. He was the expedition's assistant zoologist but the truth was he had the kind of mind that could turn itself to anything. Poetry. Politics. Dissection. Or in the case of the chequered board laid out before him, a winning strategy steeped in cold, hard logic. She scoped him and saw that Cherry was the man who had everything. He had inherited a country estate and the means with which to run it. He was good-looking and well educated. At first he was teased mercilessly about all three of these things. He had donated £1,000 from his own pocket towards the expedition's costs and despite his good manners and his willingness to do more than his share, the fellows couldn't quite shake off the idea that the money was why Scott chose him to join the *Terra Nova*. It was not. Cherry had made it clear that the £1,000 came without strings.

'I'm thinking of an outing,' Wilson started.

Birdie looked up as Cherry slid a bishop across the board.

'I'd like to get my hands on an egg or two,' the doctor said casually.

Birdie grinned. 'An omelette, is it, Teddy?'

'Emperor eggs. Penguins. They are nesting, you see. No one's ever got one before.'

The words captured Cherry's attention.

'The birds don't really build a nest, as such,' Wilson continued. 'But they are at Cape Crozier, roosting.'

'Sounds like a frolic,' Birdie said.

Cherry laughed. 'You mean now? In this?'

'It's a scientific mission. To have a penguin embryo, to examine one, I mean. It can only be done at this time of year. I'm not going to lie to you, the conditions will be rough. I came to you two first.'

Birdie's gaze did not waver. Cherry's shoulders rose only slightly. They both knew what they are getting into. It was forty degrees below and some days it had been colder. Cherry got to his feet and offered Wilson his hand.

'Thank you,' he said.

The last night at base camp, Birdie couldn't sleep. He left his bunk and sat at the table by the stove in his woollen dressing gown. The hut was lit by single lamp, hanging on a hook beside him. The air smelled faintly of pipe smoke and toast. Karina watched, settled in the warmth like a silver-white husky, waiting. The others were asleep. Slowly Birdie drew his half-written letter from his pocket and laid it on the embers where it curled and blackened. If he did not return, there was no point in upsetting Gladys Brearley, the soft, blonde woman to whom he had been composing his first and only love letter.

He told himself that burning his words was a kindness. He couldn't marry. He had his mother and sisters to support and money was tight. And besides, if things went wrong, he didn't want anyone else to know what he'd said. He leaned forward and clasped his hands over his knees as he watched the words disappear into ash. *Passion is all that matters. It is everything*, she cooed. *In eternity, the pain will go and all that is left is love.* Birdie shifted, looking straight at her. He sniffed. She could swear he could make her out, a pale wraith of a dead woman enrobed in the scent of summer berries. His gaze did not waver. She blew out the lamp and even in the pitch black she could feel him smile. Birdie Bowers was a brave man. He made a dent in the deepest darkness.

'Bless you,' he whispered, as if she had sneezed. *But this is gone. This is over,* she told herself. They ended up on the ice, singing. Insane. Exposed. She wondered if now she could walk through time as well as space. And if so, could she change what was going to happen? Could she save them? It would be restitution for killing Vince. More than that.

When Birdie got up he did not relight the lamp. He made his way back to his bunk in absolute darkness because he knew he'd have to get used to it. As he brushed past Cherry's bunk, Cherry turned over. He was dreaming of an arm around his shoulder. He couldn't say whose arm, but it was comforting. All Cherry's dreams amounted to him feeling safe. All his nightmares amounted to him letting down the others. Oblivious to the matter of which side of Cherry's dream the coin had fallen that night, Birdie climbed into his bunk. Karina settled under the table and listened as he arranged his fur-lined sleeping bag. They were a curiosity – the men Scott had brought with him this time. There was something compelling about them. Outside, the temperature rose only slightly as if to encourage these would-be heroes of the Natural History Museum. By the time they woke it was not even thirty below on the plain.

The going was harder than they expected. Of course it was – the vengeance of the continent would be felt. *Don't they know?* Karina followed them onto the ice and tried to mark the time by Birdie, who prayed every morning but what was to say he wasn't praying every night as well? Their sledges were piled high with supplies and tents. They were tough and determined. But something had gone wrong.

* * *

294

As the party approached Cape Crozier the ice ridges deepened and there ceased to be either a day or a night. The men kept walking and she could no longer account for the passage of time. On how many occasions could Wilson promise himself dinner with Oriana at Rules restaurant? How often could Cherry berate himself for almost falling asleep on his aching feet? The men were awake but this felt like a nightmare and yet she could not leave them.

The penguins roosted in the lee of a steep wall of ice that protected them on one side from the weather. Birdie climbed it, digging in his pickaxe and hauling himself over the top like a madman. Wilson and Cherry were not far behind. None of the birds appeared to notice these intruders in the darkness. In the cold, it was impossible to smell the fetid crush of the fishy-fleshed rookery but just the same, the birds could not scent the men either.

As Birdie dropped onto the ice he was not much taller than the Emperors around him. The crowd shuffled to accommodate its new member and at Birdie's feet an egg was exposed. He snatched it and handed it up to Wilson. The bereaved penguin raised his beak high and opened his mouth to make a throaty, anguished call. The group shuffled in response and again an egg popped out within reach. This time, though the bird fought back as Birdie tried to grab it. Cherry pulled a gloved hand from his finnesko mitt and pulled Birdie and the pilfered egg out of harm's way.

'You all right?'

Birdie nodded. In warmer weather – a balmy minus ten perhaps – the knife-sharp beak might have ripped the material of his gabardine but frozen not only stiff but solid to a depth of two inches, the bird was more likely to chip his beak than breach Birdie's outer layer. On the safe side of the ice wall Wilson carefully stowed the eggs inside Cherry's jacket, close to his skin.

'My turn,' he said for two eggs were not enough – they must have more.

The surgeon hauled himself over and as he did so the penguins began to rally. A fight broke out as one bird tried to replace his lost egg with the egg of one of the others. Wilson wondered if he ought to wait for the rookery to settle but having hiked for God knows how many days through the worst conditions any of them had known, nothing was going to stop him. He snatched another egg and with astonishing fluidity scaled the wall holding it in the crook of his arm. For safekeeping, he handed it to Cherry, who this time had not removed his hands from the fur mitts. He fumbled, the egg fell to the ice-hard ground and smashed. The embryo steamed for a moment and then froze.

'I'm sorry,' Cherry said. 'I'm sorry,' he repeated.

Wilson couldn't find any words of comfort. He struggled not to shout. The men huddled together a moment. From above it made a strange sight – the blackness of the birds on one side of the wall and the lightness of the men on the other, both behaving the same with eggs stowed next to their skin to keep the nascent

296

chicks alive. Wilson made Cherry hand over the eggs inside his jacket top and secreted them in his own – they had to be kept safe until they returned to the camp and they could be preserved.

'I'll go over again,' Birdie offered. He climbed up and in only a few minutes more they had three eggs and after one more foray, four.

The men were so elated at their success that they covered the ground more easily on the journey back to the camp they had set up. But after only an hour, Cherry tipped over, tripping on a deep indent. He fell on top of one of the eggs and as it smashed he squirmed at the idea. There was a dead penguin chick too close to his skin, warm and wet. This time when he realized what had happened, Wilson could not contain himself. There was no excuse. They were all exhausted. They were all cold.

'Cherry!' he shouted. 'Jesus!'

Neither of his companions had ever heard Wilson swear. Cherry felt tears welling. He couldn't even say sorry this time. He reached inside his clothing and pulled out pieces of shell and the gooey mess that it once contained. This was his nightmare. He had let the expedition down. The pieces of shell fell with a click onto the rock-hard snow. He pulled out the surviving egg in his care and Wilson took it from him.

'Three is enough, isn't it?' Birdie stepped in, optimistic as ever.

Wilson was hard-eyed but he wasn't going to make them go back. He stepped out in the direction of the camp. Three eggs were enough if it came to it but there was no further leeway.

'Be careful,' he said to Birdie.

And at that, the men pulled together and walked through the relentless darkness, heading northwards – towards the base they'd built. Towards home. This expedition, Karina realized, was an act of bravery – a dedication to their messy, foolish lives.

When she blinked, she appeared again in a makeshift hut. Wilson, Bowers and Cherry were crowded together. Birdie heated a pan of hoosh as Wilson preserved the eggs in alcohol, the three prizes bobbing about in long glass jars. When he had finished, the men ate and settled down to sleep, Wilson allowed himself to feel a sense of achievement.

Three eggs, he thought contentedly. *Three of them.*

Karina shuddered. The minute a fellow relaxed like that the weather would strike. *Don't they know? Don't they know?* Sure enough, a storm was not long coming. It whipped down the slopes of the mountain, the bastard offspring of a blizzard and a gale. The temperature plummeted. From forty below it went to fifty and then sixty under. It whistled as if it was taunting them. Wilson turned in his sleep and then there was the sound of a whip-cracking as the canvas roof of the hut blew off. Karina watched the material fly high into the darkness. Seconds later, Wilson woke to snow flurrying around his face. The wind had scooped up an earlier fall and scattered it over them. He sat up.

Cherry, beside him did the same and nudged Birdie. Bowers moved quickly, jumping out of his sleeping bag and reaching to feel around like a blind man, he quickly ascertained that the roof was not torn or damaged, but was simply gone. In its absence, the wind played eerie music around the walls. It was a strange kind of symphony and that alone made Karina shiver, for in all the years she had never heard a sound like it. It was too high a tone for the mountain to make, too thin for the wind.

'We'll never find it in this,' Birdie shouted peering into the gloom after the disappeared canvas.

He was right, she realized. Even if an unexpected dawn broke over them and the sky became light, the thick snow would mask any hope of recovering the missing six-feet strip. They'd be lucky to see that far in front of themselves. The others got out of their bags and scrambled to pick up the little stove and their scattering of possessions – cups and plates. Then they pushed out of the hut and stowed themselves in the tent beside it, uncomfortably perched on their unloaded supplies – the crates and jars they had carefully piled up inside and to which they had added the precious penguin eggs only a few hours before.

'Blizzard,' Wilson said.

She tried to call off the weather but the storm was too frantic. She could manage a nudge here and a flutter there but a storm of this magnitude was beyond her. The most she could do was to ride the weather, not change it. The wind started

299

with an adagio scoop of snow but soon it whipped the drifts into a shower of frantic all-encompassing staccato, each frozen flake like a chip of arrow sharp-flint. The wind pulled at the ropes and pegs secured in the ice and quickly it won. When they made camp the men were dog tired and now they would pay a deadly price for that. Within minutes, there was a sharp crack as the tent strained as if it was trying to cling on, but it was no use and the storm claimed it. The pegs gave way and the second canvas whipped into the darkness.

Cherry jumped up as if he might catch the retreating material but the wind was too quick and their only remaining shelter disappeared into the white and black night.

'Oh,' said Wilson, and fell heavily into a seated position.

The others couldn't hear him over the wind – this little sound of realization and defeat. They couldn't see his heart sink in his chest. Each man thought, *We will die out here without shelter.* And strangely, they made peace with that. *This*, she thought, *is even more desperate than I was on Deception Island. At least I had some kind of hope.* Without the tent it was not only that they would have no shelter. If this weather continued, they wouldn't be able to light the stove. They wouldn't be able to eat or drink. The men knew it but they didn't say so.

Cherry and Birdie sat in the snow next to the surgeon and pulled their frozen sleeping bags around them as the weather continued. It took a minute or two until Birdie spoke.

300

'We can't lie here just waiting,' he said.

He cleared his throat and began to sing 'Abide With Me'. It was his mother's favourite hymn. Wilson and Cherry joined him. At first she could barely hear them against the dark music of the storm. They sang for an hour or maybe it was two. Or more. 'Nearer My God to Thee'. 'When I Survey the Wondrous Cross'. Singing there on the mountain, in the face of death. Karina couldn't take her eyes off them. So this was what she had seen – a trip through time she had not fully understood. A horror story.

As the weather got colder they gamely dredged up more hymns from their repertoire and something at the heart of her melted. At first, she restrained herself – trying to shelter them would only prolong their flesh freezing. But in the end she couldn't help it. She lay over the three men like a blanket and shielded them as the wind cut a chill path across her back. It wasn't much but it was the most she could do. A degree or two warmer. A degree or two more hope. She wondered, would she do this for Hooker? Would she do it for Scott? No matter. There was something extraordinary about Wilson, Cherry and Bowers. They deserved to be saved.

Wilson almost fell asleep. He'd have sworn he felt warm and that angels were lulling him into some kind of heavenly slumber but Birdie snatched him back, hauling him unwillingly back into the cold. 'Praise my Soul, the King of Heaven,' he sang, right into Wilson's ear. It was one of his favourites. Wilson imagined himself in his usual pew, the stained-glass window of an angel to his right, throwing its warm light over his morning coat and Oriana, sitting beside him.

'I'm not ready for heaven yet,' he mumbled.

Heaven? Karina thought. *What on earth does he mean?* And quietly she began to sing with them.

After the storm, the men stood up. It would take days to get back to Scott's base. In England you'd walk it in a day or two and sleep in the open, but not here. Not in this. So with a long march before them and weak and frozen through as they were, they knew they would never survive for days on end without shelter. The cold would take them. It was inevitable. Karina felt their hearts drop, but again, they didn't say anything until Birdie piped up.

'It must have blown to the east,' he started and then paused, staring forlornly across the landscape, which was barely visible in the darkness, now the snow had stopped. He had not given up, exactly, but he knew the odds were long. If they were going to die they'd have to make the best of it, he thought. *If.*

Karina was not ready to let them.

'We should fan out,' said Wilson, as she whipped around Birdie's frame and led him as surely as if he was a puppy on a lead. Cherry and Wilson made a show of collecting the supplies as Karina's spectre pulled Bowers in the right direction. The frozen canvas had landed on the ice, some way off. She guided him, stumbling towards it. When he realized what it was, Birdie cast his eyes heavenwards and whispered, 'Thank you,' and it took her a moment to realize that he thought some deity had shown him the way. There at Cape Crozier, she stared, finding it difficult to accept that the men couldn't see her. She wanted them to. Death made her aware of the fault lines at the edges and they had slipped so close that she wondered that if she reached out, perhaps she could touch them, or speak to them, or even be seen. It amazed her that after all this time she wanted to.

Wilson was praying silently. He intoned under his breath, 'If it is my time, Lord, I trust myself to you.' Cherry and Bowers packed up the eggs, the supplies and the tent.

This way, she whispered, eager to get them safely onto the right path.

But Cherry had set up the stove. They'd have to eat before they could start. Of course they would. She had forgotten the needs of a body. Such an ordinary thing. Bowers broke some biscuits to boil and they scooped the porridge into their mouths like men who had thought they would never eat again.

Come with me, she whispered once they had finished.

And they did.

The men were barely alive as they tumbled over the threshold of the hut. Everyone jumped to help, trying to hide their horror at the apparitions, filthy and frozen as they stumbled in from the cold.

'Cherry looks thirty years older,' one man hissed, as he fetched shears with which to cut the uniforms from the three almost unrecognizable frozen forms. At first, they could hardly speak.

Wilson tried to restrain himself from crying tears of sheer relief. He did not entirely succeed. Cherry fell asleep on his feet. Birdie brushed up the easiest. 'I wasn't much of a specimen to start with,' he managed to joke.

Karina sank onto the floor, relieved that they had made it. The last few days she had doubted they would, wrapping herself around their shoulders and whispering words of encouragement. Wilson would see his Oriana again. Birdie's mother would be proud. And Cherry mustn't let the others down. *Keep going*, she had cooed. They had been frozen and starving and sick but they had made it.

Slowly as the story came out they were heroes among heroes. The men listened rapturous as Wilson talked about cooking that first pot of hoosh after the storm.

'Cherry cracked out double rations, lads,' he said, and the table laughed. They showed the eggs they'd brought. They admitted to singing the hymns on the hill, to thinking that they were dead men. They said it was down to sheer luck, finding the canvas that allowed them to get home in the end.

'Well . . .' Scott's voice trailed, and he couldn't continue. It wasn't often that he was speechless.

As the cook served tea and thick slabs of bread with dripping – proper *blings*, Karina thought – Birdie hummed under his breath. She smiled. She had missed his humming. He was happy now. Who could blame him? It was warm and there was food. He'd sleep forty-eight hours and wake only with difficulty. She saw him soften

304

and his legs relax at the thought of the luxury of a clean dry bunk – the glory of being alive. From his box he took out a green, woollen hat his sister had knitted. It was the same colour as her scarf had been all those years ago – the only green on the continent. As he pulled it on, he relished being alive.

Wilson too had backed away from the edge of death. The hard-won penguin eggs in their jars were stowed in the makeshift scientific laboratory at one side of the low hut. When the doctor thought about the specimens a sense of satisfaction pervaded his being. But Cherry was quieter than usual. Even cleaned up and dressed in a regulation naval woollen sweater and trousers with a dressing gown over the top, it was clear he had left part of himself on the ice.

'It was the worst journey in the world,' he admitted quietly.

The truth was that Bowers and Wilson had faced death and had not been afraid. Cherry would never recover because he had been terrified and he could not forgive himself for that. She wondered when Cherry died where his soul would reside, for he never seemed fully at ease. She peered into his childhood, as if she was pulling back a curtain. His father, long dead, had been an adventurer. 'Daddy is in the jungle, he could die any minute and you aren't eating your lunch,' a plump, rather unpleasant nanny said, as she stood over the little boy. 'No one will like you, you know, if you're selfish.'

At the mess table, Cherry hardly tasted the hot sweet tea as an uneasy cocktail of pride and shame rendered him aware of Scott's eyes upon him. He need not have worried. This kind of derring-do was exactly what the skipper required of his men, and if Scott was looking at Cherry it was because he was the one who had physically changed the most. The poor man had not yet caught sight of himself in a mirror but there was no question that his nanny would not be best pleased.

'Good show,' said the skipper, who found himself in awe of the bravery of these men and what they had achieved. He hoped one day to be able to match it. At the pole, she remembered. *Ah. That.*

Karina felt the scene begin to dim. Nothing would happen now till the light returned but still, she wanted to stay. There was no point in fighting it though – the blackness at the edges of her world, the visions that appeared and disappeared again. The way time folded. She was in the grip of the world and what it wanted to show her. It was time to go. Unwillingly, she left the men to their recovery and slipped onto the glacier. The wind had dropped and everything was still on the sound as she took the snow once more as her mantle. She told herself that she could not save every foolish hero who lost his way on the ice. It was only them. Something had touched her, almost as if she was alive again. It had been a long time.

Behind her the hut was festooned with lamps that cast shadows as the men went about their business. Back and forth, in and out, the shadows mingled as they passed one another. She was put in mind of a beehive that one of her mother's neighbours kept on Ven. Suddenly the presence of the camp seemed overwhelming. The world is right, she thought and she turned her back, walking straight into the mountain ahead. It was one way to disappear. She spread herself through the dark basalt, through its fissures and cracks and deep into the heart of the rock where the light, when it came, wouldn't find her. And she slept.

Twenty-Three

At first, she thought that she was dreaming and that someone was whispering in her ear. She turned over and then in the thick, hard silence she heard it again. An indistinct voice. It said, *Amen.* In shock, she rolled into a long crevice filled with ice and stretched along it for half a mile. She was gone too far for sound to plummet and yet this whisper found her. *Where are you?* it said, insistent, the vowels strangely long. It was an eerie, distorted sound. Uneasily, she sat up. Was it possible there was someone else here? Had somebody died? Above her, on the surface the ice shifted and creaked and she wondered if one of the men had set foot over her grave. Could that really reach her here, now, all these years later?

Then there was a rustle and she felt a stroke on her arm. An affectionate touch, skin on skin. *But there is no one*, she thought. 'What do you want?' she shouted and the rock around her trembled.

She had lived and died. She had travelled the world and beyond. She was not a woman who feared a sound in the thick of night. Yet this jolted her. It called her back to the world and once again, she had no choice.

On the glacier, the light had dawned and the azure sky stretched from Cape Evans all the way

308

to the pole. It was summer. At first, the sun was almost blinding as she returned to the biting air. Then she saw them. Far off, Scott's expedition had set off. The captain had been busy – final supplies were being laid and a route had been settled upon. *What have I missed?*

She flew overhead, curious to assess what was going on. The men were scattered across the course the skipper had set, like salt over a cooking pot. There were too many of them to make the attempt. Some would be sent back. Some were accompanied by dogs and one party had a motor, which of course had failed. They worked together to supply the storage depots, caches of oil and food along the way half-buried already by the snow. They moved like tin soldiers on a child's battlefield, a strange clockwork toy moving in concert. *He is keeping them with him on the chance that he'll choose them for the final attempt*, she thought. And indeed, the men were on tenterhooks, hope flurrying around them. Swooping low, she could see it. Every one was trying to please the skipper for he had not decided yet who would be chosen to make the final attempt. The path to glory lay open.

Thebo used to study maps in his father's workshop near the old observatory tower, in a passageway off Strogert. He had missed those afternoons, she had realized, once they left Copenhagen. He had spent hours in that office with its dark, wooden cubbyholes, sitting on a green, leather-bound clerk's stool, like a little god surveying his domain. When they had first met she'd sneak in and he'd show her the maps, talk her through the geography and explain which areas were uncharted. They had kissed, secretly when the office boy was sent out to fetch beer. New maps arrived intermittently – a man who had conducted a survey inside Africa sent a section of the Niger. Another submitted an outline of the coast of China. Thebo's father paid well. He had endowed his son with the sense that the world was a jigsaw to be pieced together. It had made Thebo long to see it.

Now, rising above the plains, Karina recalled the feeling of overlooking the curves of the landscape. Scott's party was following the curve of the earth from one direction and, far off, from another, Amundsen's men were flying across the ice with their dogs. The emotion hit her in waves. Scott's crew were anxious, desperate to prove themselves, and Amundsen and his men were wheeling with pleasure, laughing as they made their way. It was like the day Shackleton first set off – the same sense of freedom and of joy. The Norwegians had no qualms about using dogs or skis. They were enjoying themselves.

To the west, Scott was honed upon the point, the furthest south, where Shackleton and his men had planted their flag. The skipper would take immense pleasure as he passed it, the farthest south a man had ever made. He'd take even more pleasure because that man was his rival. Step by step, he relished overtaking Shackle far more than reaching his final destination and 88° 23' was suddenly more riveting than even the pole. He took measurements obsessively. He wanted to be sure when he had won. Not yet. Not quite. But it was coming.

In his sleeping bag, Cherry comforted himself that it was almost Christmas. Karina recalled him on the journey to Cape Crozier, a bundle of insecurities, and she measured him carefully. All the men were in discomfort but Cherry had not fully recovered from the earlier trip. Inside he was trembling not only from the cold but at the memory of what had happened. His spirit was bruised, far more than his body and he had done well to get this far. Scott saw it too and on the night of midsummer he told Cherry that he was sending him back with three of the other men.

The skipper issued orders to ensure supplies were replaced at each depot. Such was the endless nature of mortal need. Men hauled food with them to store, they ate it on the return and then they were sent again to resupply. Such little ants. Wilson had calculated the stockpiles required. The cold ate the men's flesh and they defended themselves with double rations. Triple rations. A soupcon of oil for the lamp might save a fellow's life. Wilson had agonized over it. Now the party was thinning out, he added up again and again. Summer rations – less than winter. Less per day than they had needed for the worst journey, though this trip was longer.

Cherry scarcely slept that last night. In part, he was relieved that he was going back. In part, he was disappointed. *There is no pleasing me*, he thought and he hoped that come Hogmanay he'd be settled.

In the morning it was bright as the party took

311

down the tents. Cherry and Birdie shook hands and Cherry shoved Birdie's green woollen hat affectionately, pushing his head to one side.

'I hope he chooses you,' Cherry whispered, low so that no one else could hear.

The decision was still to be made in the matter of the final party. Birdie smiled and did not say that he hoped so too. He never thought he'd get so close.

'I wish we had Christmas together,' he posited instead.

Birdie had secreted extra supplies for Christmas Day, though it was not quite the feast to which they would settle down if they were back in Blighty.

The four men returning watched as the eight men going on, turned away. Oates only nodded – no fond farewell as he moved off with the distinctive limp he arrived with – an old war wound. Then as the returning party finally set off back in the direction of the glacier Cherry felt his stomach turn. It was a strange sense of foreboding. *I am with them*, Karina murmured *As far as I can go.* But he did not hear her. She never seemed to reach Cherry. His mind was muddled by his nanny and his dread of not being up to snuff. He was already haunted. She patted him on the back to say goodbye and then she rose and floated with the clouds that were riding southwards with the others.

The whiteness felt endless but it was not. She knew there would come a point soon she could go no further. She realized quite suddenly that when the dark curtain fell, she did not want

Scott's party simply to pull it aside and go on without her. She chastised herself. All the years she had despised their ambition– the need to push to the pole – and here she was full of ambition herself. Perhaps it was the men. They were beguiling. Perhaps she simply did not want to be left behind. Not again.

Scott never fell asleep as quickly as the others. He had to decide on the party for the pole and however tired his body became, his mind kept him awake, mulling it over. His muscles ached when he moved, so he stayed still and reasoned it through. He had always reckoned on four men, but of the eight left, there were no shirkers or dilly-dalliers. There was not one who did not deserve a shot at glory. Even dear Teddy Evans, who Scott swore he'd keep at bay, was nothing short of marvellous. What was it that happened in this place, that there was no other obsession but the hard white silence? When he finally drifted off there was a staircase made of ice and snow and he was carrying his wife up it.

At the turn of the year Bowers produced a bottle of brandy for the men to share after their hoosh. This was against the captain's orders. It was hard enough to haul everything they needed on the sledges, never mind bringing luxuries, Hogmanay or not. Scott forgave Birdie his contraband and they toasted together. 'Good health,' they joked. 'To the pole.' 'To his majesty.' 'Happy New Year.' And that night they slept better than ever, the brandy settling their nerves.

If I had had children, I would want it to be with

men such as these. Not a liar like Thebo. Not a cheat like Hooker. But an honest man.

The next morning, the going was tough as ever. Scott was not only narrowing down the party, bit by bit, but also the equipment. As the going got harder, the skis were tougher to use. He'd never liked them anyway. A man should make his way to the destination under his own steam. All weakness was to be despised. *That old obsession.* Karina remembered the Norwegians. They were still there, far off, making good progress on their sledges and their skis. Amundsen did not carry the same burden – he'd get there any way he could. The Scandic crew were warmer, she realized. She heard their voices chiming across the mountains – the guttural sound of Norwegian interspersed with English here and there – a more international language. With words as well as equipment, they used whatever served them.

'Lashly, Evans, Bowers – stow the skis,' Scott ordered. 'Leave them at the depot and we can pick them up on the return.'

The men took a moment to take this in. The word *but* hovered on Birdie's lips. The going had been rough but it could ease at any time and the skis were a boon. He hadn't used them before and he'd come to enjoy the thrill of sliding across the ice plain.

'Sir?' Lashly, who was normally a stoker in the engine room, managed to ask the question, or as close as he could get.

'We'll do it ourselves,' Scott snapped.

Evans led the way and the men handed in their

314

skis, which were secured along with some of the supplies.

Birdie, for the first time in the expedition, if not his naval career, resented an order. Scott was wrong. He could feel it. The skis were hardly heavy kit. It felt as if he was leaving behind a part of himself – a foot, maybe. However, so deeply ingrained was the legend of Scott's fight with Shackleton, that even as a senior officer, he did not raise an objection. But he wanted to. He did not have much of a temper but what there was had been set alight at the captain's foolishness. He thought of Shackleton beside the fire in the club in London, warning him only a few months ago about the risk. When he caught Wilson's eye, the surgeon would not meet his. The skis were stowed and as the party moved off, Bowers felt the shadow of foreboding across him. He waved it off.

Karina watched eagerly. Ahead she knew there was terrain that they'd best cross using skis. Now they'd have to walk across it, slipping and tripping as they went when they could have flown. It was as if Birdie could feel the land as it rose to meet them. Karina caught a flash of his childhood home, a spectacular view from a high hill over a firth peppered with ships, and in the distance islands covered with fir trees. Just like Ven, it was green. He'd swum it once – out to Rothsay – and caught the ferry home again. He'd spent his life sailing, she realized.

How long was this taking? How long? She wondered at this, as she was pulled back towards them when they made camp for the night. Lashly boiled up Bovril and made hoosh. As they settled to sleep, she realized that Birdie had not written his journal since he was forced to abandon the skis because he did not want to betray the skipper by putting his feelings on paper. His anger had since heightened because having left the damned things behind there had been nothing but fine skiing weather since. Now, in petty rebellion, he pulled another bottle of brandy from his kit bag. It was greeted with enthusiasm.

The alcohol warmed the men. It was cold for summer, even here. There was some chit-chat – foolish talk of New Year's resolutions and what might be happening at home. Wilson knew Oriana would be staying with her parents. Lashly generally shared New Year with his cousin, a Scotsman who considered the festival more important than Christmas and insisted upon a twenty-four-hour celebration that appeared mostly to consist of drinking beer. His cousin, he thought, would only now be recovering. Birdie wondered for the umpteenth time how much the lack of skis was slowing them down but instead he told a story about a Hogmanay he spent in Burma when he was stationed there – a frenzy of curried goat and whisky.

As if he could sense the dissent of a sentiment unvoiced, Scott went back to his chart. In a couple of days by his reckoning he'd have outdone Shackleton's record. Only a couple of days.

The seamen were bluff – Crean and Lashly and Evans, all ordinary men, were amazed that they had come so far on this extraordinary adventure which surely should be the preserve of officers.

316

'We ain't seen no sign of the Norwegian, then, sir,' Lashly ventured.

Wilson's gaze flickered as he checked to see if Scott had heard the comment. There had been little mention of Amundsen's party since the telegram arrived almost a year ago, as if by mentioning the fellow's name they might give him some kind of legitimacy. The English simply assumed that they were leading the race. After all, they were used to winning. Karina, reminded, rose high above, the midnight sun lighting the sparkling snow as if it was studded with diamonds. Amundsen was making good ground on the other side. She imagined Thebo, the snake, measuring this progress with a pair of compasses. He was ahead, she realized, and the English had no idea. Wilson shook his head and Lashly said no more about it.

Scott was still to make the decision about the final party. The next day, as he walked, forcing his burning limbs on, he mumbled the men's names, so no one could hear him. His sense of fair play was hampering his decision as much as the distraction of his searing muscles. In fact, if anything, it took his mind off the pain. Four would go on and four return, but all the men who had come this far were worthy of the assault on the pole. *Lashly, Evans, Evans, Crean, Wilson, Bowers and Oates*, he thought over and over. *Crean, Lashly, Oates, Bowers, Wilson, Evans and Evans.* Then he grouped his favourites. *Evans, Bowers, Wilson and Oates.* Yes, those were the fellows, he thought, before realizing he had left out himself. *Scott. Scott. Scott.* How

317

uncharacteristic, Karina thought. But it was difficult to keep going, never mind making vital decisions about skis and crew. Perhaps it would be five, Scott decided. Perhaps five brave explorers was best.

Two days later Scott sent Teddy Evans, Lashly and Crean back to basecamp. He embraced the returning men on the ice, slapping each on the back, wishing them luck.

Karina shook her head and her hair shifted in the breeze. It was a fine summer day but there was snow coming. It was not long past midsummer and yet there was a chill on the air that was unaccustomed for the time of year. *Karina*, a voice called, tailing off as if it was being pulled away, unwillingly.

'Who is it?' she shouted. 'What do you want?' though she left what she meant unsaid. *I am the ghost here. I will not be haunted.* The world was usually so clear – what did these voices mean, coming so suddenly out of nowhere? 'Who are you?' she shouted again, but there was no reply. The air was heavy with silence. Karina watched the parties proceed. The Norwegians were still moving more quickly, making good ground. She tipped her head to one side and tried to figure out in which direction they were heading. There or back?

Karina, the voice called again. Suddenly there was a flash so bright that it made her reel, as if the sun had beamed too intensely and the slate of the world had been wiped clean. The men were whited out, their worries about rations, skis

318

and minor injuries obliterated. The voice fell to silence and she was not held by any will other than her own as below her a void opened. She clenched her fists as though she might have to fight. Then she cast around wildly, hoping to somehow make them out. Which party would make the pole? Would they arrive there together?

But that was not what was in store. Gradually, into the whiteness stepped an old man so ancient that it seemed he might melt into the brightness. He was so frail she thought she might be able to see right through him. Then she made him out.

'Joseph?' she breathed.

He looked confused. *Has he lost his mind?* she wondered. *Can he even remember?*

'You left me,' she managed. 'What are you doing here?'

Hooker peered in her direction.

'You died,' he put it baldly. It had been his voice that spoke in whispers, she realized. It was he who had woken her from the mountain. It was he who had stroked her skin. The last person alive to whom she had had a connection in life.

'You were always going to leave me,' she said, thinking she might as well admit what she knew, now he was here.

Joseph allowed only a tiny nod. 'Frances,' he said. 'Yes.' And then his eyes widened as he recollected those days, on the *Terror* – more than sixty years or was it seventy. 'The custard tart,' he said. 'It was delicious.'

It surprised her that she was beyond anger. Not

319

so long ago she would have struck him for dismissing her. Not much after that she would have been on her knees, sobbing. But today, in this bright, white place, she was not perturbed that what came into his mind was pastry and sweetened cream.

'You missed a very great love. One you would not have deserved,' she said. 'You betrayed me.'

His eyes were still recognizable. They were the only part of his wrinkled, faded body that had not changed so very much since he was the handsomest of men – the love of her life. Now they softened into clear pools of bluey green. She realized that he had his Frances and his children and his grandchildren, but he had not had her. And the fact he had materialized meant perhaps that he had wanted to. She was his unfinished business as much as he was hers.

'What happens now?' he asked.

She shrugged as the bright light faded slowly like a cloud on a breeze and Joseph peered at her spectre.

'You are very beautiful,' he managed. 'You always were.'

And it came to her that she would rather face eternity as she was than as an old woman. *It seems I am still vain.*

'Where were you happiest?' she asked.

Joseph paused, considering.

'Happiest?' he repeated as if it was an impossible notion.

'That's where you will stay,' she said.

Why she was telling him this, she could not imagine. She had had to work it out for herself.

320

'Frances is in the garden, I think. In Glasgow,' she said.

Hooker shook his head. 'Frances and her garden,' he muttered fondly. 'Well.'

He glanced behind him in the direction of the Ross Sea and those days on the *Terror*.

'Truly,' he said, 'I think it was in London. At the Royal Geographical Society. Or maybe Kew.'

She could not help but smile. No sooner had he said it than the sky darkened readying itself to pull him back, halfway across the world. Taking him away. Hooker and his heartbreaking significance. Hooker, who, when it came to it, had meant nothing at all.

As he receded, the ice reappeared and she felt a release as if she had been freed from a prison, the door simply left open for her to walk away. She lingered at the edge of the glacier, where the mountains rose. She glanced at the receding dot of Joseph's figure for only a moment and hovered as if in memoriam to her lost love. All that emotion, wasted. Then she turned her attention back to the ice plane and searched for the men.

Twenty-Four

[location] *88° 23': 97 miles from the pole*

The remnants of Shackleton's flag remained, a tattered frozen symbol. It was there, where he had turned back that Karina found herself staring into darkness. She could go no further. Scott had reached the limits of her territory. The boundaries of her world. The men had toasted. Camped. Taken a photograph. And then one by one she watched as Scott, Wilson, Bowers, Oates and tall Taffy Evans passed into the void, and she was left, there underneath the frozen, tatty flag. She could not leave. Not now. Not without knowing. Was she ever so devoted in life, she wondered. She could not now remember.

The plateau seemed too silent without the tiny party and the crush of thoughts and emotions, their private conversations and dreams. As Scott disappeared, she felt his rush of happiness evaporate on the freezing air and she realized how much she had felt through the skipper and his men. With Joseph gone, she wondered why the English still held her attention. It was as if, having been introduced to someone at a gathering, they suddenly ceased to be a friend of a friend and became a friend themselves. The most important thing about Scott was no longer that he once met Joseph Hooker. The most important thing about

Wilson was no longer that without him Scott would never have made it this far. She remembered Birdie Bowers singing at Cape Crozier and felt proud. The pole was important to these men so it had become important to her and she hoped that they would make it. Why ever not?

As she looked back along the line of food depots they had left, she felt strangely isolated. She had been trapped here for almost a century. She gazed fondly northwards, knowing that among the black dots heading back to Hut Point, Cherry was on his way. But she did not follow. Instead she settled down to wait. It was oddly uncomfortable and to pass the time, she played with the newly fallen snow, whipping it up as if she was shaking a snow globe at a fair. She stared upwards at the sky, ten years old again and once more lying on her back in Ven, examining the clouds. Whether this took an eternity or only a minute, she could not say without checking the men heading back to base, as if they were her pocket watch. Tentatively, she reached out a finger to try to push through the void, but the blackness engulfed her and when she woke, by Cherry's progress, well beyond Wilson's carefully calculated supplies at One Ton Depot, she estimated that she had disappeared for two days. He was almost at a place of safety. As the wind whipped up and the snow flurried, the flakes beyond her disappeared. Nothing blew in this direction from the darkness. Nothing came back.

Here on the cusp between unremitting light and absolute darkness she was put in mind of Marijke

323

in her more innocent days, hovering beside the window to see the boy she hoped might pass. Now, Karina waited on Scott's party to return. She was keen on them. She flew high, hoping to spy the first sign of a return. She turned away, fancying that if she refused to look, perhaps it would make them arrive more quickly. Time folded over and she fidgeted uneasily. She worried that something deadly behind the dark curtain might take them. Shackleton's flag lay still for the weather was cold, clear and settled, but what lay beyond was a sheer mystery.

She comforted herself that Wilson and Bowers were surviving heroes of the worst journey and that now it was summertime. *They will make the pole*, she told herself, for with all their difficulties, contrarieties and flaws, these men had become her heroes; that is to say, the heroes that belonged to her. The flags did not matter. The charts neither. In truth, she had never had a hero. Not one who was proven. The glory awaiting an English victory was by the by. London could not see these men as she saw them. London could not possess them. Shining. Glorious. Inside and out.

Once she looked out and saw Marijke on the rooftop. She waved and Marijke waved back. *Perhaps this is peace*, she thought. Marijke smiled. 'I found Mother,' she said. 'She was happiest at Per Hansen's house. She was there all along.' Per Hansen was Anders' father. Karina laughed. Who would have thought she was the one who would have travelled furthest? That their mother, who they thought so unhappy, had such a secret. Marijke settled down and laid her chin on her palm.

'So I could never have married, Anders. Do you see? What are you waiting for?' Marijke asked, suddenly curious as she peered into the void.

Karina shrugged. 'Men,' she said.

Marijke raised her hand, three fingers as she had done before. 'You have three of them,' she said.

'No. Two,' Karina objected but before Marijke could reply, the light faded.

The first she spotted of their return was Taffy Evans and he was a shock as he burst back into view. Evans had always been a carthorse of a man but now he was shaken, gulping the air as if he had only just surfaced from underwater. There were patches of frostbite on his face and fingertips. He had surely not been gone long enough to get in such a state. She calculated it could only have been a fortnight perhaps or three weeks at a push. Could it be more? Could it? After all, there was less than a hundred miles to go when the five of them walked into the darkness and yet Evans was changed. It came to her in a rush – he was desperate, ragged and disheartened. He had injured his hand and Wilson had twice now asked the skipper to order camp made early on account of it.

Next Oates stumbled beyond the curtain and she felt a stab of pain. He was in a bad way. Wilson, as he emerged, was more worried about Oates than himself. Oates had sustained a bad case of frostbite, particularly on his foot, and just as bad, he had not been able to keep up his kit.

325

His sleeping bag was torn and mostly sodden. When he allowed himself to wonder, Wilson could not understand why Scott chose five of them. The pole party was to be four. It had been that way all along, up to the very last minute. Everything had been calculated for four and yet, Scott had chosen one man too many. It was chance and chance alone but Wilson was looking for meaning in it. *There is no meaning.* But the doctor could not hear her, so focused was he on his calculations.

But that was the least of it. As the skipper and Birdie hauled the last of the sledges into her line of sight, she could see what they had seen – a flag at the pole that was not the jack. If she had had a heart, it would have sunk. It took her a moment to take in that Amundsen had snatched the glory ahead of them when he came from the other side of the plateau with the dogs. His sledges were faster. In this failure, she saw the measure of each man. Evans's heart flagged, for he, it turned out, was truly in it for the glory. She had not known before. Now he decided that his wife, Lois, would not be proud of him. He wanted to go home to the sweeping sandy beaches of Rhossili the hero he imagined himself to be, not this way – the man who came second.

Scott, by comparison, was tense and angry for he felt betrayed and yet he had nowhere to pin that betrayal. His men had behaved impeccably. They had done nothing wrong. They were the first to have made it to the pole under their own steam – Amundsen used dogs, after all; while ever honourable, his men had relied on themselves. At Scott's heart there was a locked box of disappointment despite that. He wondered if he had started earlier, if he had worked harder, if he had consented to using dogs. If he had chosen four, not five. He dodged the words that he couldn't help thinking. *What might Shackleton have done?*

By contrast, Birdie, Wilson and Oates were focused on their return. Step upon step. The only way. *At least it was not a close run thing*, Oates thought. Amundsen got the better of them by a month or more. They could not have made up the time.

Time? It is so unreliable.

And yet she felt disappointed. Even she.

She looked for the Norwegians – the men who had overtaken her heroes. She could not make them out any more. They were nothing to her. They were gone. All their happiness and enthusiasm and the flood of half-familiar words. How could Amundsen and his men compare to Scott's party?

Hungry, always hungry now, the English set out to follow the trail of supply depots that led back to Hut Point. But having found the exact location of the pole, somehow the men found the depot coordinates difficult to calculate. Beyond the plateau and back on the glacier, snow had fallen and the cooking oil and pemmican were difficult to find – small white hillocks in a mono-chrome landscape.

It was cold for summer and she could not mask that. Now and then a flutter of snow fell. There would be more. She could feel it on the wind.

She tried to guide them with a gentle push and nudge but Scott, in his fury, was difficult to direct. Evans kept falling like a petulant child intent on punishing himself. As she read his thoughts, it became clear that if he couldn't be first at the pole he didn't care about anything, not even his own welfare. He fell down knocking his head badly and over the days his hand got worse. Wilson privately assessed that back at Hut Point he would have to amputate it.

Then as they came off the glacier and onto the barrier after two long weeks of hard hauling with Evans falling every second day as he flung himself furiously in the direction of home, the petty officer collapsed. He mumbled words she could not catch. Wilson asked him to repeat himself and when he did so she realized he was speaking another language – a childhood tongue. Unable to discern it, the men carried him into the tent where Wilson nursed him to little avail. Karina whispered, *Come now. You must go home.* But it did no good. The force of Evans's will was beyond her. *Please*, she said, but he descended anyway. *Think of your home. Think of your family. Don't give up now.* But English was beyond him. His words sounded like the weather as they fell from his lips. Not clipped like English, but something else entirely. She watched, horrified, as his spirit left his body.

Deep in the night, Evans's spectre hovered over Scott's sleeping outline as if his happiest place might be at the skipper's side. But the dead cannot belong to the living. It is the land that owns them – each man to his own. Above, a door opened on a place that wasn't white. A long, sandy beach dripping in an orange sunset that swept in a colourful arc. Evans smiled at last. It was Rhossili and he was going home. As he was pulled away, he spotted Karina, in the corner of the tent, a thin white spectre. His eyes flashed, turning towards the skipper in consternation. *He thinks I am a wraith*, she realized. *He thinks the things that have gone wrong are my fault.* Somehow this shadow of a superstition riled her. She had done everything she could. 'I am here to help you. I stayed to help,' she insisted, but as Evans disappeared, there was a dark and silent accusation in his eyes.

They left his body, buried as best they could. Wilson packed Evans's things to take back and silently recalculated the supplies. She tutted softly and he turned. But she couldn't blame him. This place stripped everything away in the end. It laid you bare. She watched as the line of four Englishmen moved from one depot to the next. They remained animated and from high above she kept willing them on. They were weak. *Too weak*, she thought. Oates with his injured foot and Scott, with aching muscles, in a worse state than he realized. But then, she had thought that before and they had survived.

Far beyond them, back at base, a rescue party had formed. Cherry and Dimitri, the animal handler, packed sledges, to take the dogs to resupply as far as One Ton Depot. Every breath they took, the men lived in the hope that the pole had been claimed for His Majesty. At base, each kept watch – a glance to the horizon as they made their way to the hut or woken by a midnight creak, which they hoped might be the skipper returning. The party was not even late yet. Karina shuddered. The weather was relentless as ever, winter was coming. The whole of Hut Point was on edge as Cherry and Dmitri set off, imagining that they would meet the party on the way.

She found of a sudden she could not follow what the men were saying. She had lost her English and thought only in her own tongue. Then she lost even that and all she had were pictures. *The world is taking me.* She struggled against its grasp, but it was like being a bouncing ball, only able to take in what she passed in a flash. Everything fell silent. On the ice beyond base camp, Cherry stared in the direction of the returning party but there was no movement bar the empty wind. *Where are they?* Nothing was coming his way and the weather was worsening. It had been a terrible summer. Bad luck after bad luck. Blizzards and high winds. Karina flurried on the silent snows. She coasted the breezes.

In pity, she was drawn back to the tent the polar party had pitched to wait out the storm. She couldn't understand anything any more. The world was a kind of blur. Still, she could make it out. And she was relieved that there remained four of them and Birdie had picked up his skis. They talked but all she could catch were strange, slurred voices as if time was running too slowly. Each of the men was hungry and Scott realized what Wilson had known for a little while, that there was not enough oil to last – to cook and to keep warm. *Where are the dogs?* the skipper wondered, and thought of poor Blossom, all those years ago, her entrails spread over the ice. That must be a decade ago. Like Karina, his mind was wandering and the dogs were back at the base. He had sent them back. *Think*, she hissed. *Concentrate.* For without determination the party would be sunk. They had become too close, as if their bodies are circulating the same blood, pumped by four hearts, in tandem. Moving together. *What if one of them dies?*

Desperation mounting, night by night, Scott, Bowers, Oates and Wilson huddled together, sheltered from the seemingly interminable summer blizzards, clutching their stomachs just as she had, those first nights aboard the *Terror*. Trying to feel full. Ignoring the howling of her hunger. This was worse than they had expected – the worst summer weather Karina could recall. It was more difficult than they imagined and that was what had shaken them. All they had wanted was a decent shot at it, but the blizzards and snowfall and high winds weren't any more fair than Amundsen using sledges and dogs. Supplies were low and, worse, winter was coming early.

Oates was anxious he couldn't manage the pain any more. His foot was dead and blackened and he was in agony as they lurched from camp to camp. Still, what he considered the worst thing was that he would drag down the others. *A party moves only at the pace of the slowest man.* There was no question he was slowing them and there was not enough food. He'd been thinking of it for days. In the corner of the tent, he allowed himself another heartbeat before deciding it was time.

He hauled himself to his feet. When he spoke, the words were the first that Karina had heard clearly since Evans had died. *I am just going outside and I may be some time*, he said. Though she heard him, she did not understand until he had left the tent and walked, like the bravest of madmen, into the swirling snow. He left a bequest behind. A better chance. A bit of luck. As he limped on, he thought, *I was set to lose the damn leg this time anyway.*

'Stop!' she shouted as she trailed him. She tried to turn him round. His words echoed. *I am just going outside and I may be some time.* Surely there was another way. But Oates limped on – like that little penguin all those years ago.

Inside the tent, the others waited, realization dawning. Wilson stared straight ahead as if he was in some kind of trance. Scott fidgeted. Birdie could not bear it. He jumped to his feet and opened the tent flap. His green hat pulled over his ears.

'Titus!' he shouted. 'Titus.'

But Oates did not hear him. The wind was too high and he was sitting with his legs spread in front of him almost half a mile off. For the first time in weeks he felt warm. *We came to fight*, he mumbled, ever the soldier, but when the pinprick of light above him opened onto a scene it was not a battlefield but a stone bridge that came into view, its arches stretching across a wide river. A place called Putney. *These English-men love their homes.* When Oates finally saw her he smiled. It was a broad grin hiding nothing. 'You're a pretty girl,' he said, and for the first time in a long time, she laughed. She had not been a pretty girl in all the long decades. 'Putney,' she said, and Oates disappeared.

Inside the tent it was the worst day any of them had experienced. This was a kind of agony. Oates could not have survived long in his weakened condition, but they each hoped against hope that somehow he would make it back. That night they slept at best fitfully. If Oates had sacrificed himself to save them, that act was uncertain. His death was a burden, if anything – something they would have to live up to.

The next day, in a lull in the weather, Scott, Bowers and Wilson still could not find any words. Instead they took down the tent in silence and hauled everything onwards with their supplies dwindling. It was not far to go. Not far. Cherry was near here only a few days ago – ahead of them by a few miles before he shrugged his shoulders and turned back. It felt like a dream, or maybe a nightmare that they could not see what she could see. That they did not know.

She told herself that Wilson and Bowers had lived through worse not nine months before but she knew that did not mean they wouldn't die. It came back to the fact that the party could only move as swiftly as its weakest man and with Evans in Rhossilli and Oates in Putney that man was now Scott. With the others worse off, she

333

hadn't fully realized how weak the skipper had become. He always seemed inviolable but he didn't have the mettle of the men who had survived the worst journey. Not when it came to it. His muscles screamed. His teeth were loose in his gums. His bones pressed against his skin. He passed in and out of consciousness. He suffered without fully realizing it, for Scott, in his imagination, was playing to the gallery. He accepted it now as he scribbled in his notebook – a message to Kathleen. A message to the world. *For God's sake, look after our people.*

At night Wilson and Bowers whispered a plan. Would it be best to go ahead to retrieve supplies from the next depot and then come back for the skipper? They were out of oil and biscuit and pemmican. They were out of all of it. *Yes*, she breathed. She could guide them. It was all there, only a few miles north – Cherry had resupplied everything. There was cocoa, Bovril, thick blocks of dripping and oil to fire the stove.

Scott kept imagining his wife fussing. 'Kathleen,' he smiled, and told himself she'd have cook make him some toasted cheese and bring it up to him in bed with a cup of tea. It was a kind of escape though the truth was he knew where he was. He knew what was happening. Far off, at Hut Point the men at home base sent out a search party but she could feel Scott's door above the tent, waiting to open. It was too late. Wilson and Birdie were stronger, if only slightly. But she knew that they'd made not only a physical decision but a mental one too. They were a team of three. They would stay together, come what may. Still, she tried to

334

encourage them to set off but their hearts beat together in a strange three-way tattoo and she could not break its rhythm.

The grey lip of dark winter kissed the horizon and Scott laid down his pencil.

Bowers kept going back to his memory of Shackleton in the members' lounge and Wilson making him take back what he said about Scott and his decisions. He tried not to think of it – the skis and the five men instead of four. He had no strength left and what was the point anyway? As he glanced at the skipper he'd swear he could see a bubble floating above him like an escaped balloon. It looked like the inside of the Royal Society, its lamps alight to welcome members for an evening lecture.

Scott's face was pale. An old man stood behind the podium. Was it Joseph Hooker, Birdie wondered. He had seen photographs of the old duffer. Surely, though, Hooker must be dead by now. He had been reported ill before the *Terra Nova* even left. Or maybe the old man would outlast them all. Before he could ask, or comment or ponder it, the room faded away and slowly, Birdie realized, the skipper was gone.

'Wilson,' he managed. 'Teddy.'

Wilson only smiled. He had seen hundreds of corpses. He was a medical man and held out no hope that he and Birdie would fare better. He had carried everyone's worry with him. He had seen their pain clearly as well as suffering his own – each man a patient as well as a friend. Now, he decided, it was better the cold would

335

take them than they starve to death. That at least was some kind of comfort.

'We tried, Birdie.'

'Better,' Birdie insisted, 'we did it. We made the pole, old man.'

Wilson nodded.

No, she shouted but neither of them heard her. *No*, she raged but all they felt was the wind buffeting the canvas of the tent, as it had on and off for days. Karina flew high above, but the rescue party was a long way off. Too far.

Wilson started to mouth a prayer and Birdie joined him. Would she have been so brave if she had known the moment of her death? Outside the blizzard did not abate as the men clasped their hands like monks and waited for God to claim them.

Twenty-Five

Their heroes defined a person, she realized. Birdie had chosen Shackleton, after all. For some, it would be Amundsen, for he was the man who succeeded in planting his country's flag. But for many, long afterwards, it was the loyalty of Oates, walking into a blizzard in the hope he'd save his fellows or of Scott, whose last thoughts, it seemed, were of his wife and the wives and families of his men.

Karina knew there was no measure in being alone. Surely no ghost was meant to be so. Scott had Hooker now – ghosts worthy of each other. Marijke, she hoped, had their mother. Time didn't matter. Only passion. The world was a loom and its threads stretched beyond what men could see. In the end, each man got what he wanted. To Amundsen the prize and to Scott posterity. *We were each part of the landscape and part of each other, across time, like it or not.*

She wondered if anyone would find the little tent with their bodies or if the snow would pile over it so high that Scott, Bowers and Wilson become part of the barrier, as her body was part of it. Would their skin darken and their flesh shrink tightly onto their long-dead bones?

Above the tent, she watched Wilson disappear into a warm study. His friend, Ellis, was sitting at his desk. Birdie was the strongest. He would

337

be the last to go. He closed his eyes because he didn't want to see the bodies of the others. If anyone came looking, he decided, they would find them together. He tried not to shed a tear thinking of his poor mother, Emily, standing on East India Dock. How soon would she know that her son was never coming home? *Well, he'll be back there soon*, she thought as she loitered at the tent flap.

Birdie moaned. Poor Bowers. The best of men. She could hardly believe he had come to this after all the perils. Having faced death so many times and somehow always come through. Further along the route the rescue party was days away. They were far too late. She stiffened as a flower of light bloomed at the apex of the canvas and watched, thinking to wave Bowers goodbye. He was the last of them. But when she looked up he was standing beside her, staring down at his body.

'Hello,' he said, making a strange little bow.

She waited for the light to take him.

'Can you see me?' he asked.

A smile broke across her face, hopeful as a sunrise. He did not move. There was no scene waiting to take him. She wondered was Oates right about luck? Was he right about heaven? She was not sure how to answer.

'Were you happiest here? Here?' she said incredulously.

Birdie cocked his head to one side, that silly green hat on his head.

'It has been my greatest adventure. Have you come to take me . . .?' his voice trailed as he looked behind her for some kind of ladder. 'Where are the others?' he asked.

She was not sure how to explain. These things were simpler than men imagined. Birdie was expecting God and angels and heaven but all there was in death is what was best in life. The decades had been difficult, there was no denying it but now her long disappointments fell away as his gaze lingered on her hair, ever blonde and her eyes ever blue and she knew that she would not be alone now. Not ever again. Here was the third man her sister had told her about.

'I am Karina,' she told him. 'And I will be your friend.'

Epilogue

'If everyone was satisfied with himself
there would be no heroes.'

Mark Twain

1915

They did not want to see Scott's low hut
abandoned, the tins of digestive biscuits and
cornflour, half-drunk bottles of whisky,
chipped enamel plates and old books simply
left behind by the bravest of men. But the
Terra Nova sailed away. The wild winds
battered the coastline and whipped between the
planks of wood. The air froze the iron stove
and ice formed on the inside as if it would
never warm up again.

The two figures were made of light. They
stood at the summit of Mount Terror but even
from that great height they had to squint to
make out that there were two ships coming.
The *Endurance* and the *Aurora*. Bowers fell to
his knees – he hadn't seen this before. An arrival.
He hadn't been woken from eternity by the
living. Gently Karina laid a long white hand
on his shoulder.

'It's Shackleton,' he said with his head to one
side as he read the scene. 'He has returned.'

341

'What is the point?' she whispered. The pole, after all, had been conquered.

Bowers did not reply. He was transfixed.

More distinguished with every passing year, Sir Ernest was steely. Bowers smiled to see the man who once was his hero, as he took his place at the helm. There were no long speeches, no formal celebrations as the ship came into the bay. The men simply hung over the side watching the ice. They were a wayward crew, entirely different from the kind of men Scott would have chosen. Shackleton believed a man's nature was more important than his skills and a quick pass among the men on deck uncovered singers and puzzle solvers, jugglers and classics scholars – each one hardy and determined to play his part. They would not stop coming, she realized. Not ever.

Karina sighed. It was too familiar. *They won't give up until they are all dead*, she breathed. Bowers didn't answer. He sat watching the ice flow that would try to kill them and wondered if the frozen wastes were Shackleton's happiest place as well. Perhaps the two of them would have company. He leaned against Karina affectionately.

'They are going to cross it. From the Weddell Sea to Ross Island, don't you see? It's the next challenge. To go through the pole and out the other side. That ship is going to get caught in the pack ice,' he nodded towards the *Endurance*. 'You see if it doesn't,' Birdie's face curled into a scowl.

And the days passed. The darkness came and went and the light did the same. She rose with the sun. It felt like dancing. She flew on the storms. It felt like swimming. She swirled with the stars and alone, as her form stretched, she had never felt so free.

Karina stretched. She smiled at him.

'Come,' she said. 'I'll show you how to lay yourself down. We'll help them if we can.'

Author's Historical Note

History is not a matter of fact but this book is definitely fiction. The first woman did not set foot on the Antarctic until 1935 – the wife of a Norwegian whaling captain, she was called Caroline Mikkelsen, although there is some evidence of Oceanic female explorers on the continent around 650CE and Louise Séguin visited in 1773 but did not step onto the ice. There were a few female applications to Shackleton's expedition in 1914, but none were accepted and it wasn't until the 1940s that Jackie Ronne and Jennie Darlington accompanied their husbands' mission and spent a year on the ice (despite a petition signed by the men to try to stop them).

When I write historical fiction I always wonder where on earth the women were and what they were thinking. We, as a gender, are under-represented in traditional, written history, in archive material and in artefacts. For a long time, female journals and letters simply weren't valued either by women's families or by historians, librarians and archivists so they weren't always kept.

When I started writing *The Ice Maiden* I was fascinated by anger – I wanted to write a woman out for revenge – a kind of Shakespearian Valkyrie who had been scorned. The ice seemed a fitting place for that story, which I wanted to wind around the real history of the Victorian and Edwardian explorers who pioneered our understanding of the continent – every one of them a hero and yet every one of them flawed. Unlike some voyages of discovery, Antarctic missions tend to be extremely well documented. I have taken a view on these men's characters but I hope I have not denigrated their valour or their integrity by creating a fiction to tangle with the facts.

Reading Group Questions

1. Where is your happiest place?

2. Is Karina's revenge justified?

3. Is ambition always ultimately destructive?

4. How do you justify polar expeditions where there is inevitably loss of life?

5. What would you miss most?

6. Is it ever possible to conquer nature?

7. What makes the best memorial?

8. Is it important to reach the pole? Or climb Mount Everest? Why?

9. If you believe in a life after death do you live differently?

10. What makes someone a hero/heroine?

Acknowledgements

Thanks are due to many people when you choose to write long, historical novels that don't belong in only one genre. Firstly, to Jenny Brown, my wonderful agent who ever loves a challenge and never gives up. Thank you for your patience and tenacity, Jenny (and your tremendous good taste). Secondly, to those who helped along the way by reading the manuscript and offering advice: Laura Waddell, Sophie Pinkoski and Georgina Brown. Your eyes, your beautiful, clean, discerning eyes were invaluable, you wonderful people. Thank you. Thirdly, a huge shout-out goes to Creative Scotland, which funded me to research this book, including a trip to the Scott Polar Research Institute in Cambridge and the Royal Geographical Society in London. In both these places, the archivists were hugely helpful – guardians not only of information or even history but of the stuff of our culture – the sinews of us. I appreciate the time you gave me. Thank you. Any mistakes are definitely mine not yours. Thanks and apologies go to the many friends who were patient with me. *The Ice Maiden* took a long time to write and I told you all about it again and again and you didn't tell me to shut up. I have the best people around me. And on that note, thanks also go to the Goodwins for their unerring support, my darling Molly Sheridan for being unforgiving in all the detail and encouraging me to be that way too and last, but never least, Alan Ferrier, a Greenock lad like Birdie. I think you're tops.